Maybelle in Stitches

Other Books in the Quilts of Love Series

MAYBELLE IN STITCHES

Quilts of Love Series

Joyce Magnin

Abingdon fiction™
a novel approach to faith

Maybelle in Stitches

Copyright © 2014 by Joyce Magnin Moccero

ISBN-13: 978-1-4267-5280-3

Published by Abingdon Press, P.O. Box 801, Nashville, TN 37202
www.abingdonpress.com

Published in association with MacGregor Literary Agency.

The persons and events portrayed in this work of fiction
are the creations of the author, and any resemblance
to persons living or dead is purely coincidental.

Library of Congress Cataloging-in-Publication Data

Magnin, Joyce.
  Maybelle in stitches / Joyce Magnin.
      pages cm. — (Quilts of Love series)
  Includes bibliographical references and index.
  ISBN 978-1-4267-5280-3 (binding: soft back : alk. paper) 1. Quiltmakers—Fiction. 2. Quilting—
Fiction. 3. Women welders—History—Fiction. 4. World War, 1939-1945—Fiction. 5. War stories.
I. Title.
  PS3601.L447M39 2014
  813'.6—dc23

                                                                                      2013046887

Printed in the United States of America

1 2 3 4 5 6 7 8 9 10 / 19 18 17 16 15 14

For my father, a World War II veteran.
He was one of the first to land in Normandy.
We miss you, Pop.

Prologue

Maybelle Kazinski was a welderette. That's right, a welder-ette. She worked at Sun Shipbuilding and Dry Dock in Chester, Pennsylvania. Sun Ship, one of the largest shipyards in the country, boasted eight slipways and built mostly the indispensable T2 tanker but also hospital and cargo ships. Ordinarily, this would seem an unusual job for a woman, but in 1943, thousands of women went to work building and repairing the ships vital to the war effort in Europe while most of the men in the country were off fighting Nazis—including Holden, Maybelle's new husband.

Maybelle liked her job. Having begun in the sheet metal department, in only ten months she moved her way into being a first-class welderette in Department 59, working side by side with other women welding seams on the giant leviathans. And she could weld with the best of them, men included. However, some still remembered her first day on the job. She arrived wearing a pair of bright white, spotless overalls. They quickly turned grungy black and oily. She never made that mistake again.

But still, as much as she liked going to work and as much as it managed to fill the time and distract her thoughts, Maybelle carried a hole in her heart the exact size and shape of Holden. She missed him so much it hurt and longed for the day when he would come home—for good. After all, it was only right she should get to finish the marriage she had only two weeks to begin.

1

October 1943
Chester, Pennsylvania

My dearest Maybelle,

Another long day has finally come to an end. We just finished dinner. Paxton is already snoring. He can sleep anywhere. I don't have to tell you how sleep eludes me here. But, supper was good, lamb stew with potatoes and carrots. I had three helpings. I can't tell you how or where, but we actually ate supper at a real house, not a foxhole. But now, I am in our tent, shivering because it is so cold and it makes me wish even more you were in my arms. I love you, darling, and miss you more than anything. I know you are worried, but don't be. I'll be home soon, I promise. I can hear artillery off in the distance, but if I listen real hard, I can hear your voice, singing the silly song you always sang. Oh, sorry, sweetheart, I have to go now. My sergeant is waiting for me. Some sort of (censored) duty. Good night, darling.

Your Ever-Loving Husband,

Holden

Maybelle slipped the V-Mail letter into her pocket and headed off down Ninth Street toward the Sun shipyard. The main reason she had taken the job was because she thought it would help take her mind off of missing Holden. And because most of the men had been sent off to war, they needed her. As it turned out, learning to be a welder repairing huge war ships did accomplish some of her goal, but it also accomplished something else. Maybelle had become a part of a small group of army wives whose husbands were fighting in Europe. A group that worked together, laughed together, ate together, and far too often cried together. Try as they might, the wives had a difficult time refraining from long talks of their husbands and the war. There was no use trying to hide their true feelings, although each and every woman was proud as punch her husband was doing his part. It seemed to be the motto on the home front. Do Your Part. Well, Maybelle certainly believed she was doing hers.

She lived only five blocks from the massive shipyard on the Delaware River in Chester—a small but bustling suburb of Philadelphia, Pennsylvania. After Holden enlisted, Maybelle moved in with her mother. Maybelle and Holden had plans to move into one of the blossoming communities a little farther west. But for now, home with Mom and Bingo, her black mutt of a dog, was the best of all places for Maybelle. Still, she missed Holden more than anything. They had gotten married only two weeks before he shipped out for Europe. His orders came early. Six whole months early and so Maybelle and her mother scrambled to get the wedding organized in time. Pastor Mendenhall was more than accommodating. As a matter of fact, Maybelle was delighted the way the entire congregation, what was left of it, pitched in.

Maybelle could hear the shipyard whistle blow all day long from the house. The yard operated twenty-four hours a day, seven days a week. The whistle announced the numerous shift changes, lunch, starting and stopping times. She felt fortunate for having the day shift.

⸺∞⸺

Ninth Street was a nice tree-lined street with large row homes, mostly stone and wood but a few clapboard singles with small yards. Although the houses might have been identical in architecture, each one had its own personality, the mark of the owner. Just like her house, many of the homes had red-and-white service banners with blue stars indicating the number of men from that house who were fighting. Many of the houses around town displayed a black banner in honor of a fallen soldier. Patriotism was something Chester was not short of.

Maybelle stopped in front of her friend's house. She was a friend who had been her matron of honor and did more than any friend should to keep Maybelle cool, calm, and collected. Maybelle and Doris had been friends since they were babies. It was the end house on her row—her parents' house. Doris's house displayed a banner with one blue star in honor of Doris's husband, Michael. Everyone called him Mickey. They inherited the house after Doris's father passed away some five years ago. Her mother succumbed to influenza years before. Doris never really knew her and was pretty much the woman of the house since she could remember.

"Hey, Maybelle," Doris called from the door. "I'll be down in a second."

"Okay." Maybelle said with a wave.

Maybelle waited. She always waited for Doris. Doris would be late for her own funeral. But Maybelle was used to it and always arrived a few minutes early. Then they would not be late for their shift, something foreman Logan T. Frawley did not tolerate.

Maybelle watched Doris pull the front door closed. She wore a straight, no-frills dress with pretty pink flowers against a yellow background. Her hair was short, like Maybelle's. A decision they both made after hiring on at the shipyard. Long hair was not the best when working around machinery and welding torches. Doris's cut made her appear cute and flirtatious, while Maybelle often had to remind people she was a girl. Even wearing a dress to work was risky. There were posters all over the yard reminding women not to wear skirts and to keep hair tied up or short. Doris always changed into overalls once she got there.

"What?" Doris said as if she read Maybelle's mind. "I like dresses."

"Suit yourself," Maybelle said. "But one of these days you're gonna get caught in a fan or something."

"Never happen," Doris said. "We better scooch. Don't want Logan breathing down our necks." She said it every morning. Maybelle had come to look forward to it.

"Right," Maybelle said. "What did you pack for lunch?"

"Leftover meatloaf."

"I got ham—again. It's one thing about this war that's annoying. Food rationing."

"Yeah, I'll say. Everything is so hard to get. Hazel was completely out of Off-Duty Red nail polish. I had to settle for this." She wiggled her fingers at Maybelle. "Dark burgundy. Yuck."

"It's not so bad."

The two picked up the pace a bit as they crossed Front Street to the shipyard. It was a wide street with a lot of traffic and a traffic cop who directed folks in and out of the yard. His name was Wiley. Officer Wiley.

"Morning, ladies," he said as Doris and Maybelle crossed. "Have a good shift."

"Yeah, yeah," Maybelle said with a backwards wave. "Build those ships."

To Maybelle, the entrance to the shipyard, at least Department 59, where they worked always looked so disproportionate to the rest of the yard. A little, well, normal-sized steel door against a building large enough to house a battleship.

Doris located her card first. Maybelle had to wait for Big Murray Johns, one of the only men on the line. Murray wanted to go to war, but a heart murmur kept him home. He was not happy about it. "I woulda made a great soldier."

And standing over six and half feet tall and broad as an oak testified to that fact.

"Morning, Big Murray," Maybelle said.

Murray only grunted as usual and headed toward Slipway number seven.

"Always a cheerful guy," Maybelle said.

"Yeah," Doris said. "He is just way too happy."

They giggled and headed for the women's locker room. Inside they found the locker each shared with three other women. Maybelle pulled on her overalls and snagged her goggles from the many on hooks near the entrance to the actual dock where they worked welding seams.

It was a good job, a job Maybelle felt, in some strange way, rather suited for. She always was a tomboy, more eager to play baseball and climb trees than fuss over clothes and baby dolls. Doris, on the other hand, was practically absorbed with her concerns about how she looked and dressed. Even under her heavy, oily overalls and welder's shield, you could tell Doris was pretty, slight, and trim with a figure to pretty much turn any head.

Logan met them just before they took their station. "Boss said we have to get a step on. We're under quota," he said.

"Yeah, yeah," Maybelle said. "Get a step on."

Doris just let a *phttt* noise leave her mouth. "He says it all the time, doesn't he? I swear the boss just likes to get under our skin. And besides, what will happen if we don't make quota? Will the Jerries win?"

"Just get to work," Logan said from behind. "This is serious business."

"Ohhh, I'm scared," Doris said. "Look, just do your job and we'll do ours and we'll all get to Scotland before ye."

Maybelle gave Doris a punch on the shoulder. "Don't get him angry, Doris."

"Ahh, he's just a sourpuss. Never met anyone so grumpy. Besides, the ships always get launched, don't they?"

The shift went as usual. Maybelle and Doris usually worked from seven in the morning until three or sometimes four in the afternoon before the next shift came on. Sometimes they worked later depending on demand and on exactly what task they had been given. And lately, it seemed President Roosevelt was adding more and more ships to their already bulging demand.

Maybelle worked steadily, while every so often feeling for the letter in her pocket and dodging welding splatter—the sparks flew everywhere making the yard look like a perpetual Fourth of July celebration. Somehow, just knowing the letter was there helped pass the day and keep Holden close, almost home. Even though she would often remind herself anything could happen, and she really had no idea when Holden would be coming home. Or, as with the hundreds of other military wives in the yard, *if* he would be coming home.

"Doesn't it bother you?" Maybelle asked on the walk home. "How can you be so cool and so collected all the time?"

"Doesn't what bother me?" Doris asked.

"The war. All the death and destruction. We build ships so our guys can kill their guys. What sense does that make? I mean, if you stop to think about it. It's kind of crazy."

"Hitler has to be stopped, Maybelle. We're making it possible. So no, it doesn't bother me." Doris stopped and snagged a tiny rosebud still hanging on to one of Ruth Bradshaw's bushes.

"What about Mickey, then?" Maybelle asked. "Aren't you worried about Mickey?"

Doris stopped walking and looked in Maybelle's eyes. "Sure I miss him. I worry every single day, but I also pray every single day. God is watching over him and won't let any harm come. I figure as long as I keep getting letters, I ain't gonna worry. I just ain't." Maybelle could feel Doris's determination to stay brave.

"Yeah, yeah, I suppose that's best." Maybelle didn't know for sure. She didn't know much for certain except her feelings about the war, and the restrictions on gas and food and electricity. She desperately wanted the war to end. And as for God? Well, things of that nature had started to elude her. She went to church every Sunday, and if push came to shove, she would admit God was in control, but lately she had started to wonder.

"It's like this rosebud," Doris said as she picked up her pace. "I got no real guarantee it will bloom. But . . . but I believe it will. All I have to do is put it in some water and wait."

Maybelle chuckled. She wished she had Doris's optimism. But she didn't. She reached her hand into her pocket and felt the letter. Still there. Still close. She still worried.

They reached Doris's house. "All I can tell you is to try not to worry too much. Don't ask so many questions and, like the president keeps reminding us, do your part to help. I think it makes me feel like I'm fighting with Mickey, not just waiting for him to come home or for victory—which by the way is more sure than ever if you listen to the news reports."

"I do. I guess I'll try harder."

Doris kissed her friend's cheek. "Look, I'll see ya tomorrow."

"Hey," Maybelle said, "why don't you stop down for supper in a bit? Mom's making chicken and dumplings."

"Oh, boy, chicken and dumplings. I love your mom's chicken and dumplings. It's a deal."

"Great. Get changed and come by. About an hour."

———

Maybelle picked up her steps a little as she walked; the air had turned chilly as late October settled into the Delaware Valley. Maybelle thought living so close to such a huge river might be part of the reason for the cool winds in winter and the steamy zephyrs in summer. She wanted there to be a spring in her step like Doris's. Like some of the other women in the yard. They were all in the same boat, so to speak. But she couldn't shake the terrible feeling haunting her for three solid days. Every time she read Holden's letter she felt it. Every time she touched the letter, she felt it. Every time she mentioned his name, she had to hold back tears. Something was not right.

Maybelle stood a moment outside her house. She loved it. It was one of the biggest ones on the block and set off on a large lot now gone to mostly dirt and weeds. A huge oak tree grew on the side. Maybelle's father had told her it was there when William Penn first walked the streets of Chester, the oldest town in Pennsylvania. She liked knowing this. It made her feel a part of history, the way the war was making others feel, perhaps.

———

"Mom, I'm home," Maybelle called as she pushed open the front door. "Mom?"

Maybelle slipped off her boots as she did every day. The boots were heavy and made her feet hurt. Then she put her handbag on the couch. "Mom?"

Bingo came bounding into the living room to greet Maybelle. "Hello, puppy," Maybelle said. She kneeled and rubbed the dog's ears and head. "I missed you, too, boy."

"What is it?" her mother called from the kitchen.

"Nothing, just letting you know I'm home."

Maybelle played with Bingo another minute before heading up the stairs. "I'll be down in a minute," she called. "Just want to wash my face and change."

Blue jeans and flannel shirts were pretty much all Maybelle wore lately. She was comfortable and happy and saved her dresses for important things like church and the occasional party at the Canteen. She quickly washed the oil and smudges from her face and then joined her mother in the kitchen. The wonderful, enticing aroma of chicken simmering in the pot permeated the room. A smell like spring, with celery and roasted pepper, carrots, and peas. Truly one of Maybelle's favorite meals, especially on a chilly evening.

"How was work today?" Francine asked.

Maybelle lifted the lid of the simmering stew and let the steam encircle her. She inhaled. "Mom, you make the best chicken and dumplings. I invited Doris."

"I thought you would. I'm making plenty."

Maybelle sat at the kitchen table. "I had a good day. You know, same old stuff. Logan was a bear, though."

"Ahh, don't let him bother you. He's just sore 'cause he can't be fighting in Europe."

"I know, but he doesn't have to take it out on us. But yeah, it was a good day."

"Good, good." Francine dumped a bunch of confectioner's sugar into a bowl. A small white cloud drifted up.

"Whatcha making?" Maybelle asked.

"Frosting. I baked a chocolate cake this morning."

"Really, Ma? That sounds good. Where'd you get chocolate?"

Just then, Roger walked into the kitchen, yawning. Roger was a boarder whom Maybelle and her mother had living in the house. Since things had gotten so busy at the shipyard and there were so many rooms left vacant as men and women went to war, many folks rented out their beds. Some houses had two and three people sharing one bed in different shifts leading some folks to remark there was never a cold bed in Chester.

"Hey, Roger," Maybelle said. "Graveyard again?"

Roger lifted the lid on the stew. "You make the best chicken, Francine." He replaced the lid and joined Maybelle at the table. "Yeah. Graveyard. It's killing me. Except well, I probably shouldn't be saying this, but I understand we're starting some top secret job tonight."

"Now, now," Francine said. "Loose lips sink ships."

Roger snorted air from his nose. "Yeah, yeah. I ain't sayin' nothin'."

"Hey," Maybelle said. "Doris is coming by in a bit."

A grin the size of Francine's soup pot stretched across Roger's face. "That's nice, real nice. But I ain't hangin' around tonight. I'm meeting a couple of the boys down the taproom before work."

"Ahh, you and the taproom. How can you go there before putting in a full shift?" Francine asked as she tapped a large spoon against the pot.

"I can't sleep, once you hens start yakking, so I might as well." Then he smiled and kissed Francine's cheek. "See you tomorrow."

"No, no, hold on. Sit. Let me give you a bowl of stew before you go. No dumplings yet but you can eat the best part."

"Fine and dandy," Roger said. "But Francine, we all know the dumplings are the best."

Francine ladled a heaping helping of the chicken stew with carrots and peas into a bowl and set it in front of Roger. Then she tore off a chunk of bread from a freshly baked loaf. "Here you go. Eat up."

Roger was definitely charming. Maybelle had always thought so. Even in high school he could always get the girls. He moved in with her and Francine after Pearl Harbor, once the war was in high gear. Roger intended to become a soldier, but unfortunately, a small hearing loss in his left ear kept him from duty. But he stayed on at the house becoming for all intents and purposes the man of the house.

Francine pulled two cakes from the refrigerator. "Want to frost the layers, May?" she asked.

"Ah, Ma, you know I can't bake or cook to save my life. I'll just ruin it."

"I know you are not exactly a great housewife, but give it a try. You'll learn as you go. Use this wide spatula."

Roger laughed. "Maybelle is too much a tomboy."

Maybelle stuck her tongue out at Roger. "Gimme that spatula," she said. "I'll show you."

Bingo barked twice. Francine slipped him a piece of the chicken cooling on the counter. Bingo ate pretty well, considering. Table scraps, leftovers, the occasional fried egg.

But try as she might, Maybelle just couldn't get the frosting to spread evenly, and in one swipe, she took a large chunk off the top. "I'm sorry, Ma. I told you."

Francine took the spatula from Maybelle. "Sometimes I think you do this stuff on purpose."

Francine expertly reassembled the top of the cake. "Why you can't do the easiest domestic chores is beyond me," Francine said with a chuckle. "Did I ever tell you about the time she tried to make a dress?"

"Mom." Maybelle said. "Don't."

"No, come on, Francine, tell me. I can use a laugh."

Francine continued frosting as she spoke. "I can't believe you never heard this story. Anyway, it was in high school, so just a couple of years ago. She was supposed to be making a dress. A simple, no-frills dress."

Maybelle sneaked a spoonful of frosting. She then sat at the table and cringed as her mother continued speaking.

"She was going along okay, sort of, the sleeves were crooked, her seams were not straight, but at least it sort of resembled a dress. But then came the hard part. The zipper."

"It wasn't all my fault. No one really explained it very well."

Francine shook her head and spread more frosting.

"Yeah?" Roger said. "What happened?"

"She sewed it into the neck hole." Francine drew her index finger across her neck. "No foolin', my little girl zippered up her own neck hole."

Roger laughed and laughed. He smacked the table. "Hysterical! Wait till I tell the guys."

"I ain't a monkey, Ma. I'm just not suited for it. I'm better at more . . . whatcha call brainy stuff." She stood and made a hoity-toity motion with her head. "I can't help it if I got the brains in the family."

Francine elbowed Roger. "My genius daughter."

"Ha, ha, make jokes," Maybelle said. "Frost your own cake. I'm gonna go take a bath before supper."

"Can't do that," Roger said. "No hot water left. I used it all."

Maybelle heaved a sigh, "Fine. Then I'll go . . . read a letter."

"Haven't you read that letter enough?" Francine asked.

"No, it's never enough." Maybelle felt tears rush to eyes. It was hard to know if the tears were from missing Holden or from embarrassment. Probably both.

Francine set the spatula down. She pulled Maybelle close. "I'm sorry, dear. I know you miss him."

"I do, Mom. I miss him so much."

"Ahh, don't cry," Roger said. "I can't stand when girls cry. Holden is tough. He'll be home, you'll see."

2

Maybelle took the letter from her dirty overalls pocket and sat on the edge of her bed. She lightly touched the words with the tip of her fingers, and again that queasy feeling welled up in her stomach and in her spirit. "Holden, please keep your head down." Then she set the letter on her night table next to the framed portrait of Holden in his Army uniform. He wasn't what you would call tall, dark, and handsome, but he was sweet and gentle and Maybelle didn't doubt that he loved her with every ounce of his being. His nose might have been a bit too long and his ears a touch big, but a sweeter heart could not be found.

She picked up the portrait and kissed it. "Chicken and dumplings tonight." She replaced the picture and lay back on her bed atop the quilt her mother had made for their wedding present. It was pretty with blue and white and yellow fabrics all sewn together in large interlocking circles. It wasn't like a big surprise. Maybelle had watched her mother make it. She started it the day Holden proposed, but when Holden enlisted and they decided to get married six months earlier than planned, Francine dashed to get it finished in time.

Maybelle felt the smooth fabric with her fingertips. Even though it was rushed, it was perfect. Maybelle could have never accomplished such a thing. Nor did she want to. Particularly after the deep scarring left from the zipper incident. She still had the dress tucked away in her hope chest, why she didn't know. It was simply too hard to part with.

But, nonetheless, the quilt was already brimming with memories. She and Holden did not exactly have a honeymoon. There wasn't time. He was due to ship out just a day after the wedding. Francine arranged to spend the night at a friend's house so Maybelle and Holden could spend their wedding night alone. Well, mostly. Bingo whimpered behind closed doors.

Maybelle smiled at the memory. She turned and looked at Holden. "I love you so much, honey."

She reached into her night table drawer and pulled out a writing tablet.

⌐∞⌐

My dearest Holden,

 I'm lying on the quilt Mom made for us. The one we, well, you know. Mom is making chicken and dumplings. She already managed to remind me about my inadequacies as a housewife—in front of Roger Chinalewski. Doris is coming over for supper. It will be nice. I wish I could stay as cheerful as her. I don't know how she does it. Mickey has been gone longer than you and yet she still smiles and laughs everyday. She says it's because of God. I'm not so sure. Anyway, everything else around here is the same. Bingo is still digging up the backyard. Yesterday he dug up Mom's squash and pulled six tomatoes off the vine. I thought she was gonna kill him with a shovel.

I miss you too much, honey. I know what you're doing over there is important, but I wish you were here with me, right now, on the quilt. Please keep your head down and don't go taking any unnecessary duties. I'm counting the days, darling.

Maybelle folded the notepaper and stuffed it into an envelope preaddressed to Holden. It amazed her the letters ever found him, being God knows where, in God knows which foxhole or tent.

She kissed the seal and set it on the table. Still wanting a bath, she moseyed to the bathroom and tried the water. Warm. But not enough.

But it was okay, because when she came out of the bathroom she heard her mother. "Doris. I'm so glad you could come for supper. It'll be about a half hour. I'll call Maybelle down."

"Thanks, Francine. Anything I can help with?"

Maybelle started down the steps.

"No," Francine said. "I got it covered."

Maybelle joined Doris in the living room.

"I got another V-Mail from Mickey," Doris said. "He still can't tell me where he is, but he's okay. Thank God."

Maybelle spied a pile of mail on the coffee table. She hadn't gotten a letter in several days. And she knew if one had come, her mother would certainly have mentioned it. But still she flipped through the letters. Nothing from Holden.

"Mom doesn't seem to need any help," Maybelle said. "Wanna listen to the radio? It's time for Frank Sinatra."

"Oh, he's dreamy," Doris said.

The radio, a large mahogany box with a huge dial on the front, sat on the floor near the fireplace. Maybelle loved the radio. She especially enjoyed *Little Orphan Annie* and *Burns and Allen*. She tuned the dial until she heard singing she thought was Frank.

"That's him. That's him," Doris said. "I'd recognize his voice anywhere." She practically swooned.

Maybelle and Doris sat on the sofa facing the fireplace and listened.

"I'm glad you got another V-Mail today," Maybelle said.

"Nothing from Holden?" Doris touched Maybelle's hand.

"Nope. I . . . I guess he's busy, you know. They have him doing top secret stuff all the time."

"Yeah, I know. But try not to worry. You just keep writing to him. God's got him. Don't you give it a single worry thought. God's got him."

Maybelle felt her heart skip a beat. She hated thinking about it. All she wanted was for Holden to come home. All she wanted was for the war to end.

"I hate the stupid war," Maybelle said as Frank crooned "Stardust," a favorite of Holden's.

Doris was swaying a little in time with the song. "I wish they'd let us listen to music at the shipyard."

"Ahh, we'd never hear it over the noise."

"They do have those concerts from time to time, you know, with the Sun Ship band, but I wish somehow we could listen while we worked."

"Yeah, that would be nice. You should ask Logan."

Doris smiled. "You know what? I think I will."

"And you know what else," Maybelle said, as Bingo found his spot on the hearth.

"What?" Doris asked.

"I think you should join the Glee Club. You always did have a nice voice. I bet they'd love it. You sing at church."

"I thought about it, but I don't know."

"Hey, it gets you out of work sometimes."

"Maybe," Doris said. "I'll think about it."

The Sun shipyard was so large and employed so many people it was like a small city unto itself, with all the amenities, including entertainment and sports leagues. Maybelle joined the bowling league but gave it up. She wasn't sure why. She was really a pretty good bowler. "I might go back to bowling."

"Good idea. It will help keep your mind off things."

"Soup's on," Francine called. "Come and get it."

"Oh good," Maybelle said. "I'm starved."

"Me too," Doris said. "I love your Mom's cooking. I wish I could cook like her."

Maybelle gave Doris a little nudge. "What are you saying? You're a great cook."

"I suppose. I just don't get much opportunity living by myself. But when Mickey comes home, you bet, I'll be cooking and sewing and doing all the stuff that makes a woman a woman."

"Yeah?" Maybelle sat at the dining room table before realizing it had not been set for dinner.

"We're eating in here," Francine called.

"I think it's just us girls tonight," Maybelle said as they made their way to the kitchen. The kitchen was on the other side of the big dining room where Francine often set supper out when she had guests or when Roger was home, mostly because there wasn't much room in the kitchen.

"The kitchen, tonight?" Maybelle asked.

"Yeah, yeah," Francine said. "I just didn't feel much like setting the big table for just us."

"Are you okay, Mom?" Maybelle asked.

"Sure, honey." She ladled some of the chicken and dumplings onto Maybelle's plate. The aroma filled the room. Maybelle carried her plate of chicken swimming in a nice, somewhat thick broth with peas and carrots and three large, fluffy white dumplings. Maybelle had always loved to watch her mother make dumplings. There was something special about how Francine would drop heaping spoonfuls of the white, sticky batter into the bubbling stew. The blobs would sink first and then as they cooked rise to the surface. Like magic.

Francine loaded up Doris's plate and then her own.

"Thank you," Doris said. "It looks delicious."

Frank Sinatra's voice still drifted into the kitchen. All in all, it was pleasant and sweet and Maybelle enjoyed being with two of her favorite people.

Doris offered to ask the blessing.

"Now, that's sweet," Francine said. She took Maybelle's hand as Doris prayed asking first for God to protect their husbands and all the soldiers "fighting the Nazis." Then she asked a blessing on the food and Francine.

"Thank you," Francine said with a sigh. Bingo lumbered into the kitchen and sat near Francine. He knew better than to beg for food right from the table. He'd get his share soon enough but it didn't hurt to wait close by, just in case a scrap somehow made it to his mouth prematurely.

"Are you sure you're all right?" Maybelle asked as she stabbed a dumpling with her fork.

"Yes, yes, you already asked me. But I do think I'll be going off to bed a little early tonight."

Maybelle looked at Doris, who was busily chewing, and in typical Doris fashion, defended Francine. Maybelle had hoped to get some kind of agreement Francine was looking a little tired, peaked even. "She looks fine," Doris said. "No crime in being a little tired. Your mom works hard."

Maybelle glanced at the luscious-looking chocolate cake sitting on the counter. "Hey, you never told me where you got chocolate."

"Roger, of course," Francine said.

"Should have known. Roger can scrounge anything."

Once the stew plates had been cleared, Francine brought the cake to the table. It was a rare treat these days. Francine sliced three nice-size pieces.

Doris bit into hers first. "Oh, this is sooooo good."

"It sure is," Maybelle said. "You are something else, Mom."

"And now you know why I want to get to bed early tonight. I work hard around here."

"Okay, Mom," Maybelle said. "Maybe Doris and I will head down to the Canteen after dinner."

Francine smiled wide. "Fine with me. But remember, you two girls are married. No dancing with other men."

"Of course," Doris said. "No dancing."

3

It turned out to be a nice evening. The air was chilly but not too bad. The sky was bright with a gazillion stars as Maybelle and Doris returned home from the dance. They did what they usually did. They stayed mainly on the sidelines, sipping punch and watching the GIs dance with the pretty girls, even playing matchmaker from time to time. Maybelle was not much of a dancer, but Doris could definitely cut a rug.

"I can't wait to go dancing again," she had said. "The first thing we're doing when Mickey gets home is going dancing. He can swing with the best of them."

"The first thing?" Maybelle said with a smile.

Doris gave Maybelle a playful punch. "Okay, the second thing."

"Can you believe it?" Doris said when they stopped in front of her house. "The way the soldier grabbed my hand and next thing I knew we were dancing the Lindy and folks were watching."

Maybelle shook her head. "I couldn't believe it. You. Out there. On the dance floor. A married woman. Don't tell Ma."

"Ah, Mickey wouldn't mind. It was for the war effort. The GI told me his folks were in Louisiana and he was passing through on his way overseas. Probably the last bit of fun he'll have for a while."

"I guess," Maybelle said. "But we have to watch our reputations."

Doris yawned. "I think you might be a little jealous. I can teach ya ta dance. If you want."

"Nah." Maybelle pushed the thought away. "I got two left feet."

"So did that GI and it didn't stop him from having fun. And besides you have to stop being so . . . so—"

"What?"

"So Maybelle. You hide behind your tomboy image so much. You're a girl, Maybelle, a pretty young girl."

"I guess," Maybelle said. "Maybe you can teach me. I'll surprise Holden because he loves to go dancing, too, you know."

"Yeah, now that's the ticket. And then we can all go dancing when the boys get home."

Maybelle liked the sound of it. She felt for the letter, but remembered she left it on her bed.

"What's wrong?" Doris asked. "You've been falling down in the dumps all day." She snapped her fingers. "Just like so."

"Oh, I don't know." Maybelle looked into the sky. "It's just that . . . lately I've been worried."

Doris leaned against the metal fence surrounding her front yard. "About Holden? But you're always worried about him. Nothing new there."

"No, this is different. I have a sinking feeling right here." Maybelle touched the space between her heart and her stomach. "It feels like I swallowed a baseball."

"I guess we all get those feelings from time to time," Doris said. "It goes with the territory, you know. But worrying ain't gonna bring him home any quicker. And you got to ask God to help, you know that. Ask Him to keep you calm."

Maybelle sighed. "You're right. You are absolutely right."

"Sure I am," Doris said. "We have to think positive. For them, you know. They can feel it when we worry."

"You really believe that?"

Doris kicked at a small pebble. It rolled into the street. "I don't know but it helps to think so. At least for me."

Just then, the midnight whistle sounded from the shipyard.

"Oh goodness," Maybelle said. "I better get home. Mom will have a conniption fit if I'm too late."

"Okay, okay, I'll see ya in the morning."

Maybelle headed off down the street. The whistle sounded again. Long and loud. "Ahh, shut up," she said. She pushed open the wire gate and headed up the path to the front door. The house was dark.

"That's weird," she said, as Bingo came bounding down the steps. "Mom usually keeps a light on. Maybe we missed a blackout drill."

Maybelle switched on the small table lamp in the living room. Like everyone else, she had been conserving, but one small bulb wouldn't hurt.

"Hey, Bingo," she said taking the dog's head in her hands and rubbing behind his ears. "How's it goin', pooch?"

Bingo barked, but Maybelle shushed him. "Mom did say she was going to bed early."

Bingo whimpered and headed toward the stairway.

"I'm coming, I'm coming," Maybelle said. "Time for bed. I know. But maybe another small piece of cake first."

She cut a slice of cake and set it on a white plate. Then she poured a glass of milk to go with it. A full stomach always helped her to sleep. Like her mother always said since she was a little girl, "It's good to fill the empty spots before sleep."

Maybelle sat at the table. "Empty spots," she said out loud. "I got a spot about as big as . . . well, as big as the moon. What can fill an empty spot that big?"

Bingo whined and barked, this time jumping up on her. "All right, I guess we should get to bed."

Maybelle yawned. She replaced the bottle of milk in the fridge and headed off to bed. She paused a minute at her mother's door and peeked in. "Sleeping like a baby," she whispered.

The next morning came too soon. Maybelle stretched and yawned. The sun was on the rise and small swatches of light painted the room. It looked like a good morning.

But something wasn't right. Bingo usually slept on the bed with her, but he wasn't there.

"Maybe Mom let him out early."

She held Holden's portrait. "Good morning, Sweetheart." She kissed his picture. "Come home soon."

After a quick warm, not-so-hot shower, she dressed in jeans with cuffs as usual and a blue blouse. Pretty typical for workdays. Then she pulled a brush through her hair a second time and headed off to breakfast with a quick glance at the clock. Six o'clock. Her shift started at seven so she had time. But Maybelle was like that. On time for everything, all the time. Every time.

She made her way to the kitchen expecting to see Francine busy mixing oatmeal or scrambling an egg or two. But she wasn't there. The coffee wasn't on.

"Mom?" Maybelle called as a terrible queasy feeling rose in her stomach. "Mom? Bingo?"

She heard a bark. Upstairs. Maybelle dashed up the steps as the terrible feeling grew into a full-blown panic. "Mom." She pushed open her mother's bedroom door and saw Bingo on her mother's bed with his head resting on Francine's stomach. He whined and whimpered. He looked at Maybelle from under his thick, wiry eyebrows.

"M . . . Mom?" Maybelle inched closer. "What's wrong, boy? Mom oversleep?"

Maybelle looked closer. Her mother's eyes were closed, but she knew in an instant all was not right. "Mom." Tears welled in her eyes. "Mom. I . . . What happened?"

Bingo looked up and barked twice.

"Is that what you were trying to tell me last night?" An awful thought crossed her mind. She had ignored Bingo, and now it was too late. "Did you know, boy? Did you know she was in trouble?" Maybe she could have done something if she had checked a little closer.

Bingo rested his head on Francine again. Maybelle took her mother's lifeless, cold hand. "I'm sorry, Mom. I . . ." But there were no words. Maybelle sat and sobbed until Doris banged on the front door.

Maybelle left her mother and made her way to the door. She sobbed into Doris's arms.

"What's wrong?" Doris asked. "Holden?"

Maybelle shook her head. "No. It's Mom. Upstairs."

Doris pulled away and looked in Maybelle's eyes. "Is she . . . ?"

All Maybelle could muster was another deep sob. She crumbled to the floor as Bingo nuzzled her shoulder. Maybelle pulled the dog tight.

Doris sat with them. "That was the terrible feeling," she said.

4

The funeral service three days later was short and sweet. Pastor Mendenhall did a nice talk. Roger even said some words. Maybelle just couldn't. She just couldn't stand up in front of the packed sanctuary and talk about her Mom. Not then. Not yet. Maybelle was not amazed at how many people came to wish her mother good-bye and God's blessings. Everyone in town loved Francine. Roger was lead pallbearer and cried the entire time.

Francine was buried in the Chester Rural Cemetery next to Robert, her husband and Maybelle's father, who had passed away several years ago after contracting pneumonia. After Pastor Mendenhall said the final graveside prayer and the mourners filed away, Maybelle stood a while with Doris and Roger at her side.

"The doc said it was a stroke most likely." Maybelle snapped her fingers. "Just like that. I still can't believe it." She swiped tears from her cheeks. "It's not fair."

"I know," Doris said. "It's weird."

Maybelle pulled a yellow rose from one of the funeral sprays.

Roger draped his big arm around Maybelle's shoulder. "I loved her, too."

"I know," Maybelle said. "No more chocolate cakes or chicken and dumplings." Maybelle smiled. "The funny thing is I had been having this strange feeling for days. But I thought for sure it was . . . Holden was . . . you know."

Doris took Maybelle's hand. "I know. I knew what you were thinking."

"I never thought it could be Mom."

"Ahh, who can know from feelings," Roger said. "Feelings are just feelings. Can't go by them."

Maybelle set a flower on the oak casket. Doris did the same and so did Roger.

"Come on," Doris said. "They're expecting us down at Mackey's."

Maybelle pushed stray hairs behind her ears. She blew her nose into a pretty yellow handkerchief. "I wish I didn't have to go."

"I know," Doris said. "But you know what they say, funerals are not for the deceased. They're for the living. Folks want to tell you how much they care."

Maybelle started to walk toward the car that was waiting. Conroy Ferguson, a boy she went to high school with, was driving it for Fairlamb's Funeral Home. He looked good in his black suit, not the same pimple-faced, snotty boy she knew.

"When did he get so dignified?" Doris asked. "Remember him at school?"

"He grossed everyone out."

Conroy opened the back door and helped the women inside. "I'm so sorry for your loss," he said. "I remember your mom. She always treated me nice."

Conroy drove them to Mackey's, which was packed almost to the gills. Some of the folks needed to get back to the yard, some were between shifts, and a few folks had the day off, including Roger, who had taken charge of greeting folks and offering his thanks for their support.

Mackey had draped Francine's bar stool, third from the end, in black bunting and set a portrait of her on the seat. Francine, although not a drinker at all, not even beer, would like to visit the bar, sip lemonade, and watch the folks. She was always quick with a word of advice and even a reprimand if someone got unruly, which was known to happen from time to time. But mostly Francine was everyone's Mom. And everyone would miss her.

Mackey stood behind the bar, handing out cold drafts, Coca-Colas, and lemonade while friends, neighbors, some family, the few that were left, chitchatted about Francine and Robert, the war, and even a few mentions of God and Hitler.

"Here you go, May," Mackey said. "You need a cold one."

"Thanks," she said. "But maybe just a cola."

"Suit yourself," Mackey said in his Irish brogue. He was one of many immigrants who found nice work and friends in recent years. "Are you hungry? I could rustle up some cold cuts. Send Blinkers down to Pat's for a steak even." Blinkers was Mackey's lackey, not a nice word but accurate. He was fresh from prison and no one would hire him except Mackey. He did whatever Mackey told him to do, even scrub the toilets and mow the lawn, shovel snow. Whatever it took. He had a room in the back of the pub. And, as far as anyone knew, he was nothing more than an upstanding citizen who had fallen on hard times. Maybelle knew the truth, and so did Roger, who tended to watch him like a hawk.

"No, no, I'm not hungry. Not just yet."

"You just let me know if I can be doin' anything for ya."

"Thanks, Mackey."

Maybelle sipped her drink slowly as folks filed past once again offering their condolences and remembrances.

Even Old Man Flowers, the crotchety church deacon, had nice things to say about Francine. And he didn't like anyone.

"It is nice," Doris, who was sticking to Maybelle like glue, said. "All these people really cared about her . . . and you."

"I know," Maybelle said. "I really appreciate everyone coming out."

The celebration, as Mackey chose to call it, lasted until around dinnertime before the majority of the people had dribbled out. Most people came for a few minutes, while others stayed the entire time. Soon it was just Maybelle, Doris, and Mackey in the pub. Even Roger had to return to the shipyard. He didn't want to go, but Maybelle encouraged him. "Just go. I'll be okay," she told him. "Doris will stay."

"Nice funeral," Mackey said as he wiped the bar with a white cloth. "As funerals go."

"Yeah, sure was," Maybelle said. "Good turnout." What else could she say? Is any funeral really good?

"I'll say," Doris said looking around the room. Blinkers was already sweeping up, emptying ashtrays, and gathering empty bottles in a bucket. "But I'm not surprised. Your mom was loved."

Maybelle sat on the stool next to her mother's and listened to the music, the big band sound drifting around her. The sound was nice, but faraway sounding. She suddenly felt like the weight of the world had dropped on her. She grabbed Doris's hand. "Now what?" she said with pinch of panic. "Now what? I can't make it without her."

"You go home. Pick up the pieces, put things away, and keep living until Holden comes walking through the door. And then the two of you decide what's next."

"But . . . but I don't know anything about taking care of the house and what do I do with Mom's . . . you know . . . stuff?"

"Nothing. Not today anyway," Doris said. "Right now you go home, get some sleep. I'll stay with you all night."

"There's the ticket," Mackey said. "Go home. You might as well. You can't stay away forever."

<hr />

Maybelle and Doris walked hand in hand down Ninth Street. It was a glorious day, weather-wise. The sun was still high in the sky even though a chilly breeze blew in from the Delaware River. Of course, it held the faint odor of fuel oil and metal. Lining the street, the maple trees' leaves were nearly all gone. Lawns were going to seed and flowerbeds looked overrun with weeds. Even many of the Victory Gardens folks kept were starting to look tired and ready for a long winter's nap.

"You know Mom would have loved this day," Maybelle said.

"Yep, she'd be out in the garden tending to whatever was left of her vegetables."

Maybelle smiled. "Yeah, whatever the pesky rabbit family didn't swipe."

The rest of the walk, just a few blocks, was quiet. Maybelle's thoughts leapfrogged from her mother to Holden. And then back again. How she wished he were here to hold her and tell her it would be okay. And maybe if Holden were here, things would be okay. But without him, Maybelle just didn't know.

They stopped for a moment in front of the house. Maybelle looked at the red, white, and blue service banner with the gold tassels that hung in their window. The blue star was for Holden. And near it, black ribbons across the doorway.

"How long do I keep that there?" Maybelle asked.

"As long as you need," Doris said.

"Mom would hate it."

"Ha, knowing your Mom she'd make pillows or a party dress out of it."

Maybelle pushed open the metal gate and started toward the front door. "Yeah, she would."

Bingo barked. He had been in the backyard all day. "Oh, I think Bingo is going to be in a sad mood for a long time. How do you explain this to a dog?"

"Oh, they're pretty smart. I'm sure he's more worried about you than you are about him."

Maybelle swung open the gate on the backyard and Bingo bounded out. He barked and sat back on his haunches wanting a pat on the head or a scratch behind the ears. "How you doin'?" Maybelle said as she patted his big head.

Bingo seemed to smile and tilted his head.

"I know," Maybelle said. "You miss her, too. But we'll be okay. You'll see." She burst into hard sobs and held Bingo close. "I . . . I hope."

Bingo walked close to Maybelle into the quiet house. She stood in the living room and looked around. Her mother was all over the room. In every corner, every pillow and decoration, Maybelle could see her mother's hand.

"How about coffee?" Doris asked. "And I'll make us some supper in little while."

"Coffee sounds good," Maybelle said. "But I'm not hungry." She touched her stomach.

"I know, but you need to keep up your strength. I'll fix something light."

Maybelle followed Doris into the kitchen with Bingo still close to her side. It wasn't long before Doris had the coffee percolating and the room filled with the rich aroma, another reminder of Francine. Maybelle sniffed back tears.

"It's okay to cry," Doris said.

"I . . . I just don't want to cry anymore. How many tears can a person shed anyway?" Maybelle saw her mother's apron hanging on a hook near the cellar door. Her favorite, blue gingham with white trim. She had no choice but to let the tears come again as she held Bingo close to her.

"It's like that," Doris said. "I remember when my dad died. I would be going along just fine when BAM! It would hit and the tears would flow like Niagara."

Maybelle sat at the kitchen table, her usual spot, across from where Francine always sat. "It was nice of Mackey to put on the luncheon."

"Luncheon?" Doris said with a chuckle. "Was there lunch?"

Maybelle smiled. "Nah, I guess not. But it was still sweet. He offered to send Blinkers down to Pat's for me for a steak. But I told him no."

"Blinkers. Now there's a character." Doris sat at the table after setting two cups and saucers out on the counter. "Do you know his story?"

"Only that he did some time in jail—robbery I think, or rum running, maybe both. Some folks say he has mob ties, but I doubt it."

"Oh, I don't see that. He's . . . too weird for that."

"I think he just keeps to himself. Does what Mackey tells him. That's all."

The percolator stopped and Doris jumped up and filled the cups. "Here you go. Just what the doctor ordered."

"Hey, there's cookies in the jar," Maybelle said. "Mom made them."

Doris grabbed the large, red, apple-shaped cookie jar from the counter and set it on the table. She pulled the lid off. "Ahh, snickerdoodles. Francine always did make the best."

Bingo leaned back on his haunches and begged for a cookie. Maybelle complied. "There you go, boy. We all need a little snickerdoodle once in a while."

The rest of the day went slowly. Doris kept her promise and stayed all day and night. They stayed up until well past midnight talking and listening to the radio. Doris even ironed a couple of

Maybelle's shirts and managed to get some laundry washed and hung in the cellar.

"I'm so glad you're my friend," Maybelle said as the two prepared for bed. Doris chose one of Maybelle's nightshirts. She slipped into the bed next to Maybelle. "You can cry if you want. I'll be here."

"Good night, Doris," Maybelle said.

And even when morning came, Doris let Maybelle sleep and prepared breakfast for them and Roger, who had been milling around the house like a lost sheep since his shift ended early in the morning. Doris heard him come in. At first, she was startled but then remembered he was working late.

Maybelle made her way to the kitchen. She was dressed and ready for work.

"You don't have to go to work today," Doris said. "I'm sure Logan will understand."

"I know." Maybelle poured herself a cup of coffee. "I want to go."

"Suit yourself," Doris said.

The three sat quietly for a few minutes barely eating their oatmeal.

"I miss her so much," Maybelle said.

"She was kind of a mother to me," Roger said over breakfast. "My own Ma couldn't have cared less if I lived or died, but Francine"—he swiped tears—"really cared about me. She trusted me and even made me a quilt. I couldn't believe it when she gave it to me. I was . . . honored kind of, you know?"

Maybelle patted his hand. "I know. Mom loved everyone who passed through her doors and even those who didn't."

"She was the best," Roger said. "But now. What happens now?"

"What do you mean?" Maybelle asked.

Roger glanced around the kitchen as though he really wanted to avoid the question but couldn't. "Well, I don't want to sound rude or nothin' but . . . well, can I stay on? In the spare bedroom like usual?"

"Certainly," Maybelle said without hesitation. "You're not getting off that easily. I still need a man around the house."

Roger smiled. "Thank you."

"You better stick around," Doris said. "We need someone to scrounge chocolate and coffee for us."

Roger laughed. "You betcha. I can get pretty much anything. You just ask."

"Can you get me any Off Duty Red nail polish? Hazel's been out of it for days. Even the Rexall Drugs is plum out."

Roger smiled. "I'll see what I can do."

The yard whistle sounded.

Doris said. "We got to get a move on. We're gonna be late. Don't need old sourpuss Logan on our backs today."

"Ah, don't worry about him. You just let me talk to him. I'll set him straight," Roger said.

Maybelle wiped her mouth with the cloth napkin. "Yeah, we better get."

"You sure?" Roger said. "Are you sure you should be going into work? You get three days' bereavement."

"I know," Maybelle said. "But I don't want it. I don't want to knock around this house by myself all day."

"As long as you're sure," Doris said. "Let's go."

Logan was waiting at the door. Tapping his foot. "Glad you ladies could make it."

"Ahh, knock it off, Logan," Doris said. "You know it's been a tough week around here. Everyone loved Francine."

"Yeah, yeah," Logan said looking at Maybelle. "Why are you here?"

"Better ta be here than at the house." She tried to push past him, but his big foot stopped her.

"Yeah, I get that," Logan said. "But ya got two more days. Take 'em."

"No, I'd rather work."

Logan shook his head. "Okay, but if you mess up on something because, you know, your head is all in a cloud I'm gonna have ta send ya home."

Doris took Maybelle's hand and pulled her across the floor to the locker room. "Don't worry. She'll do fine."

But she didn't. Welding was harder than Maybelle thought it would be that morning. All her thoughts were on Francine and Holden. It was just too difficult to concentrate, and she was making all kinds of silly mistakes. Not to mention getting in the way of splatter. Fortunately, it landed on her heavy boots and didn't burn. So, when the lunch whistle blew, Maybelle took the opportunity to tell Doris she was heading home.

"Are you sure? Will you be okay? Alone, I mean?"

"I won't be alone," Maybelle said. "I'll have Bingo. And Roger will be sleeping upstairs."

"Okay," Doris said. "I'll see you later. I'll come by right after the shift." She lifted her welding shield onto her head. "I'm here if you need me."

Maybelle smiled. "I'll be fine. Don't worry." Maybelle looked at her friend a long minute. "You look worried."

"I'm not worried," Doris said with a little bit of squeak in her voice.

"Yes, you are."

"Okay, a little."

"Look, you go to lunch. I'm gonna write to Holden. And . . . I was thinking maybe I should start going through things. You know, her closet and stuff. Figure out what to do with everything."

"Are you ready for that?" Doris asked. "Why don't you wait for me? We'll do it together."

"Ready as I'll ever be, I think. And I'm sure there will be plenty I can use your help with."

"Okay," Doris said. "But be prepared. You never know what you might find."

"What can I find? Mom had no secrets."

Maybelle met Roger on the way home.

"Hey," she said. "I thought you would be home sleeping."

"I slept a couple of hours," Roger said. "But then I got hungry. Stopped at the newsstand for a paper and then got a hotdog."

"Any good news?" Maybelle said.

They walked toward the house together. Maybelle noticed some dark, heavy clouds were moving in overhead. "Looks like rain."

"Supposed to," Roger said. "Least it's what Gus says, and he's usually right."

"Yeah, I suppose guys who run hotdog stands need to know that stuff."

They walked another block before Roger asked Maybelle why she was home early.

"I just couldn't keep my mind on my work. I thought Logan was going to split a seam. So, I thought it would be best just to come home. I'll try again tomorrow."

Roger laughed. "Yeah, he is excitable."

Maybelle took a breath. "I like the rain. Hope it storms."

"Me, too," Roger said. "Say, would you mind if I just headed down to Mackey's? Some of the guys got a game going."

"Poker?"

"No, darts. Mackey has been teaching us. I'm pretty good. Got a deadeye."

"Deadeye?"

"Sure. It means I got good aim. Hit the bull's-eye any time I want. It's some of them other numbers I got trouble with."

"All right. Go ahead. Have fun."

"You know where I am if you need me," Roger said.

"Don't worry about me. I got stuff to do. I'll keep busy, you know."

"As long as you're sure. I'll see you in the morning then. I got the graveyard again."

"Okay," Maybelle said with a wave. "Have a good shift."

Maybelle walked on toward her house. It was getting easier, although only slightly, to go inside. First though, she checked the mailbox, taking a deep breath before opening the little mailbox door. *Please let there be something from Holden.* Nothing, just a bill from the electric company and a postcard from her Aunt Selma apologizing for not making it to the funeral. That was okay. No one liked Selma.

The living room was still filled with flower sprays given by friends and family. It smelled like the funeral parlor. And, of course, her mother's things, knickknacks and sewing box, her magazines and shoes were still right where she left them.

"Too eerie or something," Maybelle said as she looked around. Bingo, who had decided to stay as close to Maybelle as he possibly could, whenever he could, barked his agreement. "But I have to do this. I guess it's my house now. Well, mine and Holden's." If only Holden were there though, to help her through. He would know exactly what to do.

She patted Bingo's head, which when he sat was just exactly knee-high to Maybelle. "What do you say we start . . ." Tears again. "We start cleaning up."

Bingo let go a loud bark. "So are you with or against me?"

He let go a whimper and then a loud bark.

"Ok, I'm guessing you agree."

Maybelle went to her room and changed into a flannel shirt. She stopped at the bathroom to wash her face and hands. She wrapped a red-and-yellow scarf around her head.

"To keep the dust out," she told Bingo. Not as if there was ever much dust. Francine was a meticulous housekeeper.

Maybelle paused a moment and looked at Holden's portrait. She sighed. How she wished he was here. Even for the funeral, anything to help her get through, but she understood the war effort was important. Perhaps even more important than her. But still. She hated being alone. Now, for the first time in her life, she truly was alone.

Holden's last V-Mail was still on the bedside table. She read it again, maybe for the hundredth time, but it was all she had of him, this last letter. These last few words. "Why haven't you written?" she said through tears. "Did I do something to make you mad?"

She set the letter down and offered a small, quiet prayer. "Please keep him safe. Please let me hear something."

She headed to her mother's bedroom. It smelled like Francine, lilacs, and buttercream frosting. Her room was pretty, much the same as it had been Maybelle's whole life. Francine didn't change much after Robert died. The room still had the same flowery wallpaper, the heavy, dark furniture. She still kept two twin beds with a small lamp table in between and two bright quilts perfectly laundered and pressed on the beds.

Why should she have changed anything? "She likes it this way."

Francine did go through her father's things after he passed and ended up giving away his suits and work clothes. Maybelle wore his heavy shirts to the shipyard. It was fitting, after all, because he had worked there, too. A shipfitter and one of the best.

"And now it's my turn," Maybelle said with a deep breath. Bingo nosed his way into the room first and sat near the large cedar-lined closet.

46

As much as it pained her to think about it, she could rent out the room to shipyard workers. Men and women travelled miles and miles to work at Sun Ship, and many of them looked for beds to rent during the week. It would be something to look into, maybe next week. Or, she could move into the larger room. When Holden came home it would be swell to have more space and the large cedar closet. No, not yet. After the war.

"Here goes." Maybelle said. Tears threatened, but this time she talked them back. "Not now. Cry later. Just get this done."

Maybelle picked up the perfume from her mother's dresser. She sniffed it. *Chantilly.* It came in a small teardrop-shaped bottle with a tiny pink bow tied around the neck. It was packaged in a pink box, which opened in the front. Maybelle had given Francine the perfume that year for Christmas. Now what? Should she use it? Give it to Doris? Was it good for the war effort? Probably not. Not like her mother's nylons would be.

The war effort. Everything was for the war effort. There were times when Maybelle hated the war effort and this was one of them. Francine kept a photo of Maybelle and Holden on her dresser. Their wedding picture. Such as it was. Maybelle had wanted a grand wedding, to wear a flowing white gown. But there wasn't time. Instead her mother whipped together a pretty, floral print dress, and Doris helped her pick out a sweet hat with a wide brim. Holden wore his uniform. Maybelle thought he looked dashing. They were married at their church down the street. The same place where she just had Francine's funeral service. Maybelle held the picture. She would keep this, put it on her dresser.

Bingo whimpered, circled a spot a dozen or so times, and then settled down for a nap. "That's a good dog," Maybelle said.

She pulled open dresser drawers, removed the nylons that she would take to the collection bin, but left everything else in the drawers. It would all go to the needy. The only thing she found that wasn't an article of clothing was a small book of poems by

Elizabeth Barrett Browning. *Sonnets from the Portuguese.* Robert had given it to Francine. Maybelle remembered—for their tenth anniversary. Maybelle was only nine but remembered the moment well. She held the book to her heart. She would keep the poems also. But for now, she left it on the dresser.

Next, Maybelle opened the closet and a rush of cedar hit her nose. How she loved the smell. The odor meant clean and wholesome. The closet was large and contained most of her mother's clothes and a couple of boxes, and the large trunk could contain anything. Maybelle pulled the dresses from the rack and laid them neatly on the bed. She wouldn't use any of them. She'd give them all away. Next, she piled shoes on the bed. Same thing. Nothing she wanted. Then she pulled the trunk from the closet. It was heavier than she thought it would be.

"Now what on earth do you suppose she could have in here?"

Bingo, who had roused from his dreams for a minute, didn't seem interested at all.

"Long as it's not Daddy." Maybelle let go a nervous laugh. "What a terrible thing for me to say."

She flipped open the lid and more cedar odors escaped. "Well, look at all that."

The trunk was chock full of fabrics and tablecloths, small swatches of material, all different shapes and colors and designs. There was sewing materials including a large box of Coats & Clark threads. Packs of needles and a pair of scissors. Some of the material looked familiar—like dresses she had worn as a girl, an old christening dress, and a felt hat she couldn't figure out where it could have come from.

She dug deeper, setting the layers of stuff on the floor until she came across what seemed like nothing more than a raggedy piece of fabric maybe three feet by three feet made from patches and swatches of other materials. She did notice a piece of cloth she remembered as the blanket she used as a child, and some pieces of her father's shirts and old kitchen curtains.

"What in tarnation is this supposed to be?" She shook it out and inspected it more closely. "It's like she's making one big piece of material from all this little stuff."

Bingo let go a bark.

"I've never seen it before in my life." Maybelle turned it every which way, stopping when she came to a small square made from her baby blanket. She recognized the little white sheep appliquéd on to a pale blue background. Maybelle held it to her cheek. Tears threatened, and this time she let them flow.

"Oh, Mom, I think you were making this for . . . me, for Holden and me. At least I think it must be another quilt. What else could it be?"

She held it to her cheek and let her mother's memory seep into her like a warm mist. "Ahh, Mom. I bet this was next year's Christmas gift. You were making it in secret, probably while I was at the yard."

5

Maybelle folded the unfinished quilt and set it on the bed near her mother's clothes. "What am I going to do with it?" she asked Bingo. "I can't give it away. It has my baby blanket on it."

Bingo barked. Maybelle sat on the edge of the bed and touched her mother's clothes. "This is silly," she said after a moment. "I'll just find a box or even that silly old trunk and stash mom's stuff inside and take it all down to the church. They can divvy it all out as they see fit." For a moment, she felt like one of the paupers from *A Christmas Carol* selling off Scrooge's clothes.

But her eyes kept going to the quilt. At least she thought it was a quilt. Her mother made many quilts. The one on her bed and the one on Maybelle's bed were both hand-stitched by Francine. As a matter of fact, just about every house on Ninth Street, better known as Doctor's Row, had a quilt stitched by Francine. It was her way of giving back. She even paid old Doc Martin with a quilt for caring for her father right up until the end. There wasn't much money and Doc didn't want much, so Francine made him a quilt. She worked on it each and every night as Robert lay in the bed, dying.

Now, Maybelle wished she had paid more attention. But ever since the dreaded zipper-in-the-neck-hole incident, sewing, especially something as ambitious as a quilt, was the furthest thing on her list of things to do. "I'll just keep it like it is, Bingo."

Maybelle went back to the closet and looked around. All that was left was a hatbox on the top shelf. She pulled it down. It was full of hats. Churchy kinds of hats. The kind Francine wore every Sunday and little gloves, white, black, and even pink.

She would give the hatbox and its contents away. Doris might even be interested. Yes, she was pretty sure Doris would like the hats.

Maybelle knocked around the room a little while longer. She went through the lamp table drawer and didn't find anything too unusual or interesting, just a Bible and a small letter-writing pad. She went through her mother's jewelry box, really just a wooden box on the dresser. Francine didn't own much jewelry. Just a couple of gold chains and a rosary that Maybelle had no clue to its origins. Her mother was not Catholic. But still there they were, rosary beads.

Maybelle laughed. "Leave it to Mom."

And then, just as she was about to close the drawer she took a farther look and found a Valentine's Day card made out to Robert, but perhaps never received. Robert died just before Valentine's Day. Francine must not have had the heart to dispose of it. The card was shaped like a little Kewpie doll and read "I Love You from the Bottom of My Heart." Of course, the words "from the Bottom" were printed on the doll's little rear end. Maybelle thought it was cute and ever so fitting for her mom to give to her father.

Inside it was signed. "I'll love you forever, Francine."

"I love you forever, too, Mom," Maybelle said.

Soon, Maybelle felt tired and maybe even too sad to go on anymore with the chores. It was getting near quitting time at the shipyard, and she was hoping Doris would be by soon.

Again, the quilt came into view. Maybelle unfolded it and held it up. "I wish I could do something with it," she said. Bingo barked.

Maybelle heard the front door open. "I bet that's Doris. Come on, Bingo."

They headed downstairs and found Doris standing there holding a brown paper bag.

"Whatcha got there?" Maybelle asked.

"Ice cream. Vanilla and chocolate."

"Yum," Maybelle said. "Let's put it in the freezer."

Maybelle followed Doris into the kitchen. She opened the freezer door and set the ice cream inside.

"So, how's it going?" Doris asked.

"Okay. I worked in . . . in Mom's room. I'm thinking I should give most of her clothes away. Thought you might like to pick through her hats."

"Oh, sure," Doris said. "Gee, this seems a little ghoulish."

"Yeah, a little, but it's okay. I also found some other things."

"Like what?" Doris sat at the table. She picked at the ice cream.

"Well, when I opened her closet, I found this big old trunk. It was filled with all kinds of materials and scraps and sewing supplies."

"Yeah?"

Maybelle leaned against the refrigerator. "And what I think is the beginning of a new quilt."

"Really?"

"Yeah, it's kind of pretty. Made from different scraps and stuff, pieces of material and stuff from personal things, baby blankets, shirts, ties, that sort of thing."

"Oh, it sounds like a crazy quilt."

Maybelle smiled. "A crazy quilt?"

"Yeah, it's what they call them when they're made from lots of memorable stuff. Pretty sweet of her."

"I'll say. I think she might have been making it for Holden and me." Maybelle joined Doris at the table. "I don't know what to do with it now."

Doris smiled wide. "Finish it. I think you should finish it."

"What?" Maybelle said. "Finish it? You're pulling my leg, right?"

"No. I'm as serious as can be. Come on. Let's take a look at it."

"It's upstairs. In her room."

Maybelle followed Doris up the steps. Bingo still kept close to her heels.

"Gee," Doris said looking around. "I haven't been in here in a long time."

"Is it weird?"

"A little. Gee, she had some cute dresses." Doris looked through the dresses on the bed. "You should definitely give these away."

"I was gonna take them to church. I hear lots of folks go by there looking for food, handouts, that sort of thing."

"So where's the quilt?"

"In the trunk." Maybelle lifted the trunk lid and pulled out the unfinished quilt. She held it up.

"Oh, wow, it is a crazy quilt. Gee, look at all that work."

"It is pretty," Maybelle said. "But what do I do with it now?"

"You should finish it."

Maybelle laughed. "You're joking. Are you forgetting the zipper-in-the-neck-hole incident? I can't sew to save my life."

Doris laughed. "Sure, I remember. I was there. It was so funny. But this is special. It deserves to be finished."

Maybelle sat on the bed, holding the quilt in her lap. "I can't. I wouldn't even know where to begin."

"Try, you really should. You can't just toss it out or give it away or use it as blackout curtain."

"That's it," Maybelle said. "It's the perfect size to fit one of the living room windows."

"Maybelle. Don't you dare. You have to finish that quilt. For your mom."

"I don't know. I don't even know where to start and how to proceed."

"Look, you learned to weld seams in the shipyard. You can learn to sew seams at home. Start with something simple. Just make an easy square with something memorable on it, like one of Holden's stripes. I'm sure you got one or two lying around."

"I have one. But, isn't that against the law or something?"

"Nah, who would know? Just do it. Give it a go."

Bingo barked frantically. It was the same bark he used whenever Francine arrived home.

"It's like he knows," Doris said. "He knows you should finish it. He wants you to finish it." Doris patted his head. "He's a smart pooch. Come on, it'll give you something to do."

"Okay, okay. I'll give it a try. She has all those scraps of fabric in that trunk."

Doris moved toward the trunk. "I wonder why she kept it in the trunk."

"Like I said downstairs, I think she was hiding it. I'm thinking she had been working on it when I wasn't here. It might have been a gift, you know?"

"Of course," Doris said. "That's it. She was making it for you for Christmas, I'll bet."

Maybelle turned the quilt over. "Look, this square was made from my old baby blanket. And this is one of Dad's favorite shirts and this is a piece of Holden's coveralls from when he was working on the Plymouth."

Doris sniffed. "This is so sweet. You have to complete it now."

Maybelle picked up a floral print dress, yellow with pretty pink tea roses stamped on it. "Mom loved this dress. I was going to bury her in it but . . . but I couldn't stand the thought of it . . . you know."

"Use it in the quilt."

"You mean cut it up?"

Doris shrugged. "I guess. I mean what else? You could give it away but you'd never see it."

Maybelle felt her heart quicken, and for the first time in a long time, she felt a little excited about something. "I'll do it. I'll finish this quilt."

"Great," Doris said.

Maybelle took a breath. She ran her fingers over the square with Holden's shirt. "But . . . ah, this is stupid. I can't sew. I don't know the first thing about making a quilt."

"You can learn. And I'll help if you want and . . . we'll get it done."

Doris helped Maybelle bring the dresses downstairs. She found a large suitcase in a closet. They stuffed the dresses inside. "They can have the suitcase, too," Maybelle said.

Then Maybelle brought down the hatbox. Doris looked through them and fell in love with two. "Are you sure I should have them?" she asked.

"Sure," Maybelle said. "Mom would want you to."

Doris stood in front of the mirror near the dining room and placed one of the hats on her head. It was a deep burgundy color, made from something like felt, with a wide brim and looked like it could have fallen right off of Ingrid Bergman's head. Doris tilted it just so and let the wider part of the brim almost cover her left eye.

"You look very mysterious," Maybelle said.

"I do, don't I?" Doris said. "I could be a spy in this hat."

Maybelle laughed. It felt good to feel something other than grief, other than missing Holden. But it quickly passed and the same gnawing loneliness crept back.

"Say, I'm hungry," Doris said as though sensing Maybelle's sudden fall back into the doldrums. "Want to go to Mackey's for a sandwich?"

Maybelle sighed. "Mackey's? I don't know." She pushed a hand through her hair. "I don't think I want to see people. Not tonight."

"I understand that," Doris said, "but I'm hungry."

"We have ice cream. And I can make ham and cheese sandwiches."

"Sounds good," Doris said. She set the hat back in the box. "I'm gonna wear it Sunday to church."

"Come on," Maybelle said. "We still have ham and mustard."

"Got any Coca-Cola?"

Maybelle shrugged. "Not sure. Living with Roger you can never tell what will show up."

"He is a card, Roger is."

Maybelle took a ham from the fridge.

"Thin slices are best," Doris said.

"Okay, okay, thin as paper."

She assembled two sandwiches made with the last of her mother's bread. And believe it or not, she found cola hiding behind a large jar of something like relish or pickles in the refrigerator.

"Anything from Holden today?" Doris asked as she bit into her sandwich.

"No," Maybelle said. Tears threatened once again. "I just don't understand. I was getting a letter almost every day and now nothing for almost two weeks."

"Have you written to him?" Doris pulled a hard edge of the ham from her mouth and set it on the edge of her plate.

"Just a short note about Mom. But . . . it's been hard. I'm afraid if I send it the letter will hover around Germany for months and wind up in enemy hands."

"Never happen. I don't how they do it, but the army always finds the fellas. Even in the trenches they get mail."

"I guess, but I'm right here. Same place I've been for months and they haven't found me. No, there's a reason he hasn't written and—" Maybelle set her sandwich on the plate and looked into

Doris's eyes. "And I'm scared. Especially now. I keep thinking I'm all alone in the world." Tears threatened again. This time it was a mixture. A triple pack of tears for Francine and tears for Holden and tears for herself, missing Mom, missing Holden, and tears because she just couldn't seem to pull herself up and smile for longer than a few minutes.

Doris held Maybelle's hand. "I know. I also know it will get easier. You know too. Now let's break out the ice cream."

Maybelle heaved another sigh and set the unfinished sandwich aside. "Do you really think I can sew a quilt?"

Doris laughed a little. "No, at least not by yourself, but with my help and maybe some from other women at the yard you can. Besides, we're all in this together. We should work on it together."

Maybelle grabbed the two containers of ice cream from the freezer, hand-dipped by Hazel herself no doubt. Maybelle divvied it between two white bowls. "Ahh, I don't know. I can't sew to save my life. I'll just embarrass myself all over again."

"Look, winter is coming. It will give us something to do. It will help me, too, you know. I miss Mickey like gangbusters."

Maybelle looked at Doris. She was her best friend in all the world. She saw how much she missed Mickey. She could feel it in her chest and in her throat as a lump formed.

"All right. But remember, I haven't got any idea how to do this." It was now not just about finishing her mother's quilt, but also about helping Doris get through the long winter nights missing Mickey.

Doris clapped her hands once. "Good. Let's get started tonight."

6

Maybelle found it was easier to head back to the yard the next day. It was expected to be a good day as the yard Glee Club was going to be practicing for the upcoming fall concert. Maybelle was not a member of the chorus. Not only did sewing a straight seam elude her but also carrying a tune in the bathroom. But she always thought Doris should join. Doris could sing like an angel, as they say, although Maybelle wasn't quite sure how angels sounded.

Jeans with rolled-up cuffs and a light flannel shirt were, of course, Maybelle's standard issue when it came to work. She liked to wear Holden's flannels, the ones he wore when he worked on cars. She kissed his picture. "I'll write tonight, honey. I know you're out there. You just have to be."

Roger already had coffee percolating when Maybelle got to the kitchen.

"So," he said. "Feeling better? I saw the empty ice cream containers. I'm thinkin' you and Doris had a pretty big sweet tooth last night."

Maybelle nodded. "Yeah, I really am feeling better. I think having good friends close by is helping."

Roger smiled. "Eggs? I think we have four left, but I'm afraid the coffee is running out and now with . . . well, with your mom gone, rations will be tighter."

"Oh yeah, I didn't think about that. I guess all our rations will be less."

Roger poured Maybelle's coffee. "Don't sweat it. When you get the room rented out we'll do better."

"Oh yeah, I guess I better get on that. I have the room pretty much cleaned out."

"Good girl." Roger cracked the eggs into a frying pan. "Sunny-side up, for a sunny-side day."

"It's not sunny, Roger. Clouds moved in yesterday and haven't left. I bet it starts raining gangbusters any minute from the looks of it."

Roger dropped some ham slices into Bingo's bowl. He was most appreciative and wolfed them down. "You know, someone should invent food for dogs. You know, just for them. It could come in cans."

"Why don't you?"

Roger laughed. "Nah. Too much trouble. I'm just thinking it would be a good idea."

Maybelle poured milk into her cup and started thinking about renting the room. "I guess I could put a notice up at the yard."

"You could have two people resting comfortably by tonight, I betcha. I really do."

Maybelle snorted air out her nose. "I know. Hey, did you hear anything about a new defense order or something?"

"Yep, Roosevelt is ratcheting things up over there. We'll be busier than a one-armed paperhanger."

"Terrific." Maybelle looked into her coffee. "Means the war is going to last longer."

Roger flipped four fried eggs. "I know. I didn't mean to—"

"It's okay. Holden is fine. I know it now. He just hasn't had time to write. That's all." She stared out the kitchen window. The wind was moving the limbs of the oak. "At least that's what I'm choosing to believe."

"That's the ticket, kiddo," Roger said. "I bet you get a letter this morning."

After breakfast and Roger headed off to bed, Maybelle packed her lunch: tuna salad, an apple, and a small piece of apple pie. The last pie her mom baked.

She wrapped her rain scarf around her head, just in case, and checked the mail on her way to Doris's. Nothing. At least not from Holden. She let go a deep sigh, shoved the remaining mail back into the box, and headed off toward Doris's house. This time Doris was waiting on the stoop. This time, she was in blue jeans, but Maybelle could see the lace of her blouse collar peeking over her wool coat.

"Hey," Maybelle called. "What gives? You are on time!"

"Yeah, yeah," Doris said. "Don't get used to it."

Doris pushed open the wire gate. "I got two letters from Mickey this morning."

Maybelle shook her head. "Nothing. Again. I just don't get it. Do you think he's angry with me? Did I do something? Did he do something to me and feels too bad to let me know?" Maybelle swallowed. She didn't even want to think about that.

"How could you do anything to him? He's on the other side of the world hunting Nazis. I doubt there's much time for hanky-panky."

Maybelle and Doris crossed Morton Avenue. "Yeah, I guess you're right," Maybelle said.

The stream of people filing into the yard was always impressive. Maybelle felt proud to be among the newest of the women defense workers. She had read in the company monthly magazine, *Our Yard*, Sun now employed over two thousand women.

She punched in first at the time clock. They headed to their department and donned coveralls, already filthy from being worn so many times in a row. Doris somehow always managed to look good even in the thick, dark coveralls and work boots. Maybelle, on the other hand, felt and looked like a boy. But that was okay around the yard.

The two began work, dropping their welding shields over their faces. It was too hard to talk in the yard while working with all the noise. But the lunch whistle would blow soon and they could resume their gab.

Today, they were hard at work on repairing the hull of a T2 tanker ship. It wasn't a hard job but mighty necessary to the war effort. Maybelle had yet to get a chance to work on building a new ship, but with the added defense measure, she just might.

⚬⚬⚬

"I was thinking about the quilt," Doris said as she munched a nearly identical tuna salad sandwich as Maybelle's on toast. Toast was always a good way to use almost stale bread.

"The what?"

"The quilt," Doris repeated.

"Oh, oh, yeah." Maybelle moved back against the wall. On nice days, they often opted to have lunch outside along with many of the other workers. The view of the Delaware River when they could see it was actually nice. It was about a mile and half wide and deep enough to sail the huge, rugged tankers and battleships.

Maybelle and Doris could hear the Glee Club practicing from inside one of the buildings.

"They sound good," Doris said.

"Yeah, they sure do. I still think you should join."

"No thanks, I . . . I don't like singing in front of people. It's hard enough at church."

Maybelle swallowed and wiped tuna juice from her chin with a handkerchief. "Hey, did you sign up for the bowling league? The women's team needs more women."

"Oh, I don't know," Doris said. "I'm not very good."

"Well, then we're even. I'll teach you to bowl and you teach me to sew."

Doris nearly spit tuna across the yard. "Me? Bowling?"

"Sure," Maybelle said feeling almost lighthearted for the first time in nearly a week. "I'm sure the team would love to have you back."

Doris drank from a small bottle of juice. "Let me think about it." She looked Maybelle square in the eye. "Me? Bowling?"

A few minutes before the end-of-lunch whistle blew, Maybelle tossed her trash. "Listen, I'm heading over to the bulletin board. I want to post about the room. Roger says I could get renters pretty fast."

"Are you sure you're ready for that? I mean having strangers in your mother's room?"

Maybelle looked at the ground. For a moment, she saw her mom standing in front of the mirror above the dresser, admiring a new hat. Snippets of memory just kept popping up and Maybelle had to fight the grief as it swept through. "Sure. I think it's for the best. I'd rather the room have life in it than not."

"Okeydokey," Doris said. "Here, give me your can, I'll put it in the locker with mine."

Maybelle scribbled out a rental announcement on a small card provided for bulletin board notices inside the lunch room. "For rent," she wrote. "Two twin beds. One room. Women only. $6." Then she tacked it to the cork right next to the poster explaining how destructive loose lips can be to the war effort.

"You'll get takers by the end of the day," Logan, who seemed to have sneaked up behind her, said.

"Oh, Logan, you scared me," Maybelle said, holding her hand over her heart.

"Sorry. But I know two ladies who might want the room. They've been driving into the yard from West Chester and thought it'd be a good idea to rent for the winter months."

"Fine," Maybelle said, squinting into the bright sun as she looked up at Logan. "Have them come by."

"Will do. They're assigned to Wetherill, same as you. Welding tubes."

On her way to the kitchen to prepare dinner, Maybelle stopped in the dining room. It was where her mother had kept the sewing machine. Maybelle stared at the contraption. A horror in her mind, mocking her, egging her on. *Come on. Try me.*

Maybelle lifted the lid, exposing the black machine with the wheel and pulleys and the needle thing that bobbed up and down and sucked fabric under its foot like some maniacal, fabric-sucking monster. Memories of having pieces of material bunched and snagged in its grasp rushed back. And then, there was the zipper incident. She could see the day so plainly, the day she vowed to never, ever again attempt to sew. But now, she had no choice. She knew she couldn't let her mother down, or Doris or even Holden.

Bingo ambled by and sat on his rear. He seemed to smile and laugh as Maybelle touched the Singer. "It would be nice for Holden. He would be so proud of me if I actually did something like this."

Bingo barked. But Maybelle couldn't tell if it was a bark of warning or agreement.

"You'll see," Maybelle said. "I'll do it. I'll show them."

She rushed upstairs and threw open the lid of the trunk. She pulled out the quilt and a piece of fabric. She found an army private's stripe and thought she'd use that. With new determination,

Maybelle ran to the machine. She cut a square from an old, blue shirt. She found pins in a drawer and pinned the stripe to the square.

"See this, Bingo. Nothin' to it." Her voice cracked.

Maybelle sat at the machine. She remembered how to lift the foot. She saw thread peeking from under the pressure plate and gave thanks to God the machine was already threaded. What a nightmare it would have been. You needed the skill and deft fingers of a surgeon to adjust the wheel and the needle just to make it work.

Maybelle shoved the fabric under the foot. She dropped it down and started to pump the pedal. The fabric slipped through faster and faster as she pumped harder and harder until . . . as in days past, it bunched and snagged and knotted itself into a frenzy.

Maybelle sat back in the chair. She wanted to cry. She did cry because there was no way she could ever finish her mother's quilt.

Bingo dropped his head onto her lap. Maybelle patted him. "I'm just no good at this. No good at all." She ripped the fabric from the monster's jaws. "I can't do it." Maybelle replaced the lid on the machine. "Wieners," she said. "I can boil wieners for dinner. At least I can do that much."

Maybelle heaved a great sigh and went softly into the kitchen. Just as she said she would, she prepared wieners with baked beans for supper. It was easy. Francine usually fixed more elaborate suppers involving preparation, mashing, and mixing. And it wasn't as if Maybelle couldn't cook at all. She could when she wanted to. It was just not one of her favorite things to do and, unlike Francine, Maybelle worked over forty hours a week at Sun.

She boiled four wieners she picked up at the butcher on the way home and set a pot of already prepared Bird's Eye Baked Beans on the stove. There wasn't an ounce of bread left in the house, but there was still a little pie—enough for her and Doris.

Maybelle set the kitchen table with the usual white dishes and two cups for coffee. She snagged the bag of A&P coffee from the cabinet. There wasn't much left, and she wouldn't be able to purchase more until the following week. So, she opted for water with dinner instead. Doris would understand.

But much to Maybelle's delight, Doris appeared at the back door holding a bag of coffee. "I remember you were practically out," Doris said. "And I really would love a cuppa coffee."

"You are a lifesaver," Maybelle said. "I only have enough for tomorrow morning."

"That's what I thought. I wish I had more to give, but living by myself I don't have much."

Doris looked into the pots on the stove. "Oh boy, wieners and beans."

"Have you thought about renting your extra bedroom? I put a notice up for the front room. Logan saw me. He said he was sending two women over."

"Good for you. But no, I don't think I could stand having strangers in the house. I kind of like being by myself."

Maybelle got the coffee going and served the dinner, much to Doris's delight. "I just love wieners," she said. "And these beans? Already prepared for you. We live in a great time."

"Yep, just dump them in the pot. No more soaking, baking." Maybelle took a bite. "And they're tasty. I couldn't tell the difference between these and the ones my mother slaved over for two days."

Doris chuckled. "Yeah, but I wouldn't tell her that."

Maybelle had turned the radio on, so the girls enjoyed listening to the big band music filtering into the kitchen.

"We should go to New York sometime," Doris said. "Go to one of them fancy clubs they got up there to actually see Glenn Miller or maybe even that new guy Perry . . . something."

Maybelle set her chin on her fist. "Como. Perry Como. Yeah, that would be fun. Maybe when the boys get back. We'll make it a date, you know, a coming-home surprise."

"Let's do it."

After their meal, Maybelle and Doris brought coffee into the living room.

"So where's the trunk?"

"Upstairs and you can just forget about it," Maybelle said. "I ain't doin' it. No way. No how."

"Hold on," Doris said. "You have to do it. Remember? For your mom. For Holden. And . . . and for me."

"I can't. I tried to sew on the stupid machine before you got here and got the thing all knotted up and twisted. I ruined a perfectly good piece of shirt and one of Holden's stripes and I . . . just can't."

Maybelle set her cup on a small table. "Who told you to do that?"

"Me. I told me to do it. I saw the machine sitting there. It was like it was calling me. Daring me to do it. So I tried and failed and that's it. That's just it."

"Come on, Maybelle, I won't let you quit. I'm going to help. And besides, not everything is done on the machine. There's some hand-sewing involved in quilting."

And the thought made her stomach hurt. "Really. With a needle and thread? Me? I can't sew straight. I tried."

"You'll try again. Now let's get the trunk down and start going through the swatches and fabrics your mother was collecting. I bet she picked them for some good reasons."

Maybelle finished her coffee. "Yeah, Mom was sentimental like that. But, really. I can't do this."

"Let me try to help you. Just try—with me."

Maybelle looked in Doris's eyes. She could see Doris was sincere. "You really think you can help me?"

"Yep. Who taught you how to smoke? Dance?"

"You."

"Okay, then. I can also teach you to sew."

"I might need help lugging the trunk down the stairs," Maybelle said.

"Now that's good news. Come on. We'll get started right away. I bet we have the whole thing finished by Thanksgiving."

They managed to strong-arm the large trunk down the steps without damaging the walls or floors, and there it sat in the middle of the living room.

"It looks like Noah's Ark," Maybelle said.

"No, no, it's not so big. It's big enough, but don't think about it. Think about all the memories it holds and how you're going to honor all those memories in one spectacular quilt."

Maybelle swallowed and nearly choked. "Where do we start?"

"We make squares."

"Squares? Well yeah, I tried that. I cut a square and then tried to sew a stripe on it."

"Good, but it's a little more involved. Crazy quilts are all about combining fabrics to make the square."

"How do we make squares from this pile of mismatched pieces and shapes?"

"I'll show you. It's what makes a crazy quilt so pretty. We cut these irregular pieces of fabric and sew them together until we have a square big enough to add to the quilt."

Maybelle shook her head, not understanding how it could work. "And how do we cut irregular shapes of cloth?"

"Look." Doris picked up a piece of cloth. "I'll cut this into a . . . what do they call them, eight sides?"

"An octagon."

"Yeah, that's it. I'll cut this octagon and then you start adding fabric to it until it's square. Watch me. I'll make the first one. But first let me try and undo what you did with this one."

Maybelle's heart sank. "See, I told you. I said I can't sew."

Doris ripped stitches from Maybelle's mess. "Look, it's not so bad. You just forced the fabric. Let the machine do some of the work."

Maybelle took a deep breath. "I'll try but—"

"But nothing." She unraveled the square and handed it back to Maybelle. "You'll get it this time."

"There is one of my father's old ties," Maybelle said pointing to a piece of gray cloth.

"Ah, that's sweet. And this is more of your baby blanket."

"Right."

Doris cut and sewed seams together until in just a few minutes she had a piece big enough to cut an eight-inch square from. "See that's all there is to it. Then we sew the squares together to form the top of the quilt."

"Oh, I see. I think I get it," Maybelle said. She held Doris's finished square. "It's pretty."

"Now, you do the next one."

Maybelle felt beads of sweat form on her brow. "Really? Already?"

"Sure. Go ahead. I'm here to catch you."

Maybelle looked at the sewing machine. It seemed like a fierce animal, ready to snap her fingers off if she went near. "I don't know how to do it."

"You just watched me."

"That's different. Watching and doing are two entirely different things."

Doris went to the machine. "Come on, I'll show you," Doris said. "Now watch closely. I'll make this seam."

"Wish we were welding it together. That I could do."

"Wait, that's great," Doris said. "Think of it as though you are welding a seam on the hull of a ship, only you are using a sewing machine instead of a blowtorch."

Maybelle laughed. "Do you know how silly you sound?"

The music of Bing Crosby drifted around the room.

"He has such a clear, perfect voice," Maybelle said.

"You're stalling. Come on. One seam."

"Okay, okay. I'll try."

Maybelle sat at the machine.

Doris stood over her. "Oh, wait. It's out of bobbin thread. We have to refill the bobbin."

Maybelle looked at the machine. "The what? This?" She pointed to the needle.

"No, the bobbin, it's that little round thing under the pressure plate."

"Oh, well the needle is bobbin' up and down."

"Don't be so silly."

Doris slid open the foot plate and removed the empty bobbin. She looked at it and then at Maybelle. "Maybe I should do this."

Maybelle happily relinquished her seat. "Be my guest. Refill the bobbin. Do you just wind the thread around it?"

"Kind of except it would take forever. The machine does it."

Doris sat at the machine and expertly filled the bobbin and threaded the needle. "There. All set."

Maybelle was amazed at the skill her friend had. "You make it look easy."

"Because it is easy. Once you know what you are doing."

"Just because you know how to do something doesn't necessarily mean you're good at it. I mean, I might know the right keys to play on the piano, but I will never be Mozart."

Doris rolled her eyes. "Okay, fine. You'll never be Mozart, but you can sew a simple quarter-inch seam."

Maybelle sat at the machine. Doris gave her the square with a piece of fabric pinned to its edge. "Now I already pinned the front side together, a quarter-inch seam."

Maybelle laughed. "Okay. Here I go."

"Not too fast," Doris said. "Don't work the pedal too fast. Just nice easy pumps."

She stepped on the machine pedal, and the machine came to life. It sucked the fabric into it. Maybelle did her best to hang on and guide the fabric as it passed under the bobbing needle.

"Not too hard, I said. Remember, let the machine do some of the work."

Maybelle did her best, but the fabric went a little cockeyed and crooked. Her seam was not very straight.

"Okay, good job," Doris said. "Let's keep going. It will get easier."

Maybelle held up the two pieces of material she just seamed. "It's crooked."

Doris snatched it from her hand. "Yeah, it's pretty bad. Let's rip it out and do it again."

Maybelle flopped into a dining room chair nearly toppling it over. "It's futile. Impossible. I'll never learn to sew."

"You learned to weld. You can learn to sew. This is your first seam. You just went too fast. You have to slow down. Come on, try again."

"Okay, okay." Maybelle watched Doris rip the seam out. She swallowed. "That hurts."

Doris laughed and handed the two now-separated pieces of fabric back. "Now, right sides together. Pin it and sew it. Straight this time."

Maybelle sighed. "I'll try, but I ain't promising nothing."

But Maybelle never made it to the machine. She had just pinned the last pin when the doorbell rang.

Maybelle looked at the clock on the mantel. "It's nearly eight o'clock. Kind of late for callers."

"It is kind of a strange time for people to stop by," Doris said.

Bingo barked twice and rushed to the door where he stood like a sentry, just in case.

"Yeah." Maybelle shook her head. "Unless it's those girls Logan was sending over inquiring about the room. Yeah, I'll bet it's them."

"Oh, right," Doris said. "It must be the girls."

Maybelle went to the door. "It's okay, boy," she said, patting Bingo's head. "You can relax." The dog sat on his haunches, still close enough to handle any danger.

But instead of looking into the shiny faces of two young women, she was looking into the grimace of a man in uniform.

"Oh, dear," Maybelle said. "I . . . I was expecting . . . can I help you, sir?" She swallowed. Hard.

The man removed his hat and tucked it under his arm. "I have a telegram, ma'am."

7

Maybelle gripped the telegram. Her hand shook so hard she didn't think she could even read it as tears rushed to her eyes and her mind jumped to the most dire of conclusions. This was too much. Too soon. She just lost her mother and now . . .

All she could do was stand in the front entryway, hold the yellow envelope, and shake like the last leaf on an autumn maple tree. Army telegrams could only mean one thing.

Doris, who had sidled quietly next to Maybelle, slipped the envelope from Maybelle's fingers. "I'll read it. Don't panic. Yet. Let's see what it says." She took Maybelle's hand and led her to the sofa where they sat close together. Doris took a deep breath as she opened the envelope. She read:

> THE SECRETARY OF WAR DESIRES ME TO EXPRESS HIS DEEP REGRET THAT PRIVATE HOLDEN KAZINSKI HAS BEEN REPORTED MISSING IN ACTION SINCE TWO OCTOBER IN GERMANY IF FURTHER DETAILS OR OTHER INFORMATION ARE RECEIVED YOU WILL BE PROMPTLY NOTIFIED

Maybelle gasped. The room seemed to go black for a second as a tremendous pressure fell on her chest. She slumped into Doris's arms as sobs so deep and so hard surfaced from her stomach and her heart. Bingo kept close and every so often let out a soft, doggy whimper.

Doris stroked Maybelle's hair. "It's all right. It's going to be okay. They'll find him. They'll find him."

Waves of anxiety filled Maybelle as she pulled away from her friend and looked into her soft eyes. Maybelle worked to collect her thoughts. To put a sentence together.

"Missing? What does that mean? Is he lost? Is he dead? Where is he?"

"He's not dead," Doris said. "I think the telegram means he hasn't reported to anyone. They're not sure where he is, or he hasn't returned from some duty or assignment or whatever they call it. It can be awfully confusing over there, don't you think? What with bombs and bullets and men running for cover and . . ." She stopped talking as Maybelle's crying grew harder. And Bingo's whimpering increased.

"I'm sorry," Doris said. "I was stupid. I just meant it in a good way. They'll find him. You'll see." Doris pulled Maybelle closer. "It's okay. Shhhhh. Holden is okay."

"But . . . but how can you be sure?"

"Because we have to be sure. We have to believe Holden is safe and warm and out there. Alive. And because I refuse to believe God will let Holden go missing like this and not be found. God knows precisely where all His sheep are, every second of every day."

Maybelle took a deep, shaky breath. "But . . . but he could be dead. Couldn't he? They just can't find his . . . body." Maybelle stood. Her hands still shook. "He could be lying in a ditch somewhere and they can't find him. He could be injured and unable to move or find help. Oh, Doris." Maybelle slumped in Doris's arms again. "I'm scared. Not Holden. Not my Holden."

"I know you're scared. But you have to believe. You must, more than ever now, think positive, think good thoughts, and pray with every ounce of your being. I will also."

Maybelle lifted her head. She swiped tears away. "I . . . but . . . I know you are right. But . . . how? How does this happen?"

The two friends sat close for a few more minutes. Maybelle tried to find words, but there were none. Only a black hole filled with missing . . . missing Holden and questions.

The radio blared war news. The words felt like an assault. She had heard too much.

"Shut up," she cried. She tossed a book from the coffee table at the radio. "Just shut up with all your news."

Doris finally stood. She turned the radio off. "I know in my heart." She tapped her chest. "In here. I know he is not dead. He's probably on some secret mission. He will be okay."

Maybelle swallowed. "I'm hating this, Doris. I hate not knowing stuff."

"I know. I . . . can only imagine what I'd be thinking if it was Mickey in that telegram. But . . . but . . . I hope I wouldn't give up, though, you know. I hope I could be positive as hard as it can be. For Mickey."

Maybelle pulled a hankie from her pocket and blew her nose. "You're right. For Holden." She stood and moved near the mantel. "I don't know what to do. Am I supposed to do something?"

Doris shook her head. "No. You keep doing what you've been doing. That's all any of us can do. You keep doing what you've been doing until you hear otherwise."

Maybelle looked at the trunk overflowing with oddly shaped fabric pieces and the half-finished quilt. "Well, I'll tell you one thing. I'm not working on some stupid quilt anymore." All of a sudden, sewing a quilt seemed trivial and silly in the face of such an overwhelming time. Sewing a stupid old quilt would not bring Holden home.

Doris picked up the quilt and shook it out. "Yes, you are."

"What?" Maybelle practically screamed. "You can't be serious. My husband has gone missing and you want to make a quilt?"

Doris ran her palm across the smooth fabric. "It's the one thing you have to do. I think it's more important than ever for you to finish this quilt."

Her knees buckling, Maybelle sat on the couch. "Why? Why should I do this? I . . . I can't possibly learn to sew anything right now. Besides, it seems wrong somehow. Why should I do something like this, something that should be fun while Holden is . . . could be . . . anywhere."

Doris shook her head so hard, Maybelle thought it might fly off her neck. "You are going to do it for Holden, and with each square we make we'll stitch a prayer, good thoughts for Holden. Just think about the two of you snuggling into it on a frozen winter night. Who knows what will happen?" She smiled. "It's what you do."

"Oh, stop," Maybelle said. "Holden and me never needed any prompting for . . . that."

Doris laughed. "Ha, because you were only married two weeks before he shipped—" she stopped. Maybelle had burst into tears again. "But listen," Doris continued. "You are already thinking more pleasant thoughts. It's what this quilt will do for you. It's already working. "

Maybelle struggled to catch her breath. It could have been a walrus sitting on her chest, but Maybelle knew it was only sadness and fear. How in the world could a quilt, a mixed-up crazy quilt, lift a walrus off her chest? She still shook her head. "I . . . I just don't know."

Bingo dug his snout into the trunk and lifted a piece of cloth, purple with small white flowers on it. He seemed to smile as he held it gently in his mouth.

Doris dropped the quilt into the trunk. "Alright, alright, I'm sorry," Doris said. "But I thought you were made of tougher stuff than this. But if you want to give up, sit around the house, and wallow in pity and remorse then I can't stop you, but—"

Maybelle stood and pulled herself up to her full height. "All right already, geez Louise."

Doris smiled at Bingo. "Look, even Bingo thinks it's a good idea."

Maybelle patted the dog's head. "It's okay, boy, I get the idea. You can drop it." The dog left the fabric in the trunk and sauntered back to the hearth.

"I don't want to watch you sink into some awful state . . . I love you too much. God loves you too much. And Holden? He needs your strength now more than ever. Don't give up on him."

Maybelle pulled the quilt out of the trunk. She lightly touched the material with the tips of her fingers. For a moment, she thought she could hear her mother's voice whispering in her ear. *Don't give up.*

"A quilt, huh," Maybelle said. "A silly old quilt is gonna get me through this?"

"Yep." Doris pursed her lips as though she wanted to say more but thought better of it. "Stitch by stitch," she added after a moment. "We'll put a prayer on every square, every patch, every seam and stitch."

Maybelle couldn't hold back and cried. "What would I do without you?"

"Nothing. That's what you'd do and I can't abide that." Doris hugged her friend again. "Listen, we'll keep adding to the quilt and adding to it until Holden comes marching through the door. I don't care if it's twenty feet square."

Maybelle laughed. "Now that's a deal. We could end up with the world's biggest quilt."

"Yep," Doris said. "Or better yet, we could end up making a nice, regular-size quilt."

Tears stung Maybelle's eyes. "That would be better. A nice small quilt." She ran her palm over the material. "I can almost feel Mom's heartbeat in this."

"Now, I'm gonna cry," Doris said. "But hey, how about some tea? We should have tea."

Maybelle touched her stomach. "Tea?"

"And toast. With jelly. Doesn't that sound like a nice snack?"

Maybelle smiled even though everything inside her wanted to scream. Wanted to scream and tell Doris to go home. But she didn't. Doris was right. She couldn't give in to her feelings. "It does sound good. And I think Roger got that old toaster working."

Doris took Maybelle's hand. "Good. Come on. I'll put the pot on to boil. You get the toast."

"You know," Maybelle said as they made their way to the kitchen. "Food is not the answer to all life's troubles."

"Sure it is," Doris said.

Maybelle placed one slice of bread into the old toaster. It was an odd contraption with a kind of door, about bread-slice size, which dropped down. The idea was to put the bread on the door and then lift it into place against two wire grills. They got so hot they smoked and sometimes burned the bread.

"Now keep an eye on it," Doris said.

"I know, I know," Maybelle said. "I might not be able to sew, but I can work this old toaster machine. My mother said it was her mother's. It's positively ancient."

Doris set two cups and saucers onto the table. "This is nice."

"It is nice," Maybelle said as she watched smoke drift from the toaster. "The trick is to know when just the right amount of smoke is escaping. Then you open it up and hopefully have a perfectly toasted piece of bread."

A few seconds later, Maybelle opened the door and the slice of toast dropped onto the table. "Look at that," she said. "Just right."

Doris sat at the table. "Yeah, but can you do it again?"

Fortunately, Maybelle was able to repeat the toasty trick three more times, and she and Doris each had two nice slices of toast, ready for a small pat of butter and a nice helping of jam—strawberry. Maybelle loved the little jelly condiment set her mother used. She had just purchased it less than a month ago with the pennies and nickels she had been saving. It was glass with little strawberries painted on it and sat on a little glass saucer rimmed in red. For some reason, jam straight from the jelly jar always tasted better than the stuff from the canning jar. It probably wasn't true, but Maybelle would swear to it.

Strawberry had always been Maybelle's favorite, even though it was getting hard to come by. "You know," she said, still chewing her toast, "I wonder if the folks who write the magazine down at the plant would be interested in our quilt. They can write it up in the next edition."

"You mean *Our Yard*? The shipyard magazine?" Doris licked jam off her fingers.

"Yeah, they print stuff all the time about the Glee Club and the bowling leagues and the guys who go fishing. Why not our Crazy Quilt? They love stuff about our boys in Europe. We can tell them all about Holden and, who knows, maybe word will get to Washington and someone will do something to get Holden home."

Doris slapped her knee. "I don't know if it will get that far. I doubt any high muckety-mucks in the White House read *Our Yard*. But I think it's a great idea." Doris spread more jam on what was left of her toast. "I actually think you're getting the spirit." Doris wiped a splotch of jam from Maybelle's cheek with her thumb. "When life lays ya an egg, you make toast."

Maybelle smiled. She wasn't quite sure what Doris meant, but it sounded like just the appropriate thing to say. "Right." Maybelle finished her tea. But just as she thought she might be feeling a smidgen better, tears welled in her eyes. "I hate this," she cried. "Where is he?"

Doris patted her hand. "For now we are going to believe that Holden is fine. Now, come on, walk me to the door. I better get home."

Maybelle spied the telegram on the coffee table. She picked it up and read the terrifying words again. "How can a soldier just go missing?" Maybelle fell into the couch.

"Oh, now, try not to get yourself all sad and worried again." Doris sat next to her. "Think positive, remember?"

"But Holden? He—" she swiped tears. "He has such a good sense of direction. He can drive anywhere, walk anywhere. How in the world did he get lost?"

Doris patted Maybelle's knees. "Remember? We decided to believe he's not lost. He's hiding or on a secret mission."

Maybelle blew her nose into a yellow hankie she pulled from her pocket. "Maybe."

The two friends sat silently together for a few minutes until the front door swung open. It was Roger home from the yard. His hand was bandaged with white gauze.

"Hey, girls," he said.

"Hey," Doris said. "What happened to you?"

"Welding splatter," Roger said. "Burned pretty bad. I had just slipped my glove off when I got caught in someone else's way. But I'll be okay. They sent me home early though. Can't beat that."

"Oh, dear," Doris said. "It happened to me last year. Nasty. Those burns hurt."

Maybelle sniffed back tears and blew her nose again.

Roger stood in the middle of the living room. "Hey, it's not that bad. I'll live."

Maybelle looked up at him for a second and then back at the telegram. She pushed hair from her eyes now stinging with tears.

"She ain't crying about you," Doris said. She pointed to the telegram still in Maybelle's hand.

"Is . . . is that what I think it is?" Roger asked. "I'm so sorry. Here I am shooting off—oh, sorry, thumping my gums when you got—"

"Holden is missing in action," Doris said. "For almost the whole month."

Roger moved closer to Maybelle. "Ah, gee, kid, I'm sorry. But . . . keep your chin up. It's not always bad news. He'll show up. Probably lost in a cornfield or holed up in someone's house nursing a broken ankle." Roger winced and held his bum arm. "Don't you worry your pretty little head. He'll come home, wagging his tail behind him."

Maybelle cracked a brief smile. "Thanks, Roger."

"We'll all be praying. God knows exactly where Holden is," Doris said. "I'm gonna tell the pastor."

Maybelle sighed. "Fat lot of good that'll do. But . . . go ahead."

"Hey," Roger said. "It certainly can't hurt. And since when have you been down on God?"

"Yeah," Doris said. "You cut that out. God knows exactly where your husband is. And He's gonna take good care of him. You'll see."

Maybelle wished she could disappear. Just snap her fingers and disappear into thin air or melt into the couch cushion. She hadn't stopped believing in God; it was just God's timing seemed to stink. First, she lost her mother unexpectedly, and now, not a month later, Holden goes missing and could be dead in a ditch. It's why she was upset.

"Well, ain't God big enough to know I'm angry with Him?" Maybelle blurted out like she was a little kid. She did resist an urge to pout. "It's not fair."

"Life is not fair," Doris said. "But we can't stop believing God is taking care of it. It's all under His reign."

Maybelle shook her head. "Then I just pray God will find Holden, and really quick. I hate not knowing."

"I'm with you there," Roger said. "It's the not knowing that's the worst."

Doris rested her hand on Maybelle's knee. "We're all in this with you, kiddo. God's got Holden right in the palm of His hand."

Maybelle cracked a weak smile. If only she could be as certain as Doris. She shook her head. "I hope you're right."

Roger rubbed his stomach. "You know what? I'm hungry, and this burned wing is starting to throb a bit. What's for supper? Maybe I can kill the pain with some lamb stew. Got any lamb stew?"

"Oh," Maybelle said. "I didn't expect you home and sorry, no lamb stew. There's still some baked beans left, though. There's still two wieners in the pot. That's about it. We ate the last of the pie."

"Wieners it is," Roger said.

Roger headed into the kitchen whistling as he went.

"He's such a nice guy," Doris said.

"Yeah," Maybelle said. "He really is. I wonder why he's not married."

"Uhm," Doris said. "It is a wonder."

Maybelle watched a gleam enter Doris's eyes. "Uh-oh, are you thinking about matchmaking?"

"Maybe," Doris said. She snapped her fingers. "You know who'd be perfect for him?"

"Who?"

"Sally Farnsworth."

"The clock checker? Really? She's a little scrawny, don't you think? And those thick glasses?"

"Yeah, she's cute as a bug in a rug and sweet as can be. And smart as a whip. I think Roger needs a smart woman."

"That's true. Roger does need a keeper in some ways, but *Sally?* She's so persnickety and . . . don't you think she takes her job too seriously?"

"So, she likes everything to be exact, right down to the last second. I hear she gets the time from Washington, DC, every morning. That's why she's a good clock checker. She keeps them all on time, so we get paid what we're entitled."

"I know. But Roger and Sally?" Maybelle glanced off into the distance. "I don't know."

Doris picked up the quilt and folded it. "I think we've had enough lessons for one night. We'll pick it up again tomorrow."

Maybelle yawned. "Yeah, weren't you on your way home when Roger came in?"

"Yep, but that's okay. I'll just see you in the morning."

Maybelle's hands started to shake again, but this time she willed them to stop. Shaking like a leaf would not bring Holden home. "Okay, I'll see you tomorrow. I'm tired, too, and I don't have to tell you that it's been a rough evening."

Doris hugged Maybelle. "I know." She paused a moment. "Say, do you want me to stay the night? I hate the thought of you sitting up all night worrying and crying and staring at Holden's picture and reading that telegram over and over."

Maybelle shrugged. "But I think that's what I'm going to do. I doubt I'll sleep a wink, and I hate that I'd be keeping you up, too." Maybelle glanced toward the kitchen. "And besides, Roger is here. He won't let me tumble over the deep end."

Doris yawned this time. "Okay, as long as you're sure." She pulled Maybelle close for another hug. "It will get easier, you'll see. And please try and get some sleep. Maybe some warm milk."

"Okay. It might help."

Doris shook her head. "Nah, I know you too well. You are gonna sit up all night trying to figure out how you can get to Europe and go find him yourself."

This time Maybelle chuckled. "I hadn't thought of it but—"

"Now don't be silly. Your place is right here at home and at the shipyard. You let God find him. He will."

"Okay, you better get on home," Maybelle said.

"Think about Roger and Sally and how we can get them together." Doris picked up her handbag. "Now look, I'm gonna go straight home, take a bath, and go to bed. I'll see you in the morning. And I will say a prayer for Holden. I know he's out there."

"Okay," Maybelle said, feeling her spirits deflate once again.

Doris stood on the porch. The winds had definitely picked up. It was downright cold. "Glad I wore my coat." She looked at Maybelle who was standing in the doorway. "Promise me you won't get yourself in a bad way over this. Holden is safe."

"Okay." Maybelle said when she heard a tremendous clang coming from the kitchen.

"Oh dear," Maybelle said. "Roger. Sounds like he dropped some pots. I hope he didn't hurt his arm even more."

Doris shook her head. "I'll let you deal with him. I'm going home."

8

Maybelle sought every excuse she could to keep from heading off to bed. She let Bingo out and watched from the back door as he went about his nightly routine including rooting out a raccoon from behind the back hedges and getting his snout clawed. And Roger was as good as any reason to linger in the kitchen. She sat with him for a good, long time. She poured him a glass of milk and got his supper for him.

"Thanks for doing this," he said. "I guess these burns are more trouble than I thought."

"You're welcome," she said as she dumped what was left of the beans onto his plate. "We haven't any bread left."

"Rats," Roger said. "It was one thing when your mom was around. She always had bread."

Maybelle felt the hairs on the back of her neck rise up. "Well, I am so sorry," she said with more than a tinge of annoyance. "I'm not my mother." Maybelle slammed the pot onto the stovetop. Bingo let go a loud bark, obviously not accustomed to displays of frustration. Maybelle leaned over the stove feeling steam rise, not from the kettle but from her brain.

"Hey, you," Roger said. "I didn't mean anything by it. I'm sorry."

Maybelle hung her head. She really wasn't angry at Roger. And it was true. When Francine was alive, there was always bread. "Look, I'm sorry. I guess I'm a little on the edge." Bingo stood near her, as close as he could. "And what you said reminded me of things, and not just about Mom, but other things like Holden and the fact I am pretty much a useless lump when it comes to anything domestic."

Roger set his fork on the plate. "I'm sorry, kiddo. But look, first of all"—he chewed a piece of wiener and swallowed—"you are not a useless lump. You're your way. And that stuff about Holden? Yeah, well it is tough news. Your husband's gone missing. But he'll come home. You'll see. And in the meantime, we buy bread. Not a problem."

Bingo barked probably just to make sure they knew he was there.

"Right," Maybelle said. Once again, all the domestic stuff seemed to bite her right in the throat. She'd never learn to bake bread, make cookies like Francine, or even sew a straight seam. What good was she? But she swallowed her feelings. "Thanks. I know you're right. It's just that . . . oh, never mind."

Maybelle looked at Roger. The pain from Roger's splatter burns was obviously bothering him. "Let me get you an aspirin for the pain."

"Thanks, it would help. Maybe two. Can you take two aspirin?"

"Yeah, you're a big guy."

Francine had always kept the aspirin in the cabinet with the water glasses—easy access. No running upstairs when a headache struck. She dropped two aspirin into Roger's palm and filled a glass with cold water.

Roger smiled and swallowed the medicine.

"I guess I should get to bed," Roger said. "I'll clean up the pots and dishes in the morning, if you want me to."

Maybelle smiled. "No, I'll do it. You got that bum wing."

Roger stood. He kissed her cheek. "You know, you're like a sister to me," he said. "So it's kind of like my brother is missing. But, he'll be okay. We have to believe that. I'm right here with you."

"Thank you, Roger," Maybelle said. "It means a lot."

Roger excused himself and headed off to bed but not before Maybelle remembered. "Hey," she called to him. "I might have the front room rented real soon, so don't be surprised if you see two strange women walking around the house."

Roger stood between the dining room and kitchen. "Good to hear. And besides, I'm used to strange women walking around the house." He smiled a sheepish smile. "I'll be sure and get more milk and coffee from now on."

"And chocolate," Maybelle said as sneaky tears welled in her eyes.

"Of course, chocolate," Roger said. "Good night."

Maybelle straightened the kitchen for the morning while Bingo slept nearby. She washed the pots and put them away. The dishes she washed but left them to air dry on a towel on the counter. She paused a moment before shutting off the kitchen light. She would give anything, absolutely anything to be slipping off to bed with Holden now.

"Come on, Bingo, let's go to bed. At least I have you."

———————

Maybelle sat on the edge of the bed, still in her street clothes, in the darkened bedroom holding the telegram. Only a single dim bulb burned in the lamp on the nightstand. She kept reading it, hoping maybe she had read the wrong words, that maybe it was saying Holden was found safe and unhurt, or reading it slowly, wishing the words would change into the words she wanted to read. But no, the words always read the same. She must have read them a dozen times, maybe three dozen times. Missing in action. Missing in action.

As the clock struck eleven thirty, Maybelle thought she had better try and get some sleep, if not sleep, then at least some rest. But changing into her nightgown seemed like almost too much of a chore. Now she carried the weight of missing her mother and missing Holden, but in a new and scary way. She missed him when his letters were still arriving, but at least she knew he was alive.

Maybelle set the telegram on the nightstand and took Holden's portrait. She held it to her heart and then her cheek hoping she could feel the love she knew he had for her. Listening for his voice, remembering some of the last things he had said to her, like "Chin up, darling." And "I'll be home soon, I promise."

As long as she could still hear his voice and remember how much he loved her she could believe Holden was alive and simply lost as they said, lost like she got lost on her way to Cape May, New Jersey. That's it. It's all it meant. Holden was only lost, not gone.

Maybelle took a deep breath and found enough renewed energy to change into her nightgown and robe thinking Holden was merely lost. The room was cold. War meant rations. Rations for everything, including heating fuel, coal. It was still too early in the season to turn the heat on. She'd wait until the last possible moment to switch on the boiler. This she had learned from her mother who could squeeze every last bit out of her ration stamps. Francine knew exactly what to buy, when to buy it, and how to use it. Maybelle could learn. Sure she could. And how proud would Holden be when he arrived home to discover that Maybelle had become such a confident woman.

She washed her face with ice-cold water, brushed her teeth, and went back to the lonely bedroom. She retrieved Holden's last letter from the bedside table and read it again and again until she couldn't see through her tears anymore. It was one thing to ration coal and butter. But tears? No, she would cry as many tears as when wanted, when she wanted. After all, God had them counted and would turn them off when He was good and ready.

Bingo, who had been waiting patiently for Maybelle to finish her bedtime routine, jumped onto her bed. She would let him sleep there tonight. His big head rested on her lap as she sobbed. "I miss Mom. I need Holden to be all right," she cried. "And I can't sew!"

Bingo whimpered. Maybelle could feel the pooch's unwavering devotion as she rubbed his head. "You're a good dog, Bingo." Bingo looked up at her, and Maybelle could see the sadness. She was convinced that her dog could feel emotion, and Bingo understood something was terribly, terribly wrong. And he would stay by her side as long as necessary.

"He'll come home," she said. "Right, boy? We have to think good thoughts. Positive thoughts. Holden will come home."

Bingo let go a gentle bark and nudged her hand. Maybelle figured he was telling her she would learn to sew also. After all, all things are possible through Christ.

Maybelle must have finally fallen asleep because the next thing she knew the sun was on the rise and in another few minutes, she would be late for work if she didn't get a move on. Bingo leapt off the bed and made a beeline down the stairs. He hadn't left her side all night, and, boy, did he need to go out. In the past, Francine would often make a two-in-the-morning trip downstairs and let him out, not so much with Maybelle's way of doing things. Or not doing things.

She pulled on her robe—it was still quite cold in the room—and found Bingo at the back door, sitting on his haunches asking to go outside. Cinching her robe, Maybelle gave a swift kick and opened the back door. The door often stuck at the bottom. Roger had been promising to take a plane to it, but as yet, it was still not done.

Bingo wasted no time finding a good spot to do his morning thing. Maybelle closed the door, sighed deeply, and went back to the now lonely kitchen. She remembered how Francine would have coffee percolating by now, but now it was her job. Not that she objected so much; there would just be a lot of change to get used to.

She opened the freezer and found a paper bag with three slices of bread inside. Aha, surprise bread. Why not? Maybelle decided on toast with jam again except this time she was not able to time the bread so well and ended up with burnt toast she scraped off into the sink. But given the time, she had no choice but to wolf down semi-burnt toast with butter and jam.

"When life gives you an egg, you make toast." Doris's words rushed back and she smiled. She smeared butter and strawberry jam on the toast, thinking how silly her friend was, but also how thankful she was Doris stood with her. And said silly things like that from time to time. As she sat gulping coffee and eating toast, she remembered a portion of Scripture she didn't even know she knew. It was something about standing in the gap. "That's it," she told herself. "Doris is standing in the gap for me." It was the gap between her and Holden, a gap between feeling good and able to work and settling into a state of despair. She didn't want to, not really. But she knew it would be a battle as those sneaky tears threatened once again.

Bingo barked twice, a signal he wanted to come inside. Maybelle pushed open the back door, and the dog hurried past her to his bowl. Maybelle looked around for something to feed him. There wasn't a single leftover wiener, but she found one questionable egg and a hunk of old cheese in the refrigerator. She quickly made a mixture of oats and egg and cheese and called it breakfast.

"There you go, boy. Eat up. I haven't time to fuss." Bingo looked up at her appreciatively. She knew Bingo stood in the gap also. Bingo lapped up the food, grateful for anything to eat. The war was tough on him also.

"I'll try to get more wieners," she said. "And eggs."

Next, she prepared her own lunch for the day. A slice of the old cheese and a bit of leftover ham. It didn't look very good, but it was all she had. She would have to find a way to prepare more meals, so she had leftovers for Bingo and for lunch. Perhaps what she needed was not so much help with a quilt as help with the household.

By six thirty, just thirty-five minutes after she woke, Maybelle was ready to leave for work. She chose blue jeans and a blue blouse. She wrapped a scarf around her head, laced and tied her work boots. Everything felt heavier than usual. Even her heart. She pulled the front door closed and let go a heavy sigh. "Out with bad air." She took in a deep breath. "In with the good." "Just keep breathing," she thought as she took her first steps into the new day.

She headed down the walk to Doris's house. Doris was late, as usual. But it actually helped Maybelle feel better. She liked the routine of waiting for Doris. It gave her a minute to enjoy the street, the large houses mingled with row homes with wooden porches and gable roofs. She remembered how she and Holden, high-school sweethearts, would walk the streets, hand in hand, counting stars and smooching. Holden liked to take Maybelle to the Chester Rural Cemetery where they would sit and smooch and talk about the future and how many kids they would have. It was there he proposed. "Maybelle," he had said. "Now I know I got to ship out soon and I got no bloomin' idea what is waiting for me over there, but I sure would be most happy if I knew you were waiting for me back here. So, Maybelle? Will you do me the honor of becoming my wife, now, today even, before I have to leave?" Then he remembered to breathe.

Maybelle was not surprised. She had expected the proposal and didn't care one lick it had come in the cemetery. But still and all, Holden had practically poured his entire heart out to her and she quite simply fell more in love with him then, sitting on the tombstone under a half-full moon, and said, "Yes, Holden. I will be your wife. I will be here waiting for you when you come home, Mrs. Holden Kazinski. Your bloomin' wife."

Then they kissed, and Maybelle felt things she had never known she could feel, things that started in her toes and raced like electricity through her body.

There was no engagement ring, not then, but just for the time being, Holden found a small key ring in his pocket and slipped it on Maybelle's finger. Then he kissed her full and hard and sloppy. "I hope you won't live to regret this."

Maybelle laughed. She had never felt happier. But now, as she waited for Doris, an almost unbearable sadness waited with her. "Please bring him home," she whispered. "Please? We had so many plans."

Maybelle let go a big sigh. But now he was lost, and now all their hopes and dreams could be shattered. She shook her head. Doris was right. She couldn't keep thinking about it. Best to let go and concentrate on the day ahead. On work. On making good welds and helping with the war effort. The soldiers depended on her and so many women like her. She could not give up.

"Yo, Doris," she called like they did when they kids. "Come on, we're gonna be late."

Doris pushed open the front door. "Hey," she called. "Keep your shirt buttoned."

Maybelle swung open the iron gate and let Doris through. "It's about time. I swear you'll be late for your own funeral."

"Sorry, Miss Always on Time," Doris said. "I had to tweeze my left eyebrow a little more."

"You always got some excuse, every morning. Ever think of getting out of bed a little earlier, to allow for tweezing and such?"

Doris twisted her mouth and looked into Maybelle's eyes. "I ain't gonna argue with you today. Now let's get on."

The two set off down Ninth Street as always.

"Nice day," Doris said, looking into the sky. "I thought I heard rain last night. But today looks fine. Bright and clear. Not a cloud in the sky."

"I thought I heard some rain, too," Maybelle said. "I really thought it was gonna storm, but just nice, quiet rain."

"Well, it sure looks like it's gonna be a swell day, now," Doris said.

"I suppose," Maybelle walked ahead a few paces.

Doris caught up and took her hand. "How are you doing today? Get any sleep?"

"No, not really, maybe a little. It's just . . . just so hard. I stayed up with Roger for a while. Gave him some aspirin for his arm."

"Yeah, I know what you're going through is hard," Doris said. "But let's stay positive. Remember our motto? Positive thoughts."

"I'm trying. Just keep reminding me, okay? After all you are in the gap."

"The gap?" Doris said. "Oh, you mean the gap. From the Bible. I guess you're right. I'm standing in the gap for you. And I'm proud to do it. I know you'd do the same if it was me with a lost husband."

"Oh, don't even say that," Maybelle said. "Tempting fate and all."

"Ah, I don't believe in that malarkey, but you're right, I shouldn't even think it. Nothing but positive thoughts for us."

"Yeah, I was remembering how Holden proposed to me. He's such a gas. In the cemetery."

"Who cares?" Doris said. "Long as he proposed."

"Oh, I ain't complaining. Fact is, I think it'll make a nice story to tell our kids and grandkids."

"Good idea," Doris said. "You'll see. You two will be making those babies sooner than you know. You'll see."

Maybelle laughed.

"What's funny?" Doris asked as a skinny, stray dog sauntered by.

"I just thought of something," Maybelle said. "Right now, Holden might be missing in action. But pretty soon we'll be kissing in action." Then she laughed.

"That's a good one," Doris said. "Kissing in action."

They crossed Morton Avenue and headed onto the shipyard property already bustling and hustling with workers scattering and walking every which way. The yard never stopped, operating twenty-four hours a day to build and repair those mighty vessels so important to win the war. And everyone who worked there understood that. And everyone who worked there was as proud to help. Maybelle knew this, and every time she walked onto the Sun property, she felt her back straighten. Proud to be a shipworker.

"Say," Doris said, still holding Maybelle's hand. "I've been thinking about the quilt."

Maybelle pulled her hand away. "Ah, stupid old thing. I don't want to do it anymore. I just can't. It seems silly now. And like I said, I cannot sew to save my life."

"Don't be a stick-in-the-mud," Doris said. "You're doing it, you have to. Even your dog thinks it's a good idea."

Maybelle was just about to protest, but Doris wouldn't let her.

"Now what I was going to say," Doris said, "was we should get some of the other welderettes together tonight. At your place. The ones who can sew and we'll get started. I think four should do. A real quilting circle." A chill wind off the river whipped around them. Maybelle pulled her coat tight. A nice, warm quilt would be something to look forward to in the coming winter. She thought of Holden—wherever he was—and wondered if he was cold.

"You're not gonna drop this are you?"

"Nope. I think it's a terrific idea and will be good for you. Like a tonic."

"Four welderettes?" Maybelle said as they entered the building. "Really? But, I don't know."

"Four, including us," Doris said. "So we just need to find two. I think it's a great idea. I was thinking we should invite Janice Petrillo. She is always sewing stuff—leastways she's always yakking about what she makes—curtains and all."

"Didn't she sew the curtains in the Canteen?"

"Yeah. And they're pretty, especially with that lace at the bottom. She's really a good sew, sew-er."

Maybelle rang in her time card. "Seamstress. What you just said is spelled S-E-W-E-R and it spells *sewer*, as in down the drain."

"Yeah, yeah, seamstress," Doris said with a chuckle. "So, I ain't so good at English. Anyhoo, then I thought the new girl, what's her name? She works next to Janice, usually, likes to wear the fancy bandanas around her neck, the ones with all the colorful swirls and junk. Lois . . . Lois something or other. I forget. I only formally met her the one time and for just a second or two."

"Yeah, I know who you mean. She's real tall and thin, blonde hair. Kind of pretty with an hourglass shape."

"She's the one. A real bombshell. We'll ask her. She looks like she can sew," Doris said. "Don't you think?"

Maybelle shook her head. "I guess. Just ask her."

They walked past Logan who was looking stern as usual. "Morning," he said in his usual gruff voice. A voice most of the women had come to understand was pretty much show. All bark, no bite.

Maybelle and Doris snagged their welding shields from the rack.

Doris needed to raise her voice because the noise level had risen dramatically. "Yeah, Lois. She's new and might could use some friends, ya know?"

"I doubt it, she's gorgeous. I'm sure all the guys would love to be her friend."

"She's married," Doris said. "At least, I think she is. Why would a single woman want to work at the shipyard?"

"There's lots of single women here."

"Really?"

Maybelle took her spot. They would have to talk later, at lunch. She'd be laying down a bead weld to a ship's hull recently in for repairs. Tack welding had become Maybelle's least favorite operation at the plant. She'd much rather weld seams or even inspect pipes, but maybe, given all that's going on, a less critical task was best.

Maybelle didn't want to let on to Logan anything was wrong. After the mistakes she made when Francine died, this was all Logan needed to send her back to sheet metal where she'd drill holes for bushings. Now that was a loathsome job in Maybelle's mind.

She lit her torch and set to work, dodging a little splatter and sparks as she worked. There was something comforting about the sound of the torch. It was kind of like a rush of wind and heat. But it was hard to keep her thoughts from turning to Holden. Fortunately, Doris was there to watch her and help her keep her mind on the work with a few well-timed nudges.

She worked steadily but had to work with all her strength to keep her mind from wondering to Holden.

—◦◦◦—

It was not a usual day at the shipyard. One of the things about working in a place as large as Sun Ship and Dry Dock was that among the thousands of employees, there were a lot of talented people, from singers to artists, hunters and fisherman, athletes, and apparently seamstresses. And this day, the Sun Ship band was set to entertain during the lunch hour. According to a poster hanging in the lunchroom, they had a number of big-band tunes rehearsed.

"Come on," Doris said. "Let's get a good seat. I just love it when the band plays."

It was quite a treat, and most folks enjoyed the concerts. But today Maybelle would have preferred they didn't play. She was trying not to dredge up any thoughts of Holden, and the band just made it harder because it seemed every song they played reminded her of Holden. Holden or Francine.

Particularly, "Juke Box Saturday Night," the Glenn Miller song that she and Holden liked to dance to even if Maybelle couldn't really dance. For a tall, lanky, string bean of a fellow, Holden could cut a rug with the best of them. He mostly enjoyed swing dancing and often tossed Maybelle around like she was rag doll. But Maybelle didn't mind. She kind of liked it, and of course, any time she was in Holden's arms was a good time. Doris and Mickey, on the other hand, were not the best dancers, well, Mickey anyway. He had two left feet, as they say, and both were fashioned from concrete. Doris often went home from the dance hall with sore toes.

"Maybe I should have just worked through lunch," Maybelle said as she watched Doris snap her fingers and sway with the music.

"Why's that?" Doris asked, still moving to the sounds. "Music is good for the soul. Just relax. We'll be back to work soon enough."

Maybelle looked out over the river. "I feel like I need someone to repair my seams, you know. Too bad a broken, sad heart can't be welded like the hull of a ship."

"I know," Doris said. "I've had days when I felt like that, like I wanted to just keep working and working. I thought it would make missing Mickey easier. It doesn't. And besides skipping lunch is against the rules. The bosses say you need a break, and we still need a chance to talk to the girls about joining the sewing circle. I think I see them—over there." Doris pointed toward the back of the crowd.

Sewing circle. Maybelle shook her head. If anyone had told her one day she would be joining a sewing circle, she would have laughed her head off.

Maybelle agreed to stay, and even when they played "Juke Box Saturday Night" the second time, she managed to stand tall and even swayed a bit with the music without giving in to tears and to what she was beginning to consider annoying feelings. How she wished she could just shut them off completely.

As the band wound down from the midday concert, Doris suggested they make their way through the crowd and speak with Lois and Janice.

"Okeydokey," Maybelle said. "But you do the talking."

They had to bob and weave their way through the applauding lunch crowd.

Doris grabbed onto Janice's arm. "Say there, got a second? We have a question."

Janice spun around quickly, as though Doris caught her completely off guard. "What?"

"I'm sorry," Doris said. "I didn't mean to startle you. It's just the crowd and all."

"Oh, it's okay," Janice said, holding her hand to her heart. "I'll live. You're Doris, right?"

"Yes, and this is Maybelle." Doris draped her arm around Maybelle's shoulders.

"Hi," Maybelle said.

"How'd you like to join our little sewing circle?" Doris pointed her thumb to Maybelle and then back to herself. "We're making a quilt. A kind of special quilt. And I heard you can sew."

For a second, Maybelle got a kick out of the conversation. It was like they were lining up a gang to pull off a bank heist.

At first, Janice seemed to laugh. Like she was incredulous. But then she said, "Really? Me?"

"And you," Doris said pointing to Lois. "Both of you. We heard you gals are pretty good seamstresses."

Maybelle said nothing. She only stood by Doris's side and nodded.

"What's with her?" Lois said. "Cat got her tongue?"

Doris shushed Lois and whispered in her ear. Maybelle watched, as Doris no doubt explained to Lois there was a perfectly sound reason for her to be acting in such an apparently antisocial manner. For an instant, Maybelle felt annoyed. Why shouldn't she be sad and unhappy? She certainly had every right in the world to feel the way she did. And how on God's green earth was a sewing circle going to make anything better?

Lois put her hand on Maybelle's shoulder. "Gee, kid, that's rough. I'm sorry and even more, I'd be proud to help out on this here quilt project. I'm quite a handy seamstress. Make all my own clothes."

Janice, on the other hand, happily agreed in a more quiet tone. "What a gas. I'd love to join your little quilting bee," she said. "And I am sorry to hear about your husband."

"Thanks," Maybelle said. "And thanks for joining the sewing circle. It's really Doris's idea."

"And it's a good one. We all need a little kindness from time to time. It's your time. But you'll see. Things will look up."

"Yeah," Lois said. "Which reminds me, I hear Frank Sinatra might be coming by the dock one day. Who knows"—her voice raised two octaves—"today might be the day."

"Sinatra?" Doris said. "No foolin'?"

"Nope. No foolin'," Janice said. "Might be today. It's all the talk in Wetherill Plant."

"Ahh, it's just a rumor," Logan said as he passed by. "They been sayin' that for weeks. Sinatra coming to Sun Ship." He waved the notion away. "What gives? Why would he come here?"

"It's not so far-fetched," Janice said. "Remember when the strong man came?"

"Oh, yeah," Doris said. "The guy who could bend steel pipes with his bare hands. He was amazing."

The girls laughed. "And he was so scrawny. He must have had some help," Janice said.

"Or them pipes was made from rubber," Lois added.

"Anyway," Doris said. "I think we got our little sewing circle. We'll get started tonight. Just come on down to number eighteen North Ninth Street. It's the big house on the corner with the huge oak."

"Oh, yeah," Lois said. "I seen it."

"Good deal," Doris said. "We'll see you then."

Maybelle and Doris made their way out onto the tarmac where workers were scrambling about and the smells were strong—oily, metallic odors—sometimes made Maybelle sick to her stomach. She sat on the ground and leaned against a cold wall. She unpacked her lunch. They only had ten minutes left before the whistle blew. It was late in the year, the sun still shone warm, but it was definitely fall when the wind blew. Still, Maybelle didn't mind. The rush of cool air kept her thoughts from sticking on Holden. She opened her lunch can and stared at the old ham and a thin slice of Swiss cheese. She bit into the ham. It was tough and terrible. She pulled the ham out of her mouth and tossed it and the sandwich. "Let the mice and cats eat it."

Doris laughed. "Hey, I was talking to Mitch, one of the clock checkers, the other day when my card was messed up—you remember, right?"

Maybelle nodded as Doris offered her a sip of hot coffee from her thermos.

"He told me Mom, you know the big fat cat living in the yard, had another litter, seven kittens. Maybe you should get one. I might."

"Bingo wouldn't stand for it," Maybelle said as she stared over the top of her cup at the expansive Delaware River. It was wide and long and apparently just right for shipbuilding and launching ships.

"They say she must have had fifty litters and caught over five thousand mice. The cat gets around." Doris laughed.

Maybelle let go a soft chuckle. "Yeah, I'll say. Holden and I wanted to start a family, right away, when he got home." She gave Doris the cup back. "Thanks."

Doris smiled into Maybelle's now teary eyes. "You will. Don't fret." She screwed the lid onto her thermos. "So, first we weld seams, and then tonight we sew them. You'll see. It will be fun. Get your mind off your troubles."

They could hear the band from where they sat. They were playing the "Stars and Stripes Forever." Sun Ship was nothing if it wasn't patriotic.

"They must have stuck around for an encore," Doris said. "It's nice."

The lunch whistle blew and the workers headed back to their posts. Maybelle felt a little draggy, but once she was shielded under her welder's mask and holding her torch in her hand, she felt relieved. It was easy to hide and cry behind all the equipment. Seams of steel she could understand. But tonight? Quilting? Every time she thought about it, she imagined sewing the quilt to her pants.

9

Before the girls arrived, Maybelle did her best to get the house in order. She had noticed about a quarter-inch of dust on the mantel and the end tables the instant she walked through the front door. Francine had always taken care of the house, but now, along with everything else, this responsibility was hers. Not that she minded, but housework, like sewing and other domestic chores, was just not high on Maybelle's priority list. And for the first time, she felt a little frustrated her mother did everything for her. Her stomach growled with hunger, but she would eat later.

After she let Bingo out the front door, she found the dust cloth and set to work. She dusted her mother's portrait. The one on the mantle. "I don't know, Ma. I sure wish I knew what I was doing around here. When Holden comes home, I am going to make one terrible housewife."

But she managed to clear the place of dust and clutter and get the living room tidied for the sewing circle. Next, she tackled the front room, in case the new boarders decided to show up, though there was not much to do. She and Doris had the room pretty much cleared. Maybelle got clean sheets from the hall closet and set them on the beds. She figured the boarders could make their own beds—

how they liked it. Otherwise, there wasn't anything to do. She stood in the doorway and let a memory flood back. Francine, sitting at the small vanity applying her makeup. Maybelle remembered how often she stood in the doorway and watched her mother's face in the mirror. Even after Maybelle's father died, Francine wanted to look her best—even for a short trip to the butcher. She wanted to ask her mother to teach her about cosmetics and straight nylon seams and such, but as she stood there looking into the room she realized that Francine might have liked being the expert around the house and wasn't quite ready to pass that on to Maybelle.

"Oh well," Maybelle said out loud. "I guess it's not too late to learn."

After one last look around the upstairs, she let Bingo back inside and headed for the kitchen where she found a note taped to the refrigerator. It was from Roger.

"I decided to go to the yard. Went shopping. Made stew. In fridge."

She patted Bingo's head. "He's a good guy, Roger is." She pulled open the refrigerator door and found the stew. It looked like beef with potatoes and carrots. She found fresh eggs and milk and cheese, apples, tomatoes, and zucchini, no doubt from her neighbor Mrs. Frawley's garden. The Victory Gardens would soon be going to seed and weed as the winter moved in. So she was thankful for this bit of vegetables.

She even found a small package of chocolate on the counter and a loaf of freshly baked bread, no doubt from the Athens Bakery— Roger's favorite place in downtown Chester. He once said he could live on the smells inside.

While the stew heated on the stove, she set herself a plate at the table. She would have a nice dinner. Lord knows, she was starving. And she would share with Bingo, who seemed plenty eager to snag some of the stew.

Maybelle flipped on the radio and listened as the dulcet sounds of Bing Crosby filled the room. She'd take Bing over the new young whippersnapper Frank Sinatra any day. She laughed. A famous singer like him coming to Sun Ship. That would be the day.

Maybelle filled her bowl with stew and another for Bingo. But she let it cool in the fridge. "I'm sorry," she said. "I should have just given it to you cold. Now you have to wait."

Bingo sat back on his haunches and whimpered.

The stew was delicious. "Roger sure can cook. I can't figure out why the guy isn't married. I mean most men wouldn't even think about cooking, let alone making a whole stew."

The doorbell rang just as she dropped her empty bowl into the sink. "I bet that's the sewing circle girls." Doris never knocked. She would have just walked inside.

"Or, hey, it could be the new boarders."

Maybelle stood behind the door and played a little game. She bet herself a hot soak in the tub later, it was the boarders.

Yep. There they stood, two young women. One short. One tall. Both a little older than Maybelle.

"Halloo," said the taller of the two. "We're Rachel and Marybeth, your new tenants." They each held a single, worn suitcase.

"Oh, hi," Maybelle said. "Logan said you'd be coming by. Nice to meet you."

"Likewise, I'm sure," said the shorter one.

Maybelle stepped aside and let the women inside.

"I'm Rachel by the way," the tall woman said as she looked around.

Maybelle smiled. "And you must be Marybeth."

"That's right," she said. "Marybeth . . . Chewtalewski." Then she sniffed as though she had been crying. Maybelle chose to ignore it.

"Nice to meet you, too," Maybelle said. She paused a moment, looking the women over. They seemed the friendly sort. Yard workers, so they must be okay.

Maybelle showed them to the room. "Here you are. Nothing fancy but it's clean. The bathroom is down the hall on the left. We have a schedule posted."

"Good," Rachel said. "This is nice. Very nice."

Marybeth dropped her suitcase and stood in the middle of the room looking like she was about to burst into a Niagara of tears.

"Oh dear," Maybelle said. "Are you okay, honey?"

Rachel put her hand on Maybelle's shoulder. "She just found out her husband, Ricky, is MIA."

Maybelle felt a wave of compassion wash over her. She didn't waste a second and went straight to Marybeth. She took both her hands and looked into her bright blue eyes. "Marybeth, I know what you're going through. I just found out my Holden is . . ."—she held back tears of her own—"missing."

With that, Marybeth seemed to crack a small smile, or more of an expression of relief. She nodded her head. "Thank you," she said.

"Well, ain't that nice," Rachel said. "You two got something in common."

Maybelle didn't think Rachel meant it to be as crass as it sounded.

"That's right," Maybelle said.

"No, I mean it," Rachel said. "I been hoping someone would come along who can understand what Marybeth is going through. So this is a good arrangement, don't you think?"

"I do," Maybelle said. She put her arm around Marybeth's shoulders. "I do know how hard it is, but we have to stay strong—for our husbands."

Marybeth only nodded, still seeming to be ready to burst into a flood of tears.

"Now listen here," Maybelle said, choosing to let the moment pass. "I got some friends coming by this evening. We're making a quilt of all things, and you are both invited to join our little sewing circle, if you like." She looked especially at Marybeth, thinking it might be good for her—if what Doris said was right and making a quilt can be good for anyone in the throes of grief.

Rachel burst into laughter. "Sewing circle? I can't sew to save my life."

"Me, neither," Maybelle said. "But just so you know, you're welcome. They're gonna teach me."

"Thanks," Marybeth said. "Maybe another day, we have an early shift."

"Yeah, we thought we'd head down to that little pub on the corner first though. Do they have sandwiches?"

"Mackey's? Sure, the best roast beef in town. When he has it. Just tell him you're staying with us, and he'll take good care of you."

"Alrighty then," Rachel said. Marybeth still had not moved much.

"Don't worry about her. She's just feeling a little lower than usual tonight. It's her husband's birthday."

Maybelle felt like she had been punched in the stomach. Must be hard. Fortunately, Holden's birthday was months away.

"It's why I'm taking her out," Rachel said. "Help pass the time. Get her out of the blues if I can."

"Okeydokey," Maybelle said. "Holler if you need anything. Rent is due first of the week. Just put it in the candy jar in the kitchen. There's usually plenty of towels in the linen closet. Hope you don't mind a dog. His name is Bingo. He's really very sweet and listens well. So if you don't want him in here, just tell him. He'll scram."

"Thanks a lot," Rachel said. "I'm sure we'll be comfy."

"Oh, and then there's Roger. The other boarder."

"A man?" Marybeth said. "You rent to a man? Isn't that . . ."

"Ahh, don't worry about him," Maybelle said. "He's like a brother. Takes good care of us and can scrounge pretty much anything we might need. Roger has lived here for years."

"Don't give it another thought," Rachel said.

Maybelle went to her room before going downstairs. She sat on her bed and peered into Holden's picture. Then she retrieved the letter, the last letter Holden had sent. She didn't need to read it. She had it memorized, but she just felt closer to him to see his writing and to hear his voice through the letter. Then she kissed the portrait.

"We're making a quilt," she said. "Can you believe it?"

She could almost hear Holden laughing. And it seemed to make the evening just a little bit sweeter.

"You'll be home soon," she said.

The doorbell rang.

"That's Doris for sure," Maybelle said. "And those other girls."

Maybelle dashed down the steps and opened the door. It was Doris standing there with Janice and Lois.

"Come on in," Maybelle said as she pulled open the door. "We might as well get this party started."

The girls laughed.

Doris went in first, followed by Lois and then Janice.

"Doris tells me you can't sew," Lois said as she looked around the room. "Nice place."

"Thank you," Maybelle said. "And yeah, that's right, I don't sew. Maybe a button or two."

Doris draped her arm around Maybelle's shoulders. "We'll get her sewing like a regular Paris seamstress in no time."

"That's right," Janice said. "Like a regular Paris seamstress."

Maybelle laughed. "I doubt it. But come on in anyway. Make yourselves comfy." And it was then Maybelle realized she had not planned any snacks or drinks. Sometimes she just didn't know where her brain was.

Fortunately, Doris, who always thought of everything, brought a sack of cookies. Maybelle could make coffee.

"I brought snickerdoodles," Doris said, jangling the bag.

"Terrific," Maybelle said. "I'll just run and put coffee on."

"Sounds good," Janice said.

Lois smiled. "Coffee does sound good."

The three women, Doris, Janice, and Lois, sat on the couch, which seemed to bend and grimace under the weight.

"It's an old couch," Maybelle said.

"So tell us about the quilt," Lois asked in her high lilting voice Maybelle could hear in the kitchen. "Doris said your mother had started it before she passed."

"Yes," Maybelle called, as she measured out grounds. She plugged in the percolator, assembled cups and saucers on a tray, and sailed a quick prayer. "Help."

Maybelle headed back to the living room as the coffee percolated. Bingo loped into the room carrying an old leather shoe.

"Oh, look," Lois said. "A dog. Isn't he beautiful?"

"Thanks," Maybelle said. "He's a big sweetheart. His name is Bingo."

Bingo barked and then settled near the fireplace.

"He can't wait until it's cold enough to have a fire," Maybelle said.

"So," Janice said. "I'm dying to see this thing. I love crazy quilts. They have such neat stories behind them."

"Everything is in the dining room," Maybelle said with a nod to Doris.

"I'll get it," Doris said. She pulled the trunk closer to the couch. "It's all in here. Scraps, swatches, needles, thread."

"What about a machine? Do you have a sewing machine?" Janice asked.

"Yes," Maybelle said. "It's over there. In the corner." She pointed into the dining room. Francine had used the dining room as a center for many activities. Not just eating. Sewing, bill paying, letter writing, and even reading sometimes.

Lois went over to inspect it. "It's a nice one."

"Thanks," Maybelle said. "It was my mother's. She loved the thing like it was her child. I hope I don't break it."

Lois laughed. "Nah, never happen. These machines are sturdy. Built to last forever."

"Kind of like the ships we build," Janice said. "Can you believe it—a bunch of women are building ships. What a gas."

Doris chuckled. "I'll say. But I really like working at the yard. And it passes the time."

Which was the cue for all the women to share more details of their husbands' military duties.

Janice and Lois, and even Doris, had all received a new V-Mail, which made Maybelle a little sad. It was hard not to let the tears fall. But she soldiered on and listened to Lois tell about how her husband, Johnny, would be coming home by Christmas. Doris was expecting Mickey about the same time, and the girls wondered if they'd be on the same ship.

"We should get them to meet," Lois said. "I'll write to Johnny and tell him to be on the lookout."

"Good idea," Doris said.

Janice's husband had just been home on a little furlough and was now on his second tour. He was stationed somewhere in Germany. But for most wives, the exact details were kept secret. Like the women would go around blabbing details and war secrets. Nonetheless, they respected the loose-lips-sink-ships policy of not discussing war things.

Maybelle, of course, did not have news as rosy. "I keep reading Holden's last letter," she said. "It helps me get through. I can hear his voice."

"We understand," Janice said. "But he'll be home sooner than you know. You just gotta keep the faith."

"That's why working on this quilt is so important," Doris said. "It's kind of a tribute and a pastime at the same time." She laughed. "You know what I mean."

"Sure do," Lois said. "And just think about how much fun it will be to snuggle with Holden on those cold winter nights under it, you know."

"Yep," Maybelle said. "Holden and I have no trouble snuggling—if you know what I mean."

The women laughed. They all knew.

"Let's get started," Lois said. "I can't wait to see what we're working on."

Doris opened the trunk. It overflowed with the colorful scraps and rolled-up swatches of fabric, old shirts and blankets, sheets, trousers, handkerchiefs—neatly laundered, of course.

"And what is this?" Doris said, pulling out a large, albeit chewed-up piece of cloth—blue with tiny snowflakes appliquéd onto it.

"Oh, it's a tablecloth," Maybelle said. "My mother made it—of course."

Janice took the edge of the cloth and ran her fingers along the snowflakes and the hem. "Your mother was a good seamstress."

"She was," Maybelle said with a lump in her throat. Seeing all the fabrics and remnants brought floods of memories and feelings. A habit she was beginning to detest. How long would it be before she could think of her mother without getting sidetracked by some memory or thought or feeling? "A trait we most definitely do not share."

"Okay, so where is the quilt?" Lois asked.

"It's over there." Maybelle pointed to the sideboard in the dining room. The quilt was folded and sitting on top.

Janice stood up and went into the dining room. She returned with the quilt. "This is gorgeous. A real crazy quilt. This is going to be fun to work on."

Maybelle smiled as an even larger lump formed in her stomach. She hated sewing. She hated everything about sewing and was starting to think she was about to embarrass herself beyond all recognition.

"What's wrong?" Lois asked, apparently picking up on Maybelle's change of mood.

"Look, I hate to sew. Why don't you girls do it? I'll watch."

"No," Doris said with a tinge of frustration. "We're doing this mostly for you. You have to help. We won't let you fail."

"Did you tell them?" Maybelle asked Doris.

"Tell them what."

"About me and the great sewing catastrophe in high school."

Doris screwed up her face and glared at Maybelle. "Well, I wasn't going to."

"Well, now you have to," Janice said. "What catastrophe?"

Maybelle folded her arms across her chest.

"Want me to tell?" Doris asked.

"Nah, I'll do it. It was really a simple mistake."

Doris cracked up. Maybelle glared back. "Sorry," Doris said.

"Well, it was. We were making these dresses. Pretty simple. Just . . . just . . . " Maybelle was searching for the correct word.

"Simple, straight dress. Nothing fancy," Doris said. "I wore mine to the spring dance with a pretty sweater I knitted."

"Show-off," Maybelle said.

"So, tell us what happened," Janice said.

"Wait," Doris said. "We need coffee and cookies first." She and Maybelle went to the kitchen. Maybelle poured coffee while Doris arranged her snickerdoodles on a plate.

"Why do you like to embarrass me?" Maybelle asked.

"Ah, come on, you're not really embarrassed. It's just a funny story. Help break the ice."

Maybelle carried the tray. "Break the ice or convince them I'm an idiot."

"Either way," Doris said. "Come on, just tell them."

Maybelle set the tray on the coffee table. Janice and Lois each took a cup. Janice added a splash of cream as did Lois. Maybelle always saved the cream from the top of the milk bottle for coffee. It was so smooth and sweet. No need for sugar. Which was scarce anyway.

"So," Janice said. "Tell us what happened. You sew it to your skirt or something?"

"Worse than that," Maybelle said. "I sewed the zipper into the neck hole."

Lois spit her coffee across the room and laughed so hard Maybelle thought she might take off and spin around the room.

Janice nearly split a gut also. "How on earth did you do it?"

Maybelle shrugged. "Look, it just happened. I zippered up my own neck hole." And for the first time she laughed about it. "I guess it was kind of funny."

"Yeah, Mrs. Leland scolded you good. She even held it up for the whole class to see."

"She wouldn't give it back to me to fix," Maybelle said. "Not right away."

"Why?" Lois asked.

"She said she wanted to show her friends," Maybelle said with a sad tone. "Truth is, I found it in the display case in the school lobby right alongside the girls' basketball trophy. It was humiliating."

Janice and Lois got a hearty laugh.

"So where is it now?" Lois asked.

"It's here. In the house. I brought it home—eventually. I think it should be hanging in the Art Museum in Great Blunders of All Time Hall."

"All right, all right," Doris said. "I say we just get started on the quilt."

Maybelle sipped her coffee. "I still think you guys should do it without me. I'll just mess it up."

"Come on," Janice said. "You'll be sewing like a professional in just a few hours. We'll teach you everything we know. And hey, no zippers to worry about." Then she laughed.

Maybelle took a breath. She really didn't want to be part of the sewing circle. She really wanted to just sleep and eat, go to work, and wait for word from Holden. But how could she disappoint Doris and now Janice and Lois? After all, they were waiting too.

"Let's start by choosing some materials for Maybelle to cut and piece together and pin," Lois said. "Pinning is easy. You'll like pinning. Quarter-inch seams. Just remember it. It's important that all the seams are a quarter-inch. No bigger, and definitely no smaller, because it will unravel and pull apart and be sloppy."

"All right, already," Janice said. "Just show her how to pin the pieces."

That was when Maybelle heard a noise on the steps. Doris must have heard it also.

"What's that?" Doris asked.

"Oh, I should have told you. The new boarders arrived a little while ago. Marybeth and Rachel. They work at the yard. Their husbands are in Europe. Same as ours. They said they were going down to Mackey's for a bite."

"Oh, good," Doris said. "I'm glad you got the room rented."

"Yeah," Janice said. "I hear a lot of folks make some extra dough renting their extra rooms to shipyard workers."

Maybelle nodded. "It's a good deal. Anything for the war effort."

Doris removed a black shirt from the trunk. "Okay, back to the quilt. Cut this up into a shape, like a hexagon, you know six sides." She set the fabric on Maybelle's lap.

Bingo barked.

"I can do it," Maybelle told the pooch. "I think."

But then she looked at Doris like she had just sprouted corn from her ears. "Hexagon? How? How do I cut a hexagon and I know they have six sides but . . . how?"

"Eyeball it," Lois said. "Or look." Lois grabbed a piece of newspaper and expertly cut a hexagon. "Use this as a pattern."

Maybelle took the pattern and set it on the material.

"Now pin it." Lois said.

Maybelle could at least pin the pattern to the material. Which she did, only sticking herself once, but she chose not to complain or make it public knowledge. Bingo, fortunately, had sidled nearby, and she was able to hide her pain behind his big head.

"Good," Doris said.

"What's next?" Maybelle asked.

"Now you start adding fabric to the hexagon until you have a piece large enough to cut an eight-inch square," Lois said. "Easy as pie."

Maybelle couldn't make a pie to save her life—or her country for that matter either. "How?" she asked. "How do I add fabric to this . . . this hexagon?" Maybelle's attitude toward the project was not exactly enthusiastic.

"Pick some pieces, like this—" Lois held up a small yellow fabric that looked torn from a blanket. "Put right sides together. Pin at a quarter-inch and then sew the seam."

"I'll pin but someone else will have to operate . . . the machine."

"You operated it in high school," Doris said.

"And look where it got me." She drew her finger across her neck. "Zipper. Remember?"

"Look," Lois said. "I bet it wasn't easy to cram the zipper into the neck hole. So look on the bright side. You made the machine work and do what you wanted it to."

"It was a little bunchy," Maybelle said. "The zipper didn't exactly fit."

Janice cracked up again. "I bet it didn't."

"Fine," Doris said. "I'll run the machine. But you'll have to learn eventually."

The evening didn't exactly go along swimmingly. Maybelle stuck herself several times with the pins. Three times her seam allowance was more than a quarter-inch and once too small. Lois turned out to be quite a taskmaster.

The women worked for a while longer. Mostly it was okay. Maybelle managed to piece together enough fabric to make two squares to eventually be sewn onto the quilt. Of course, the others were cutting and sewing like crazy, like they were born with quilt hands or something, but still, Maybelle couldn't help but feel a little happy with herself. She tried and that's what was important. And the project did help keep her mind occupied.

"Too bad they don't let women be foremen at the yard," Doris said after they had gone for the evening. "Lois would make a great one."

Maybelle laughed and flopped onto the sofa. She looked at the mantel clock. "It's ten o'clock. Holy cow."

"Yeah," Doris said. "I better get home to bed. We have to work in the morning."

Work? Maybelle felt like she had been working all night. But, and she wasn't about to tell Doris, she did feel a little morsel of satisfaction having cut and pinned the squares. Two squares in one night and she didn't pin the fabric to her pants once. Quite an accomplishment.

The squares were stacked and ready to be added to the quilt. Lois had spread it out on the dining room table where she decided it should stay until finished.

"We should put all this away," Maybelle said.

"Nah, let's just leave it," Lois said. "Make it easier."

"Can't," Maybelle said. "I need the dining table for the renters."

"Oh yeah, that's right," Lois said. "Sorry. I didn't think about that."

Maybelle nodded. "They should be back by now. Except, they were celebrating Marybeth's husband's birthday."

"Birthday," Doris said. "That's rough."

"Yeah and it's not all. He's MIA also. She's taking it pretty hard. Rachel wanted to try and cheer her up."

"Still, I don't blame her for having a rough night. Her husband's birthday, moving into a new house. These are some rough times."

"Sure are," Maybelle said. "I will be so happy when this war is over."

"We all will," Doris said. She folded up the quilt and set it on the trunk. "It will be fine to put it away every night."

"I know," Maybelle said. "I guess Lois just likes things her way."

"Okay. Well, good night," Doris said.

Maybelle hoisted her tired body from the couch and walked Doris to the door. But before she could pull it open, the door swung open and there stood Marybeth and Rachel.

"Oh," Maybelle said. "I thought you two would be in bed by now."

"We should be," Marybeth said. "But Rachel sure likes to yak. And that Mackey can talk your ear off."

Maybelle chuckled. "He sure can."

"But you won't meet a sweeter guy," Doris said. "By the way, I'm Doris. Maybelle's best friend."

They exchanged introductions, but Doris wasted no time getting on her way down Ninth Street toward home. Maybelle watched from the porch. She could watch Doris practically all the way home.

When she went back to the living room, she saw the new girls admiring the quilt.

"This is great," Marybeth said.

"Sure is," Rachel said. "You're making it?"

"Well, the others mostly. I'm in charge of pins."

Marybeth laughed. "I love to sew. Made this dress I'm wearing."

"And mine," Rachel said.

The women looked at the quilt a few moments longer. Maybelle explained the meaning behind some of the squares and colors and materials before suggesting they get to sleep.

"Logan hates it when we're late," she said.

"Sure thing," Rachel said. "Good night."

Maybelle checked things in the kitchen before heading upstairs. The percolator was unplugged and Bingo was in the house. But where was Roger? He should have been home by then.

"He's probably at the pub," she told Bingo. "Some of the guys like to go out after the shift."

Bingo barked. But just then the back door swung open.

"There you are," Maybelle called.

"Hi, Maybelle," Roger called. "Sorry I'm a little late. Got to talkin' down there. You know how it is."

"Oh, hey, it's none of my business. How's the arm?"

"Better. Hardly noticed it all night." Roger pulled open the refrigerator. "Mind if I heat up some stew? I'm starved."

"No, go ahead. I think I'll head off to bed."

"Sure thing, say how did the sewing thing go?"

Maybelle felt a smile stretch across her face. "Good. I made two squares."

"Not sure what that means," Roger said. He dumped stew into the same pot Maybelle used. "But congratulations."

"Thanks," Maybelle said. "And by the way. The new boarders moved in tonight. Marybeth and Rachel. They're very nice."

"Oh, good," Roger said as he stirred. "Nice to have a full house again."

Maybelle yawned. "Well, good night."

"Good night," Roger said.

Maybelle dressed for bed. She was very tired after all the pinning and cutting and sewing. She hadn't dared try the machine. But she knew she would have to sooner or later. Bingo sat near the bed. "Think I can handle it, boy?"

Bingo barked and leaped onto the bed. "Don't get too comfortable. Once Holden gets home, I think you're going to get evicted."

Maybelle slipped under the covers, and all of a sudden, a wave of foreboding washed over her as she pulled the blanket up. She looked at Holden's portrait. "Please be safe."

10

The next morning was filled with hustle and bustle. The new renters were up and ready for work, but also quite hungry. Maybelle suggested oatmeal. Even Roger was up early. He was on the early shift but didn't get a day off in between as usual.

"And I can't be happier," he said as he sat at the kitchen table. "I hate working nights."

"Good," Maybelle said. "I know working nights can be hard."

Marybeth and Rachel found their way to the kitchen.

"The quilt looks good," Marybeth said. "Hope you don't mind, I took a peek."

"Oh, thanks." Maybelle poured oats into the boiling water. All she could do was hope for the best where the oatmeal was concerned. She stirred and stirred until Rachel came to her rescue. "Let me help with that. You get the coffee on."

"Coffee," Roger said. "Now that sounds good."

"Oh, I'm sorry," Maybelle said. "I need to introduce all of you."

"You must be Roger," Marybeth said.

"The one and only," Roger said.

"Well, it's nice to meet you," Marybeth said.

"Sure is," Rachel said.

"I hope you girls are comfortable here. And if you need anything, just let me know. I can usually get my hands on things hard to come by."

Maybelle watched Rachel's eyes light up like the Fourth of July. She even raised her hand and waved like a little schoolgirl. "Oh, can you get me a pair of nylons," Rachel said. "And red nail polish? I haven't seen red nail polish in weeks. What's the color everyone is using . . . it's called . . . oh, I forget but I'll find out."

Marybeth slapped Rachel's shoulder lightly. "Don't be rude. We just got here."

"He asked," Rachel said.

"Off-Duty Red," Roger said. "I'll see what I can do."

A guffaw the proportions Maybelle had not heard since Mackey fell off the bar stool and the entire pub broke into laughter, escaped Marybeth's mouth. "Now how in the world would a big, burly guy like you know a thing like that?"

Roger sipped coffee and smiled. "I'm in the scrounging business. I know many things."

Maybelle filled bright yellow bowls with oatmeal. Everyone, including Bingo, got a bowl. Of course, she left Bingo's to cool on the counter.

"Thank you," Rachel said. "I'm not used to having someone serve me breakfast."

"Don't get too used to it," Maybelle said. "There will be plenty of mornings when you'll be on your own."

Rachel nodded. "Maybe I can make breakfast for everyone one morning."

Now that sounded like a plan Maybelle could live with. "Sure thing. Be my guest."

Rachel batted her long eyelashes at Roger. "If you can scrounge some eggs and bacon."

Roger smiled. "You never know."

The conversation grew quiet as everyone was busy eating oatmeal until Rachel mentioned the quilt.

"I think what you're doing with the quilt is really neat," Rachel said. "It's kind of important."

Important. Maybelle had not thought of the quilt as being important. But as she sat at the table stirring a little more brown sugar into her bowl of oatmeal the thought did cross her mind. Maybe there was more to making the silly old quilt than she considered before.

"In what way?" Roger asked. He had finished his oatmeal and taken the bowl to the sink.

"Would you set Bingo's bowl on the floor?" Maybelle asked.

"Sure thing. Does he like brown sugar?"

"No, just some milk."

"I think it's important," Rachel said, "because it symbolizes how much we want our boys to come home. Back to the comforts of a loving wife and mother, sisters, brothers, you know—it's about family."

Maybelle had to think about it for a second or two. But Rachel was correct. The quilt, the crazy quilt with all the family memories sewed into it was about family, everything the boys were fighting for. She felt kind of proud.

Marybeth finished her breakfast and carried her bowl to the sink. "I heard they're getting ready to launch the new ship soon."

"They are," Roger said, taking his seat again. "As a matter of fact, they are choosing the sponsor at lunch today."

Bingo burst into the kitchen and lapped his oatmeal like he hadn't eaten in days.

Maybelle watched a glance pass between Rachel and Marybeth. "How does that work, anyway?" Marybeth asked. "I mean how do they choose who gets to sponsor a ship?"

"Luck of the draw," Roger said as he folded his hands in front of him. "They put names in the hat and pull one out. That's it. Not much to it at all. Then some dame gets dressed up and smashes a bottle of champagne, which is really not champagne, against the hull of the ship and off she rolls down the slip as the band plays. I've seen a dozen of them."

"It's still an honor," Maybelle said. "And I think it's really good they choose the workers."

"Unless they have some important person around to do it," Roger said. "But you're right. It's usually a worker and always a woman."

"How come?" Rachel asked, still chewing her oatmeal.

"Tradition," Maybelle said. "Not sure why else. But it's always a woman."

"Pretty neat," Marybeth said. "Maybe it'll be one of us."

Maybelle snorted. "Us? Highly doubtful. Sometimes I think those drawings are rigged."

"You can never tell," Roger said. "Anyway, they're choosing at lunch today. So make sure you're there. You can just never tell."

Bingo moved near Rachel and sat. Then he begged with his paws up and tongue out, no doubt looking to clean the last of Rachel's oatmeal. Maybelle scraped what was left of the oatmeal in the pot into Bingo's bowl. "Here you go, fella."

The dog happily lapped up the sweet grains.

Maybelle opened the refrigerator. "What shall we make for lunch? Not too much in here."

"I know something you can make," Marybeth said. "And it's ration-free."

"What's that?" Maybelle asked. "Anything ration-free is appreciated."

"You take carrots, cabbage, celery, cucumber, onions, parsley and if you have them green peppers. Mix it all together with mayonnaise if you can get it."

"Or make it," Rachel said. "Marybeth and I made these sandwiches all summer long. Delicious."

"Yeah," Marybeth said. "Then you spread it on bread, add a sliced tomato or two and there you go."

"It does sound good," Maybelle said. "Only one problem. I got no cucumbers, parsley, onions, or celery."

"I'll see what I can do," Roger said.

The girls laughed.

"Guess we'll settle for jam and apples."

Marybeth and Rachel helped pack the lunch cans while Maybelle rinsed bowls and set them on the counter. She looked at the clock.

"We better be going," Maybelle said. "If you girls want to run ahead, it's fine. I need to stop for Doris."

"Okay," Marybeth said. "I wonder how she does it."

"Does what?" Maybelle asked.

"Lives all by herself."

"Oh, she's fine, and besides, she spends most of her time up here."

"That's true," Rachel said.

Marybeth and Rachel headed off to the yard ahead of Maybelle. She lingered a few seconds longer to make sure all the curtains were drawn in case of a blackout and the doors and windows were closed. Maybelle pulled the shade down on the living room window and thought of Francine. She couldn't help it. This had been her mother's responsibility and even her joy. Maybelle just didn't have the drive her mother had for domestic things. And if her work on the quilt from the night before was any indication, she was completely unsalvageable. She was beginning to understand why her father often said Maybelle should have been born a boy.

There must be something she could do. Some talent. Some interest beyond welding and being Holden's wife. After all, she and Holden wanted children, but would it be enough? Maybe Maybelle wanted more.

She sighed and pulled open the front door, lunch can in hand. What kind of a mother would she make? She didn't even know about cabbage, cucumber, parsley, and carrot sandwiches. It would not have even occurred to her to make them.

Maybelle headed down the street to snag Doris as usual. The air was crisp as the end of the month drew near. The leaves had turned vibrant reds, yellows, and orange. Particularly the sugar maple out in front of Doctor Pemberton's home and office. It always turned first and was always the brightest. Maybelle loved to see it each fall. Only this morning, she longed even more for Holden to be with her. He at least understood her and appreciated her qualities—whatever they were. And he didn't even like cabbage.

Doris stood at the gate, waiting, even tapping her foot like a nervous Nellie. A sight rarely seen.

"Hey, you're early," Maybelle called.

"Nah, you're late." Doris pushed open the gate.

"I am? I have so much more to do in the morning now with the new boarders and . . . and Mom not being here. I better get up earlier, I suppose."

Doris draped her arm around Maybelle's shoulder. "You poor kid. You'll figure it out."

"Thanks."

"We just have to find a way to get the army to find Holden," Doris said. "And quick!"

"Yeah, wouldn't that be great?"

The friends walked on across Morton Avenue as usual and made their way with many other workers into the plant. Other than the sponsor drawing scheduled for the day, there was nothing terribly unusual going on. Even Logan barked his usual orders as the women passed.

"Get a move on, ladies. We have ships to build."

Maybelle slid her helmet onto her head. "See you at lunch," she told Doris.

Doris nodded as the two set to work on the giant gray bulkhead.

The lunch whistle blew and the workers eagerly scrambled to the lunchroom. The bosses were ready to draw the name of the new sponsor. It could be anyone that day.

"Hey, maybe they'll call your name," Maybelle said to Doris. "Wouldn't it be fun? Get all gussied up and slam the bottle of champagne on the ship and then watch her roll out to sea."

Doris practically shivered. "What a thrill." She nudged Maybelle. "You never know, though. They could pick you."

"Me?" Maybelle swallowed. "Nah. Never. I'd be so . . . embarrassed to stand up in front of all them people."

Doris gave her another shot in the arm. "Aww, you'd do great."

It was a monumental sight every time a new ship was released to the sea. The gigantic ships always dwarfed the spectators but not the resounding applause or the patriotic songs from the Sun Ship band.

Maybelle and Lois made their way to the staging area. The day had grown chillier as fall had finally taken its grip on Chester. Maybelle pulled her coat around her, glad she had stopped at the locker to grab it. Doris, on the other hand, said she'd skip her coat. But she was sorry now, well, for a moment, until the crowd gathered. "This is exciting every time," she said.

They always drew the names outside where a large crowd could gather and usually near the slip where the new ship sat. A giant leviathan, five hundred feet long, almost seventy feet tall. Huge and magnificent and built by many hands.

The room drew quiet as Maizie Pervis, one of the clock checkers, stood with Mr. Pew, the owner of the shipyard. She reached her hand into the jar and pulled out a folded piece of paper.

"Maybelle Kazinski, Wetherill Plant," Maizie called out.

Maybelle didn't react right away. She stood there with the others waiting for the applause. Waiting for some signal the winner was on her way to the podium.

"It's you," Doris said. "Oh my, my goodness. It's you. It's really you. You won."

Marybeth ran up to her. "Congratulations, Maybelle. You won."

"Me?" Maybelle pointed to her heart. "But how? Why?"

"Go on," Doris said. "You deserve it."

Maybelle pushed her way through the crowd, receiving pats on the back and congratulations until she reached Mr. Pew who stood like a proud peacock on the podium.

"Maybelle Kazinski?" he said.

"Ye—yeah. I mean yes."

"Congratulations. You will help launch the *SS Liberty*, Monday morning at 9:00 a.m."

Maybelle swallowed. All she could say was, "Wow." And, "Thank you."

Mr. Pew took her arm. He spoke into the microphone. "We understand your husband, one of our fine fighting men, has gone missing in action somewhere in Germany," he said.

"Yes, but how did you know?"

"Oh, Sun Ship likes to know about soldiers, and besides, a little bird told us."

Maybelle looked out over the crowd. She tried to spot Doris, but she was short and lost in the sea of workers. Maybe it was Roger. Yeah, Roger was the little bird. Her heart swelled with both pride and thanksgiving and a smidgen of melancholy. It was a great honor, but perhaps the honor was bittersweet.

"Thank you," Maybelle said again. And then the band struck up "Stars and Stripes Forever" as Maybelle made her way back to where she thought she left Doris. Except it took another five minutes to find her. Doris had gone outside.

"You fink," Maybelle said. "You arranged this whole thing. I thought it was Roger, but it was you, wasn't it?"

"Now, now," Doris said, biting into her ham sandwich. "I just told them about Holden. You know how they like to honor our guys. So they put your name in the hat. The fact that Maizie picked it is, well, a gift from God. You deserve it."

Maybelle sat on the cold ground with her back against the wall underneath a sign reminding the workers again not to talk about their work. This one read "Loose Lips Might Sink Ships" and had an image of a ship sinking into a blue sea.

"I guess it will be fun," Maybelle said.

"Yep, and who knows maybe Pew will use his influence to get the army on Holden's case."

"Nah, what can a shipbuilder, even a rich one, do? But that's a nice thought."

With the sound of the band playing in the background, Maybelle and Doris finished their lunch before they headed back inside the plant. Maybelle was greeted with more congratulations and a couple of sneers from other women who wanted to be chosen. When she saw her standing all alone, Maybelle thought briefly of giving the honor to Susan Weinberg, whose husband was killed, but Doris wouldn't let her.

"This is your day. You lost your Mom and your husband is missing."

"Not to mention the quilt," Maybelle said. "It's pretty traumatic." She laughed.

Doris laughed also. "Yep. Which reminds me, I thought I might bring some of my fabric over tonight. Maybe we can make it a real crazy quilt, parts of all of us while we wait for our men."

"Good idea," Maybelle said. "Maybe we can all share it." It was a good idea. Maybelle knew how important the quilt had become. More and more, so it seemed, as each day passed and their husbands were away.

"Yep," Doris said. "I found one of Mickey's hunting shirts. I'll bring it."

"And anything else," Maybelle said. "Mickey is important, too."

11

In the evening, Maybelle actually felt better about getting the house in order for the sewing circle. The idea of being a ship's sponsor was starting to sink in, and, well, she was happy. For the first time in a while, she felt something like happiness emerging in her spirit. It had been a long, long time since she found herself smiling without feeling forced.

She changed into another pair of jeans and a pretty yellow blouse. It had always seemed too sunshiny to wear lately, but as she looked in the mirror while fixing her hair, she thought she looked nice. No, she would never be a raving beauty like Doris. But she didn't need to be.

Even Marybeth noticed as they passed in the hallway. "You look so pretty," Marybeth said on her way to the bathroom.

"Thank you," Maybelle said with a smile.

She went to the kitchen to put coffee on and found a tray of brownies. Roger must have whipped them up. "God bless him," she said as Bingo made yummy noises like he couldn't wait to bite into one of the luscious desserts. "Sorry, fella," Maybelle said. "They're not for you."

But she did find a little leftover stew, which she gave Bingo along with a scrambled egg. "This should tide you over." She patted his head.

She assembled cups and saucers and napkins on the table.

Roger, who had been in the backyard, entered the kitchen.

"I didn't know you could bake," Maybelle said. "You are just full of tricks."

"I love to cook," he said. "Your Mom just never let me."

Maybelle smiled. "Yeah, she was kind of partial to her kitchen."

"Well, enjoy them. I'm heading down to Mackey's. Nothing like Friday night at Mackey's."

"Have fun," Maybelle said.

"Oh, hang on," Roger said. "Congratulations on the sponsorship. It's really a gas. Don't be nervous and make sure you smack the bottle squarely or it won't break and can be pretty embarrassing."

"Oh, I hadn't thought about it," she said pulling a large knife from a drawer.

She cut the brownies into neat squares and set them on a plate. She popped popcorn and dumped it into a large bowl. Her butter ration had run out, so they'd have to settle for butterless popcorn.

The bell rang, and Marybeth, who had beaten Maybelle to the door, answered it. "Hey, Doris," she said. "Welcome."

"I smell chocolate," Doris said. "Where did you get chocolate?"

Maybelle, who was holding the plate of brownies, shrugged. "Roger made them. Need we ask more?"

Doris dropped the bag she was carrying on the floor and grabbed the plate from Maybelle. "Roger is a pip."

"He sure is. He's always coming up with something."

"He'll make some woman a fine husband," Doris said with a mouthful of brownie.

The girls gathered around the dining table. Doris set up the sewing machine. Rachel was still upstairs. A minute later, the doorbell rang. It was Lois and Janice.

"Hey, congratulations again, you lucky dog," Lois said. "What an honor."

"Thanks," Maybelle said. She was still holding the tray of brownies. "Oh, they look good," Janice said, taking one.

"We're in the dining room."

Janice and Lois followed Maybelle into the room.

"So why isn't he married?" Marybeth asked.

"Why isn't who married?" Doris asked.

"Roger," Maybelle said. She set the tray on the table.

"You know, I've often wondered that myself," Doris said. "He's such a good guy."

"Maybe we can find him someone," Lois said. "There's got to be someone at the yard. It's a big place."

"Oh, no," Maybelle said. "Don't go matchmaking. He'll find someone when he's ready. He just ain't ready."

Marybeth picked up a piece of shiny fabric with flowers all over it. "What's this?"

"That, believe it or not," Maybelle said, "is from my mother's wedding dress. She couldn't afford a fancy white gown so she got married in a pretty dress."

Maybelle set it aside.

"I bet she was gorgeous," Marybeth said. "Just gorgeous."

Rachel finally joined the group. She looked like she had just woken up. "Sorry," she said. "I think I dozed for a bit. Have a headache. Sometimes the shipbuilding business can be so noisy. And who's gorgeous? Me?" She touched her hair and struck a pose.

"No, not you," Marybeth said. "I mean, I didn't mean you're not gorgeous, because you are. We all are. We were talking about Maybelle's mother." She displayed the shiny fabric. "This is from her wedding dress. What a gas. Not your traditional white."

"Yeah," Maybelle, who was glad she was just sitting and not pinning or cutting, said. "I was just saying, she couldn't afford a white gown and so she wore this really pretty flowered dress."

JOYCE MAGNIN

Lois waved a half-eaten brownie toward Maybelle. "You know, she was like a trendsetter. I bet if one of them fancy Paris fashion magazines got wind of it, flowered wedding dresses would be all the rage."

Doris laughed. "Are you crazy? *No* way. White is tradition."

"Ahh, the world is changing," Janice said. "Once our boys kill Hitler and end the war you'll see, things are gonna change. I think women are gonna start striking blows for independence. You'll see. We have minds of our own, you know."

"All right, all right," Maybelle said. "Now is not the time for political debate." Although she did like the notion of being her own person, making her own choices, maybe even having a career. It was hard to admit and she hadn't even told Doris, but lately she was thinking about what she would do if . . . if the unspeakable happened and Holden never made it home.

Maybelle went to the kitchen and poured coffee. She didn't want her mood to change again. She hated how easily it was to go from feeling good to feeling sad. But perhaps it was that way for many people these days. Except Doris. Doris never seemed to be on the down side.

She lifted her eyes to heaven. "Help me be more like Doris more often. Feeling good feels so good."

"Coffee," she said as she carried the tray into the small dining room. Doris was fast at work on the machine, and the others, even Marybeth and Rachel, were fast at work making squares. This was going to be one large quilt. But that was okay.

Soon the small group was fast at work on the quilt. They had grown quiet, each lost in her own thoughts and maybe memories. Doris was working with the hunting shirt she had brought, and Lois suggested Maybelle try making a square using her mother's wedding dress.

"Oh, I don't know," Maybelle said. "I don't want to ruin it."

130

"You won't ruin anything," Lois said. "I'll keep an eye on you."

Maybelle did her best, cutting and pinning, but the sewing machine was still little more to her than a snarling, vicious dog with snaggly teeth. Try as she might and with Lois hovering over her, she could not get the fabric to ride smoothly under the needle foot the way the others did.

But Lois helped with the patience of a saint. "Don't worry, hon, you'll get it."

"I still want to know why Roger isn't married," Marybeth asked out of the blue.

Doris was ripping one of Maybelle's seams. "I hear he got his heart broken and never recovered."

"Really," Janice said. "Do tell."

"Not much to tell," Maybelle said with two pins in her mouth. "He was all set to marry some young doll, when poof." She snapped her fingers.

"Poof?" Lois said.

"Left him standing at the altar." Maybelle sipped coffee and cringed as Doris ripped another seam. "Anyway, it's what my mother said. Everyone is pretty tight-lipped about it."

"In front of God and everyone?" Lois said. Her voice a note or two higher than usual. "Just left him there? At church?"

"Yep," Doris said. "I heard she ran off with some sailor who came in on one of the ships. A ship Roger himself had helped build. Now, ain't that a kick in the teeth."

"Wow, it is rough," Janice said as she pulled a needle through a piece of yellow fabric. "I'd thought I'd appliqué a pretty rose on this piece."

"Oh, nice," Maybelle said. "The rose is from my grandmother's favorite apron. I remember it like she was still standing in the kitchen stirring lamb stew."

"Really?" Janice said. "This was the house you grew up in?"

"Yep. It was my father's parents' house. My grandfather built it. He was a doctor and wanted a place big enough to act as a hospital, if needed."

"Wow, now that's cool."

Maybelle glanced out the window at the now-black night. There was a time when she would have liked to become a nurse or a doctor, but it just didn't seem to be in the stars.

"So what happened?" Lois asked. "I mean with the girl. Did she leave town?"

"Well," Doris said. "I heard the character she got mixed up with turned out to be a real rat."

Janice shrugged. "Maybe he's waiting for her."

"I highly doubt it," Maybelle said. "He said he'd never, ever talk to her or see her again. No matter what. Broke his heart."

"Well, you just never know," Lois said. "I, for one, could never do that to a fella. She just never loved him is the truth of the matter. She just never loved him."

"But he sure loved her," Doris said. Maybelle watched as Doris's eyes grew dreamy and far away. She must have been thinking about Mickey.

"I think we should talk about the launch tomorrow," Lois said. "You must be so excited, Maybelle."

Maybelle took a deep breath. "I am. I guess. It's not such a big deal. Lots of girls get picked. It's just my turn."

"But still," Lois said, "imagine it. Standing up there with all those people looking on, the band playing, and then you get to say it, 'I christen thee the *SS Whatevertheynameit.*' And WHAM!"

"Go on," Doris said. "You can admit it. You know full well you're excited. You don't need to be so shy."

Maybelle snipped some long strings from a quilt square. "All right, all right. I'm excited. What should I wear?"

"Oh, that's easy," Doris said. "Something you can change into real quick before lunch and change out of and back into your overalls after lunch."

"So maybe just a simple dress?"

"Yeah, a cute dress," Janice said. "Preferably *without* a zipper in the neck." She laughed.

"All right, all right, can we forget about it now?"

"Maybe your pink dress with the pretty blue collar and belt," Doris said. "And those blue pumps."

Maybelle smiled, but her smile quickly turned into a frown. She snapped her fingers. "Rats. I forgot. I don't have a single pair of nylons. I just donated them all."

"Oh, it's not a problem," Lois said. "I got a pair you can use. I got an extra pair for the weekend. Just in case we go dancing down at the Canteen."

Maybelle was relieved. "Thanks."

The group worked for a little while longer until Marybeth yawned and Doris started to get the giggles.

"Hey," Rachel said. "Did anyone else hear the yard might be going to six days soon? Could mean the war is ending."

Marybeth laughed. "Nah, it's a rumor. But I heard they're taking on more work."

"Yeah, I heard it, too," Maybelle said. "I highly doubt they'll close the yard for one full day. I heard they just got another government contract. More ships."

"Hey," Lois said. "If so, maybe we'll all get a chance to sponsor."

"They aren't making *that* many ships," Maybelle said.

"I'm still pretty happy for you," Doris said. "If anyone deserves the honor, it's Maybelle."

"Yeah, it's rough about your husband. No word yet?" Rachel asked.

Maybelle shook her head. "No, but it's only been a week or so." Maybelle glanced at Marybeth. "How long as your husband been—"

"Six months." Marybeth looked away. "But I still have hope. He's gonna come home. I just know it. In here." She tapped her heart. "In here, you know."

"That's the spirit," Doris said. "We have to keep believing. All of us."

"Yeah. It's tough, but I refuse to let go of hope."

"Good girl," Doris said. "We all have to hang on to hope. I know I do."

Maybelle felt a tug in her heart. It was the first time Doris even hinted at feeling anything but positive about the war and Mickey.

The clock struck ten. "I guess we should quit for the night," Doris said.

Rachel yawned. "Yeah, I'm tired. I am going to sleep late tomorrow. I love having a day off."

"And don't forget those nylons," Lois said. "I'll leave them in the bathroom."

"Thank you," Maybelle said.

Maybelle began dropping pieces of cloth into the trunk as the others helped clean up the workspace for the morning.

"I think it would be best if we kept the dining table clear," Maybelle said. "It's a little cramped in the kitchen."

"It's okay," Lois said. "Cozy."

"Nah, I think we should keep it clear in here."

"Suit yourself," Lois said.

Bingo bounded into the room. He was covered in mud.

"Oh no," cried Janice. "Get that mutt out of here. He'll wreck the quilt."

Bingo jumped and barked.

Lois practical threw herself on the quilt. "Get him out!"

"Why is he covered in mud?" Doris asked.

Maybelle ran to the window. "Because it is pouring rain. We were so busy gabbing and sewing we didn't hear it. Boy, it's really coming down."

"But how did he get outside?" Maybelle asked.

She grabbed the dog by his collar just as he was about to leap onto the quilt. "See that?" Maybelle said. "He knows a comfy spot when he sees one. Come on, Bingo, it's the mud porch for you."

Maybelle had to drag the dog through the kitchen where Roger was standing eating a sandwich.

"Roger? Did you let Bingo out?"

"Sorry," he said. "He got past me too quick. He really had to go."

"He almost ruined the quilt."

"Oh no," Roger said. "I plumb forgot you gals were doing that. Well, I am really sorry. How's it going?"

"Fine, but could you keep him in here until we get cleaned up in there?"

"Sure, I'll even wipe his feet and towel him off."

"Great. Use one of the old towels on the mud porch."

"Well, aren't you sounding like the woman of the house," Roger said.

Maybelle pulled herself up to her full height. "Yeah, I guess I am."

Roger took Bingo by the collar. "Come on, fella, we don't want to get into trouble."

Maybelle returned to the group. They had everything pretty much cleaned up.

"We got a lot done tonight," Doris said.

"We sure did," Marybeth said. "This is fun. I am really glad you invited us."

"Me too," Rachel said. "Thanks for including us." She put her arm around Marybeth's shoulders. "It's been good."

"We love having you. But for now I think we should all say our good nights."

The group stood for a few seconds almost as though no one wanted the evening to end. Maybe they didn't. Maybe facing the world was not as preferable as sewing memories.

"Come on, Doris," Janice said. "We'll walk you home."

"Thanks," Doris said. "Just down the street."

"There's a couple of bumbershoots near the door," Maybelle said.

"Thanks," Janice said.

Doris took Maybelle's hand. "I knew this would be good for you. You seemed so strong tonight. I'm proud of you."

"Thank you," Maybelle said. "But right now, maybe with everyone leaving, it feels like I'm slipping."

"It's okay. Just ask God for strength. He'll give. All we need to do is ask."

"Then why won't He bring Holden home? I keep asking for that."

Doris grinned. "I don't know, but you have to believe and keep on believing even when you don't want to. He will, you'll see. In His time."

"I wish I was so sure," Maybelle said.

"You have to believe," Marybeth said. "You just have to. Until I get another telegram telling me that Ricky is . . . well, you know, gone forever, I'm hanging on to hope. Hope is all we got."

"Right," Doris said. "Hope. It's not loose lips that sink ships. It's lack of hope."

"Hey," Rachel said in a little louder tone than her usual quiet voice. "I got an idea. I think we should call our quilt *the Hope*. Don't you think? We should name it."

Maybelle felt a twinge of excitement. They name important things. Why not the quilt? "Sure, why not? I mean all those pieces we're sewing have some hope connected to them. I think it's important."

Lois smiled. "It sure is important. Even if it's not important to anyone else. It's important to us. To this group."

"Capital idea," Doris said. "*The Hope.* I like it."

"Then it's settled," Maybelle said. "Tonight we christen the quilt. *The Hope.*"

"I don't think we should slam a bottle of champagne on it," Janice said. "But this is good enough. To *the Hope.*" She raised an imaginary glass in the air.

Maybelle pulled open the door as her friends filed out. Marybeth and Rachel had made their way upstairs.

"Don't get too wet," Maybelle called just as the rain seemed to pound harder. She closed the door after watching them as long as she could. Before a swift cool breeze kicked up.

She went into the dining room and ran her hands over the quilt.

The Hope. If only she could believe.

12

Before she headed upstairs to rinse out the nylons, Maybelle went to the kitchen. Roger was at the table eating a brownie. Bingo was at his side, wide-eyed and wishing for a taste. Just a taste. But Roger refused. "Chocolate is not good for doggies."

"Did you hear any of that?" Maybelle asked.

"About the quilt?"

"Yeah. We named it."

"Why not?" Roger shrugged. "They name ships. They name dogs and roses and even houses. Why not the quilt?"

"*Hope*," Maybelle said. She placed coffee cups in the sink. "We're calling it *the Hope*."

"Good. I think that's good." Roger yawned.

"Yeah, I'm tired too. What do you say we turn in?"

"You go on," Roger said. "I'll get the lights and check the doors and windows."

"Thanks. Don't forget the shades."

"I won't."

Maybelle patted Bingo's head. "Come on, boy. Bedtime."

Lois left the nylons in the bathroom just as she promised, and already washed and hanging over the shower rod. Maybelle touched them. "Not a single run. I hope I can return them in as good a shape."

After brushing her teeth and pulling a brush through her hair, Maybelle changed into a warm nightgown and slipped into bed. Bingo was already there snoring like a stevedore.

Maybelle reread Holden's letter six times before finally rolling onto her side to sleep with the letter still in her hand. She missed him so much she could hardly breathe. Her mood had definitely changed. She had hope. At least she thought she had hope but why? Why couldn't they find him? How does a soldier get lost?

She turned onto her back as tears ran down her cheeks. She sobbed gently and listened to the rain pelt against the side of the house and dance on the roof. "Hope," she whispered. "I hope you're safe, my darling. I hope you're warm. I hope you're not getting rained on." She swiped away tears and then kissed her fingertips. She blew the kiss into the air. "I hope it reaches you, honey."

But sleep wouldn't come so easily. She sifted through so many thoughts and feelings her heart raced. She hated the war. And sometimes, she hated that Holden had signed up and volunteered to go away. But after a minute, she reeled her despicable feelings back because she also understood why he went away. It would be a safer world because of men like Holden. And for them she was thankful. She was proud. But as the rain seemed to let up, her concerns didn't.

She couldn't help but nurse the same feeling of foreboding, of something terribly wrong and Holden right smack in the middle of it. She wondered how Doris did it. How she seemed to go blithely on as though there was no war and Mickey was simply away—on a vacation or something.

Bingo, with freshly cleaned feet and dried coat, was resting comfortably on her other side. He was warm and comfy, and Maybelle felt happy. She knew that her tenants were warm and that Roger, the man of the house in so many ways, in spite of the brownies, was willing to tackle the hard stuff and keep things going until Holden returned. Yes, she had much to be thankful for. Many blessings had come her way. Blessings along with the struggles. She'd count the blessings.

———

When morning finally did arrive, the rain had turned to clear skies, yet there was still a chill in the air. But it made for a nice, brisk Saturday morning. Perfect for hanging clothes on the line. That's what Francine would say. Maybelle got herself out of bed, washed up, and changed into work clothes, even though she had the day off. She would work around the house and outside the house. Lots of laundry to do.

Bingo bounded down the steps before her and slid into the kitchen like the gangly puppy he once was. She plugged in the coffee pot and set about getting oatmeal prepared for Marybeth and Rachel, who still had to go to the yard. She even made ham sandwiches and found two still solid, fresh apples to toss in their pails. Roger had managed to find a lovely cooked ham the night before and left it in the refrigerator like a Christmas present.

It would be a good day, she decided. She would get lots done and it would bring her hope. Or so she wanted to believe.

Marybeth and Rachel made it into the kitchen begging for coffee.

"You lucky duck," Marybeth said. "How'd you get a day off?"

"Just my turn. I was working three weeks straight without a single day off."

It wasn't unusual for the workers to work straight six-day shifts for days without a day off. Most of the time the employees had scheduled off days, but when production was high, no one was ever certain. A day off could be taken back in an instant.

Rachel sat at the table. "Oatmeal again?"

"Sorry. I gave Bingo the last egg."

"What?" Rachel protested.

"Oh, give her a break," Marybeth said. "It was just one egg. Fat lot of good it would do you. Oatmeal is better. Sticks to your ribs."

Maybelle filled their bowls. "Look, I found raisins."

"Oh, sweet treat," Rachel said. "They will help."

"And I already packed your lunch cans. You each got half of the one leftover brownie."

"Thanks," Marybeth said.

"Yeah, thanks," Rachel said.

The women happily ate their breakfast, while Maybelle stood by feeling very much like the woman of the house. An actual caretaker. Maybe she could get used to it.

Marybeth wiped her lips and stood. "Come on, girl, we better shake our tails. Don't need old Logan breathing down our necks."

"All right already. Can't I finish my coffee?"

"No time," Maybelle said. "You better git."

Maybelle watched from the porch. For an instant, she thought she might have felt what Francine felt all those years, a kind of joy at taking care of others. She knew she liked that feeling. To care for others. But welding ship hulls left little room for that. No, she'd put her energies into hope. At least for now.

After the kitchen was spotless, and the living room tidy enough for drop-in guests, not as if she had many, Maybelle thought she'd tackle the bedrooms and try to work on laundry. Francine loved her new washing machine, bought from the Sears Roebuck catalog just that summer. Roger installed it and showed her how to work it. Now it was Maybelle's job.

She gathered some clothes and set to work. Maybelle was never fond of doing laundry. Oh, she'd rinse a few things out in the sink, but actual laundry was daunting. But she had finally run out of fresh clothes. The machine was a strange-looking thing on four legs requiring her to first fill the tub with water. Hot water.

She filled a pitcher several times, added a cup of clothes washing powder, and then crammed a small bundle of clothes into the tub. She had seen Francine operate the contraption, but this was her first time solo.

Next, she flipped a small switch on the side of the Maytag and the thing growled into action, agitating the clothes. Water and suds slopped out all over the kitchen floor. She kept pushing the clothes back inside with the giant tongs made especially for the washer. But still it gulped and slogged and soap was on the floor and she nearly slipped and broke her back more than once.

Maybelle pushed her hair out of her eyes. She wanted to kick the dastardly beast.

The machine continued to churn. Then she remembered there was a small panel, a lid of sorts to flip over the tub. But, by then, it was too late. Suds dripped down the sides of the machine, the floor was wet, and Bingo had slipped into it with muddy feet and was now tracking it all over the place. And the machine stopped. It was now time to wring and rinse. But first, she kicked Bingo outside.

With a great, huge sigh, Maybelle pulled a blouse out of the tub and put it through the automatic wringer. She repeated the process with the next blouse, a pair of pants, and two socks and was just about to attempt squeezing a towel through the wringer when the doorbell rang. "Oh, dear God, please let it be someone who knows how to do laundry."

She dashed to the front door as Harry James sang "I Had the Craziest Dream" through the radio. "Only it's not a dream," she said.

Maybelle pulled open the door. It was Doris. In tears.

"What's wrong? What happened?" Maybelle's stomach churned like the washing machine. She took Doris's hand and led her to the couch. Doris was by now sobbing almost uncontrollably.

Doris sat on the couch, her knees pressed tightly together and her hands in her lap clutching a yellowed slip of paper. Telegram paper.

"What is it?" Maybelle asked.

Doris said nothing. Maybelle pulled the telegram from her hands and read:

IT IS WITH DEEP REGRET THAT WE MUST INFORM YOU YOUR HUSBAND SERGEANT MICHAEL SWIFT HAS BEEN REPORTED KILLED IN THE LINE OF DUTY IN GERMANY LETTER TO FOLLOW

Tears rushed to Maybelle's eyes. Her stomach clenched like she had been hit by a wrecking ball. She dropped next to Doris and hugged her. There were no words to say. Not then. Not at this difficult moment. They cried together for a good long time.

Bingo sidled next to Doris. He set his big, black head in her lap. Doris patted him and sobbed.

The next few minutes were silent. Maybelle simply had no words to say. It was Doris who finally spoke.

"Why him?"

"I don't know," Maybelle said. "Do you know what happened?"

Doris shook her head. "Not yet. He was supposed to be home right after Christmas. I was going to save the tree and keep the presents wrapped. I was going to—"

Maybelle held her closer. "I know. I know."

"What am I going to do now?" Doris said. "What am I supposed to do?"

"I don't know. I don't know."

"The officer gave me a black banner. A black banner. I'm supposed to drape it over the door." She blew her nose into a hankie she pulled from her sweater sleeve.

"You don't have to." Maybelle pulled Doris even tighter. They sat again with nothing to say.

And then it struck her. She had thought not knowing if Holden was alive or dead was the hardest thing in the world, and now she knew for sure. Knowing Mickey was dead was terrible, but at least Doris's worrying was over.

"Look," Maybelle said. "I don't know what we should do next, but I do know this. You are going to stay here. Right here with me while we figure it all out."

There was not much to do the rest of the day. They shared the news when the others arrived home.

"Oh dear," Marybeth said. "This is awful. Just awful."

"I'm sorry to hear this," Rachel said.

Doris sobbed even harder. "I don't understand. He was set to come home. One more week of—" She sobbed into Bingo's head. "Then on to Paris and then home. That was the plan."

Maybelle, who had gone to the kitchen to make coffee, returned. "I think you should eat something."

Doris shook her head. "I'm not hungry."

"Coffee at least. Soup. Something. You need your energy."

"Maybelle's right," Rachel said. "You need energy now. The next few days will be rough."

"But don't you worry," Rachel said. "We'll take care of things at the yard. You just stay put."

Maybelle did her best to make Doris comfortable that night. She avoided talk of Mickey as much as possible but knew they would have to discuss the arrangements. None of the members of the sewing circle had experience in this. It wasn't until Roger returned home they learned about procedure.

"The army usually buried the dead soldiers in military cemeteries overseas," he told Maybelle in the kitchen. "They don't return the bodies to home. Not always."

"Really?" Maybelle had not known this. "Then what does Doris do?"

Roger shook his head. "Man, this is rough. I say we throw Mickey one helluva party down at Mackey's. It's what he would have wanted."

"That's the ticket," Maybelle said. "But how do we tell Doris?"

Roger took Maybelle's hand. "Come on. I'll do it."

Doris was still on the couch and still crying, but in smaller sobs. Marybeth and Rachel were doing their best to comfort her.

"How about a cup of tea?" Marybeth asked.

Doris sniffled and nodded.

"So here's the thing," Roger said.

Doris looked up at the big lug of a man. "I say we throw Mickey a party. Give him a proper send-off."

"What?" Doris said. "But how? I don't even know when he'll—"

Roger sat near her and took her hands. "Listen, darlin', the thing is, the army probably already buried old Mickey, with full honors no doubt, overseas. It's how it's done."

"Really? I . . . oh, that's what the officer was telling me," Doris said. "I could hardly hear him."

"Of course not," Roger said. "Now you don't worry your pretty little head over nothin'. You let old Roger Dodger take care of everything."

Marybeth whispered into Maybelle's ear. "The bodies don't come home?"

"Not always," Roger said. "Maybe someday. But it's more efficient just to take care of this over there. I know it stinks."

In the evening Doris stayed close to Maybelle. She had no family except the people at her church, and Roger was making sure word was delivered there. "Not sure how they'd feel about coming to the pub for a wake," he had said. "But we're doing it."

"Mickey would have loved it," Doris said. "I'll take care of the stuffed shirts at church."

"Good going," Roger said. "You have to keep your chin up and move ahead. That's what Mickey wants for you. Chin up. Full steam ahead."

After dinner, which was more wieners and beans, Maybelle suggested working on the quilt. "Come on, it's way more than my quilt now. It's for all of us. We have to make it to honor Mickey, too."

Doris didn't eat much, but Maybelle managed to convince her to try. "I don't know how all this works," she said. "I just know how I felt after Mom d . . . di . . . passed. It gets easier."

So they sewed well into the night. Maybelle called Janice and Lois, who came over even though they had made other plans for their Saturday night. It was important the whole group was together. "You bet," Janice said. "We army gals got to stick together. We take care of each other. You bet we'll be there."

Doris cried most of the way through her squares but laughed when Maybelle managed to sew her own shirttail onto a quilt square. And for once, Maybelle thought her incompetence was a good thing.

"God is good," Doris said finally. "I know God is good. I know He will help me through this." She sniffed into a hankie. "My hope is in Him. For things to come and I'll see Mickey again. On the other side of the Jordan. I know I will."

Maybelle believed her, mostly. But she also knew Doris was trying to convince herself at the same time.

13

The next morning Maybelle told Doris she would take over the plans for Mickey's wake. It wasn't until then, on their way to the pub, she learned Mickey had no family other than Doris. This made Maybelle a little sad.

"He never talks about his family," Doris said. "It's like they never existed."

"That's sad," Maybelle said. "Do you even know if they're still alive?"

Doris shrugged. "I think they are, but I have no idea where."

Doris, although strong and filled with a peace Maybelle could not understand, was really not able to follow through with many of the details. And to tell the truth, there wasn't that much to do. Mackey did practically everything, and Roger made the arrangements for the food—everything from potato salad and cold cuts to cheesesteaks, which Roger got from Pat's down on Passyunk Avenue, hotdogs, and even lasagna baked by Alice Crumble, one of the welderettes.

Doris, of course, had taken bereavement days off from work. Maybelle was amazed at how the yard workers banded together at times like this and wished Doris could be there to see. There was so much help offered, she had to start turning people away.

The wake was to be Thursday night, a good night in Maybelle's opinion. Just about everyone was available to come. Mackey made arrangements for extra chairs and tables. Unfortunately, it was not the first time he had done this.

"But," he told Maybelle, "it's one area I wish I didn't have so much expertise."

So, Maybelle dressed in black, well, mostly in black, a dress her mother once wore to a friend's funeral. Maybelle headed to Doris's house. She had gone home on Monday after spending a couple of days with Maybelle.

"I have to go sooner or later," she had said. "And I'll be okay."

"You be sure and come right back if you have to," Maybelle told her. Maybelle knew all too well what it was like to walk through the doors of a house where one family member was missing. But this must be harder. It has to be harder. Maybelle had Roger to comfort her and even Bingo was source of strength.

Before she left for the wake Maybelle looked at the quilt. It was far from finished but getting bigger every day, maybe too big. Almost comical, but it was okay. They vowed to keep going until Holden came home or . . .

And then, in a flash of inspiration, Maybelle folded the quilt. She stuffed it into a wooden box, an orange crate she found on the mud porch. Bingo let go a loud yelp.

"For the quilt. I'm taking it to the pub."

Maybelle walked down the street. She felt very solemn and sad as she went. The sky was darkening but not quite dark yet. Clouds had been threatening nearly all day, but so far no rain. And the winds were barely noticeable. Just the usual breezes off the river.

Doris's door was open so she walked inside. Doris was there, dressed, ready to go, and in Maybelle's opinion, looking quite strong and gorgeous as always. But it wasn't a bad thing. It wasn't as if Doris was simply able to push Mickey from her mind. Doris just had an inner strength and stamina, stamina of soul to weather any storm. This, Maybelle knew, was something Doris had begun to cultivate after Doris's mother passed away so young, leaving her and her father to fend for themselves. And then when Doris's father died, also still too young, Doris took over the house and learned to maintain many things. She was every ounce a pillar.

"Are you ready?" Maybelle asked.

Doris, who was holding a simple black-veiled hat in her hands, stood. She didn't seem to notice the crate. "Just a moment." She stood in front of the mantle mirror and adjusted the hat just so.

A pretty war widow. That's what they would call her.

Maybelle took hold of Doris's hand as they left the house. "You amaze me," Maybelle said. "I'd be a wreck. A total wreck."

Doris shook her head. "No you wouldn't. You'd be surprised at just how strong you can be."

Maybelle squeezed Doris's hand. "Maybe."

"I pray you never have to find out. By the way, what's in the box?"

With a glance back toward the house, Maybelle stared the black banner across her door. There were so many black banners in town it was hard to keep count. But this one, this one counted for many things.

"Come to think," Maybelle said, "we all met in high school, didn't we? At least you and me and Holden were in high school. Mickey just kind of hung around."

"Yeah, he was staying above Doc Pemberton's garage. He left school early and got a job fixing cars."

"Yeah, he could fix anything," Maybelle said. "He was kind of an engine genius. At least Roger said so. A real genius."

"Yeah, the guys at the garage are sure gonna miss him."

They crossed over Morton Avenue.

"Did you never ask him about his folks?"

"Once. He said he didn't want to talk about it. So, I never asked him again. I figured maybe someday he'd tell me what happened." She shrugged. "Guess I'll never know now."

They crossed the street. "Yeah, sad. I wonder if they'd be proud to know about Mickey's sacrifice—it's what the officer called it. A sacrifice."

The girls walked on toward the pub. Maybelle noticed a line of people outside Mackey's.

"Wow, look at that," Doris said. "Everybody loved Mickey. Do you think they're waiting to get inside? Is it that crowded?"

"Maybe," Maybelle said. "I don't think there was any sweeter guy. Everybody loved him, so it stands to reason he'd have a lot of friends."

Maybelle shifted the crate to her other arm.

"What is that?" Doris asked. "I asked you already."

"The quilt. I know it's not finished yet, but I thought we'd hang it anyway. Since it has some of Mickey in it, you know." Maybelle swallowed. "Sorry, that didn't come out right. But you know what I mean. His hunting shirt."

"I know what you mean. Thanks for bringing it. It's a good idea."

Maybelle felt a shiver. It was hard not to think of Holden. How she wished he were here. Holden loved Mickey more than anyone—except Doris, of course. They were best friends, like brothers. Mickey taught Holden a little about cars, and Holden sold him some life insurance. Seemed weird now.

"I wish Holden was here," Doris said, reading Maybelle's mind.

"Me, too. He'd get the joint going with stories about Mickey. He had a hundred of them."

Doris sort of laughed, maybe at a quick, passing memory.

Roger was standing outside the pub. He caught Maybelle's eye and rushed toward her.

"Come on you two, let's get you inside." He kissed Doris's cheek. "How are you holding up?"

"Okay," she said. "I'm doing okay."

Maybelle looked down the line of people, friends mostly from the yard and the neighborhood. "Quite a turnout," she said.

"I'll say," Roger said. "Hope we have enough food."

The pub was crowded and loud. Maybelle kept hold of Doris's hand as they waded through the sea of people. Everyone wanted to offer their condolences to Doris, which she graciously accepted. But Maybelle knew it would end up being a long night. And Doris might grow weary of accepting niceties. She knew. It can be tiring.

"Let's find a place to hang old *Hope*," Maybelle said. "Maybe Mackey has an idea."

"Good idea."

Maybelle approached the bar. Mackey, a tall, thin man with bright eyes and dark hair, stood smiling.

"Hey," he said. He held out his hand to Doris. "I am so sorry, Doris. Mickey was a good guy. One of the best. A winner on all accounts."

"Thank you, Mackey. He really was one of the good guys."

Just then, Maybelle noticed Doris had gone into survival mode. Saying what she needed to say, but with not a lot of feelings attached. It was the safest place to be.

"Say," Maybelle said. "We were wondering something."

"What's that?" Mackey asked.

Maybelle pulled the quilt out of the crate. "Doris and me and some of the girls from the yard are making this . . . this crazy quilt. It's made from memories."

Mackey's forehead wrinkled.

"No, let me explain," Maybelle said. "It's made from bits and pieces of materials from important things. Like this—" she pointed to the square with Holden's stripes. "And this is from my baby blanket."

"Ahh," Mackey said. "Ain't that sweet."

"Ah, come on, Mack," Roger, who had appeared near Doris, said. "It's really sweet. They even got a piece of Mickey's hunting shirt on it."

"Oh, I get it," Mackey said. "Yeah, I guess it is kind of nice."

"Anyway," Maybelle said, "I was wondering if we could hang it somewhere. In honor of Mickey."

"And all the guys," Doris added. "All the soldiers who sacrificed."

"How about here," Mackey said. "I'll just hang it here over the mirror."

"Good idea," Maybelle said. "Not like anyone will need to use it."

"Nah, it just gives the place depth or something. At least it's what they tell me."

He climbed onto a stool and with Roger's help hung it on two nails.

"You don't mind a little hole do you?" Mackey asked.

"Nah, I'll bet someone will sew them up like new."

Doris smiled "Yeah, Lois can sew anything and make it like new."

Maybelle looked around the pub. People certainly seemed to be having a great time of it. The cheesesteaks were, of course, going fast. And still, people were filing past Doris to offer their thoughts. A few brought flowers and cards arranged on a table near the door. Mackey had thought of pretty much every contingency.

He set up a small place where people could say a few words about Mickey at the appointed time. Doris only had a few pictures of him, one in his uniform, of course, and two more taken during more peaceful days. One of the pictures was placed on a bar stool. Mickey's usual spot. Second from the end. Not that Mickey drank a lot. He enjoyed an occasional beer, but mostly he liked Mackey's for Mackey and for the friendships and conversations.

"That was taken when we went canoeing down the Brandywine, remember?" Doris said pointing to the photo. "He was a such a goof."

"Yeah, we had a blast," Maybelle said, looking at the image of Mickey in the canoe with Doris. She and Holden paddled their own canoe that day and managed to capsize it. But it was okay, just another reason to hold on tight to Holden.

The sounds inside the pub were joyous—just the way Mickey would want. But when the time came for people to take turns eulogizing Mickey, the mood shifted. Several friends told stories of Mickey and offered their deepest sympathies to Doris.

"He was a fine young man," Mrs. Caldwell, who ran the corner grocery, said. "Always had a good word to say." She looked toward the heavens. "Thank you, Mickey, for keeping us safe from all them dang fool Nazis. We'll never forget."

Doc Pemberton showed up and said, "Mickey lived above my office. He was such a handy guy to have around. The lad could fix anything. Even my X-ray machine." He seemed to get choked up. "Thing is, I miss him. He was sort of like a son to me."

The memories went on for quite a while until it was finally time for Doris, if she wanted to say something. She seemed a little wobbly so Maybelle helped her. She stood at the small podium, hanging on to the sides as Maybelle stood behind. "Thank you all for coming. I'm . . . overwhelmed by all your kindness. Mickey was a good man, a good husband, a good soldier." She sniffed back tears. "I will always love him."

And with that, Lance Ludlow, the trumpeter with the Sun Ship band blew taps, and Roger presented Doris with a small American flag. She and Maybelle sat as people left in silence. Maybelle kept looking toward the door, half expecting to see Holden burst through, but no. Finally, all the well-wishers departed and Doris and Maybelle walked home hand in hand, missing their young men.

14

The following week wore on like an engine filled with molasses. Maybelle was becoming increasingly anxious to hear something, anything, about Holden. Every walk to the mailbox was painful; every walk to work was even more painful. She was glad for her work at the yard and looking forward to the launch Saturday, but still, it all felt hollow without Holden. And now, with Doris feeling so blue, the wind had definitely gone from her sails.

Janice and Lois did their best to cheer the group up, even suggesting a night at the movies.

"Let's go," Janice said at lunch on Wednesday. "We can all use a break. Something different. Especially you guys." She was, of course, referring to Maybelle and Doris, who were two peas stuck in a very bedraggled pod.

Doris was not too interested at first. "Ahh, all they play are war movies," she said while eating a tomato sandwich. "I don't think I can handle a war movie."

"Me either," Maybelle said.

Then Logan wandered past, obviously overhearing the conversation. "*Frankenstein Meets the Wolfman* is playing down at the Boyd."

Maybelle's ears perked up. "Are you serious? Frankenstein?"

"Come on," Lois said. "It'll be a gas."

And so they went. Just a couple of days after Mickey's wake. Maybelle did think it was a little strange, but as it turned out, the movie was just what the doctor ordered. The theater itself was what Maybelle really liked—the art deco architecture with neon and flash. The name BOYD in huge block letters towered above the theater, drawing attention to the marquee proudly proclaiming *Frankenstein Meets the Wolfman.*

Even though it was supposed to be scary, the women didn't really find it so.

All in all, the plan worked. Both Maybelle and Doris had gotten out and about in town with its hustle and bustle even on a Wednesday night. Maybelle especially enjoyed the smells, cinnamon and sugar from the bakeries and cigarette smoke mixed with perfumes and popcorn and the occasional fuel smell from the cars whizzing down Eighth Street.

But on the walk home they ran into two soldiers on leave heading into town for a little R & R. Maybelle recognized one of the men from the block. They looked so smart in their uniforms.

"Terrance Wicket," she called. "Terry, it's me, Maybelle."

The soldier turned around and greeted the girls with hugs and even kisses. A well-placed kiss on Doris's lips caused a bit of snickering from some passersby. She promptly pushed him back, but still, she smiled.

"How's it going over there?" Maybelle asked.

"It's rough," Terry said. He looked down at his shiny shoes. "Real rough."

Maybelle could see it in his eyes. War was not pretty, and this sweet young man she used to play baseball with was scared.

"I'm sorry," she said. She wanted ask about Holden, but what could Terry possibly know.

"Say," Doris said. "It's a long shot, but you know Holden, Holden Kazinski, is overseas."

"Yeah, yeah," Terry said. "But there's so many guys, you know. It's not like we catch up."

"It's all right," Maybelle said. "It's just . . . just that he's missing in action and—"

"Wow," Terry said. "That is rough."

"Yeah," said the other man. "Most of those guys never make it—" But Terry punched his arm before he could say anymore.

"It's okay," Maybelle said. "Some of them come home."

Terry planted another slap on the back of his friend's head. "Come on, you idiot, let's go."

Maybelle kissed Terry's cheek. "It's okay. Have fun."

The women walked on in silence until Lois broke the ice. "Gee, that was unfortunate."

"It's okay," Maybelle said. "Really. I can't avoid people until Holden comes home or I get word he's . . . been killed. It's okay."

Doris slipped her hand in Maybelle's. "I'm proud of you."

They stopped at Maybelle's house on the walk home.

"Want me to come in for a little while?" Doris asked. "It's not that late."

"Nah, it's okay," Maybelle said. "I think I'll just hit the hay."

"Are you sure?" Doris asked. "Because I can stay. Are you sure meeting those guys didn't upset you?"

Maybelle kicked at a twig. "Look, trying to avoid soldiers around town is like trying to avoid oxygen. I'm okay. But I do think I want to just be alone."

"Okay," Doris said. "Call me if you get too lonely."

"You, too," Maybelle said.

They said their good nights and Maybelle started up the walk. Seeing the guys in uniform was tough. It was hard not to remember Holden in his neatly pressed uniform, holding his cap with both hands in front of him on the porch, saying good-bye. She had wanted to go to the bus depot with him, but he said, "No. I want to remember you here. In front of the house. On the porch with the sun glinting off your hair." Then he kissed her long and sweet.

Maybelle started up the porch steps. She stopped and touched her fingers to her lips and closed her eyes. She could still taste his kiss. She decided it was worth the price of the movie.

After work the next day, the sewing circle gathered to work on *Hope* after a couple of days off, which in Maybelle's estimation was a good thing. She picked up the house pretty well, made sure Bingo had something to eat, and even managed to set the sewing machine up before the others arrived.

"Now see, Bingo," she said. "I am learning."

Next, she set out the fabrics and supplies and even had coffee percolating and a tray of cinnamon buns Roger got at the bakery downtown. "It's going to be a good night." Then she slipped Bingo a piece of a delectable bun, which he pretty much inhaled and then had the audacity to beg for more.

Maybelle patted his head. "Later, boy. Later." Bingo headed for the hearth, circled five times, and lay down to rest.

Lois arrived with some of her own fabrics including a baby bib she had hand-sewn.

Doris picked it up. "Oh, this is so sweet. I love the little lamb."

"Thank you," Lois said.

"I didn't know you had a baby," Maybelle said as she set the tray of cinnamon buns on the dining table. The circle decided to vote

Roger an honorary, nonsewing member of the group as long as he supplied the sweet treats.

"Her name is Roberta, named for my father," Lois said.

"And she is just cute as a button," Janice said.

"Well, where is she?" Doris asked.

"Oh, she loves spending time with her grandma." Lois snagged a bun and headed to the dining room.

Maybelle couldn't help but entertain a twinge of . . . something. Jealousy? Maybe, but something more. "Okeydokey," she said pushing the feeling away. "Let's get started."

The next knock on the door was Janice. Marybeth and Rachel made their way downstairs but opted out of joining the circle that evening.

"We would rather go to Mackey's," Marybeth said. "Hope you don't mind."

Maybelle did feel a little disappointed. After all, they had made a commitment. But she didn't express it. "It's okay. We understand."

"Sure," Doris said, biting into one of the warm buns. "This is delicious. Roger, I suppose?"

"Yep," Maybelle said.

"Well, good night," Rachel said.

"Good night," Maybelle said. "Have fun."

Soon the group was busy sewing and cutting and pinning. Lois's lamb made a nice addition.

"How come you never told us about your daughter?" Doris asked.

Lois shrugged and looked away. Then she looked back and touched the lamb on the square she was working. "Not sure, really. The truth is, I suppose that I felt guilty."

"Guilty?" Doris said.

"Yeah, about needing to work and not taking care of my own kid."

"Maybe you could bring her to the yard. They have babysitting and you'd get to see her during lunch and breaks," Maybelle said with a smile.

"Maybe," Lois said. "I'll think about it."

Doris squeezed Lois's hand. "It's okay. We understand. But you should think about bringing her with you."

Lois swiped away tears from her cheek. "It would be nice to feed her lunch."

"That's the ticket," Maybelle said.

Lois stabbed her needle through the fabric. "I will definitely think about it."

Maybelle wiped tears away also. "All this talk makes me miss Holden even more."

"Yeah, I know what you mean," Doris said.

There was a long, sad silence until Roger walked into the scene.

"Hey, kids," he called. "How's it going?"

"Fine," Maybelle said. "It's going fine."

But Lois burst into tears, dropped her square, and dashed out the door. Janice went after her.

"What'd I say?" Roger asked.

"It's not your fault," Doris said.

"Oh, good, I mean I know I'm ugly, but geez." Then he laughed.

"Wow," Maybelle said. "This is really becoming something. Who would have thought a quilt could bring out so much in people."

"What do you mean?" Doris asked.

"Well, I guess I mean it started out to be just my mother's simple quilt and now look at it. It's part of all of us. You might say all our lives and dreams and wishes are stitched into it." She touched the little lamb. "I don't think my mother could have ever even imagined. Least of all imagined me working on it."

"And you're doing great," Doris said. "The last seam you sewed is nice and straight."

Maybelle thought she was just saying it, but she thanked her just the same.

"Should we do anything about Lois?" Maybelle asked. "She seemed so upset."

Doris shook her head. "I don't think we can."

Maybelle bit a long thread with her front teeth. "Am I wrong? I just . . . just don't know about having a baby here."

"A baby?" Roger said. "What on earth are you talking about?" He sat at the table and picked up an already-cut hexagon. The fabric was purple and soft, almost like silk.

"Did you know Lois had a little girl?" Maybelle asked.

He shook his head. "No, I didn't. And gee, I know everything."

"Well, she does," Maybelle said. "She had to leave her with her mother, so she could work and stuff."

"Man, that's tough," Roger said. "But she's not the only one, I'm sure."

"Yeah," Maybelle said. "I guess we're all missing people. Lots of people. Even little babies."

Doris snipped some string and then smoothed the square she was working with her palm. "Ahh, she'll make it. Her husband is coming home in a few weeks, isn't he?"

"That's right," Maybelle said. Her mood lifted. "Now I feel better. A little."

"Don't let it get you down," Roger said. "A baby in the house would not be a good idea."

"Ever?" Maybelle said.

"Now I didn't say that," Roger said. "When you and Holden start a family, well, I'll be right here to be Uncle Roger."

Maybelle smiled. It was a good thought. She glanced at the front door. Soon. He's coming home soon. He has to.

The circle worked until just a little before nine. Rachel and Marybeth had returned from Mackey's and joined the conversation, which had moved from shipbuilding to husbands to how much they all wished the war would end. And even to discussion about ration stamps. Maybelle detested rationing, but she did her part with as much joy as she could.

"It's all to help the men," Doris said as she finished her last square for the night. It was made from old neckties once worn by Maybelle's father.

"Are you nervous about the launch on Saturday?" Marybeth asked.

Maybelle shook her head. "No, not really. Well, maybe a little."

"You'll do great," Doris said. "Nothing to worry about."

Maybelle had hoped she wouldn't have to talk much about the coming ceremony. She felt strange accepting the honor after what Doris had just been through.

"I wish Doris was doing it," she said.

"No," Doris said. "This is your ship. I want to see you smack the bottle. You deserve it as much as anyone."

"Yeah, I never bothered to go to a launch before," Rachel said. "But wild horses won't keep me away this time."

"I hear the ladies who launch the ships get kind of close to the men who sail on them. They write letters and stuff," Rachel said.

"Really?" Maybelle said. "I hadn't thought about it. But come to think of it I guess it makes sense." She ran her fingers through her hair. "It's kind of neat."

"I doubt you can write to all of them on board, but maybe a few," Doris said.

"I will check into it," Maybelle said. "For sure."

Doris yawned wide. "I think we should call it a night. I'm sleepy."

"Yeah, me, too," Maybelle said.

Doris stood and folded the quilt. "It's getting bigger and bigger."

"Yeah, I'll say," Maybelle said. "But you know, I really love it now. Not sure if I like sewing any better, but I do love this quilt."

Roger yawned also. "I think what you ladies are doing is terrific. And I think the quilt belongs in a museum or something." Then he said good night. "Early shift."

They cleaned up the scraps amid light conversation and laughter. Rachel and Marybeth said their good nights.

"Sleep tight," Maybelle said.

"Don't let the bedbugs bite," Rachel added.

Doris sat at the kitchen table and picked at what was left of the cinnamon buns. "These are so good."

"Tea?" Maybelle asked. "Or do you want to go home?"

"Tea sounds good. I don't feel like going home just yet."

Maybelle filled the teakettle. "How are you doing? Really?"

"I'm okay," Doris said. "God is good. He'll get me through this. It's just all the war talk and talk about babies now can get me down sometimes. I try not to let it, but sometimes, it's just impossible. But I am trusting God will help me. He always does—come what may."

"How can you say that?" Maybelle said. "How can you say God is good after He let your husband die?"

"Because God is good. No matter what. Bad things happen, but I know it's all part of His plan."

"Mickey's death is part of a plan?"

"Yeah. Mickey died for no better cause, right? I know Mickey's okay with it. And I'll be okay too. I just miss him tonight."

"But . . . but aren't you angry? At least a little? I think if Holden turns up . . . more than missing, you know, I'd be so angry."

"Maybe a little. But not at God. It's not His fault. I have to take comfort in it." Doris reached across the table and grabbed Maybelle's hands. She held them tight and looked into Maybelle's eyes. "I have to."

Maybelle felt tears rush to her eyes. She couldn't hold them back and sobbed while still holding her friend's hands. "I miss Holden so much I can't stand it. I wish I could hear something from the army or him." She sniffled. "I'm angry, Doris. Angry at the army. How could they lose him?" She pulled her hands free and wiped her eyes and nose on a cloth napkin.

"We won't stop thinking the best. And praying for the best until we know something for certain." Doris scraped the last of the gooey, sugary goodness from the tray just as the kettle screamed.

"I wish I believed like you," Maybelle said. She grabbed a pot holder and lifted the heavy kettle. She poured the boiling water into waiting cups with the last of the tea. "I hate rationing. This is the last of the tea, the kind in the little bags anyway."

"You can choose to believe or not," Doris said. "But I think if I were in your shoes, I'd have a hard time keeping the faith, too. Sometimes I think I got the better deal."

Maybelle carried the cups of hot tea to the table. "I'm glad you said that. I thought there was something wrong because I had the same thought."

Doris dropped a single sugar cube into her cup. "Not knowing is worse than knowing."

Maybelle sighed. She looked into Doris's eyes and smiled. "I love you so much. You will always be my best friend."

Doris stirred her tea. "So, do you know what you're going to say tomorrow?"

"Say? I have to say something?"

"Sure. All the sponsors say a short speech."

"Ah, man," Maybelle said. She took a sip of tea. "I hate talking to crowds. I can't. I thought I just had to smack the bottle and wave good-bye."

"It's not a long speech. Just tell the people how proud you are to do it. I'm sure someone will coach you."

"That would be good, if someone tells me what to say."

"Sure, just say a few words and then take the bottle and say 'I christen thee the *SS Liberty*' and smack."

Maybelle smiled. "Now I know I can slam a bottle of wine against the hull of the ship. It'll be pretty hard to miss."

"And they suspend it from a rope. Nothing can go wrong."

Maybelle smirked. "This is me, remember? If anything can go wrong around me, it will."

"Not a chance tomorrow. I definitely do not think Mr. Pew will let anything go wrong."

Bingo sauntered into the room, sat down, and yawned a huge, smelly yawn.

"Whoa," Maybelle said. "What have you been eating?"

Doris yawned. "Why are yawns so catchy? Even dog yawns." This time she tried to shield the gaping yawn, but it was to no avail. "Listen, I guess I better be getting home before I keel over right here. And besides I can't wait to see you in a dress."

"I wish I could wear my overalls." Maybelle felt her eyebrows lift like a gothic cathedral. "After all, I wore them when I welded the seams on that ship."

Doris shook her head. "No need to get all in a swivet. Wear that dress we talked about. You'll be so pretty. And you get changed a few minutes before lunch."

"I guess that will be okay. I just hate dresses and nylons and all that fuss."

Doris put her hand on Maybelle's shoulder. "I know, I know, but you would look a little silly in front of all those people, including the big bosses in your coveralls and welding shield, now wouldn't you?"

"Yeah, yeah, I know."

Maybelle walked Doris to the door and watched as she made her way down the dark street. "See you tomorrow," she called with a wave.

"A dress." she said as Bingo slipped his head under her hand for a scratch. "I have to wear a dress."

15

The next morning Maybelle woke to a chorus of wind through the trees. Rain had not been called, but October in her neck of the woods could bring just about anything, including a rare snow shower.

"Oh, good," she said giving Bingo a little nudge to get off the bed. "Launching a ship in the rain."

A launch is never postponed on account of weather.

Maybelle swung her feet over the side of the bed. She took Holden's picture and kissed him good morning. "Today, I get to be in the limelight, honey. I'm a little nervous." But as she gazed into Holden's bright eyes, she felt a wash of calm. "Wish you could be there."

After a quick shower and dressing in regular work clothes, she chose the dress Doris had mentioned along with the little hat. She also thought to find shoes, lady shoes, not work boots. "How silly would that look?" she asked Bingo. She hadn't worn either the dress or the shoes, and certainly not the hat, since before Holden left for Europe. Bingo stood nearby and whimpered as though he, too, knew it was Holden's favorite.

"The last time I wore this was when we went to the movie *Casablanca*," Maybelle said. She held the dress up to her neck and looked in the mirror. "Here's looking at you, kid."

Bingo barked.

"Well, now what? Doris is right. I can't wear it to work. The launch is at twelve thirty and I have to weld seams first."

Maybelle looked around the room. "I guess I can carry it in a suitcase, but that's stupid, isn't it?"

Bingo stuck his nose in the closet. The suitcase, also unused since she and Doris had an overnight in Ocean City, New Jersey, after high-school graduation.

"I guess it'll be okay. Doris would say it's okay."

Maybelle pulled out the suitcase and set it on her bed. She popped it open and discovered she had left a small box of saltwater taffy inside. She lifted the box out and tears welled in her eyes. "I meant to give this to Mom and forgot."

Holden had to leave quickly and suddenly. The taffy was the last thing on her mind. And now . . . now she couldn't even give it to Francine. Bingo whimpered.

"I know. I'll just leave it in the living room. Whoever wants it can have it. We'll share."

Maybelle carefully folded the dress and set it in the suitcase. She found the nylons Lois lent her and also set them carefully on top of the dress, and last, placed the little hat with the delicate white veil. It was the most girly thing Maybelle owned. "Please, God. No runs in the nylons today." Walking around a shipbuilding plant in nylons could be dangerous. She could get caught on practically anything. She stuffed the shoes into the small pocket in the suitcase lid.

She carried the suitcase downstairs and set it near the front door.

"Don't want to forget that," she said.

Then she headed into the kitchen to make yet another batch of oatmeal. There just wasn't much else to make except bacon and eggs, and they were too expensive for so many mouths. She looked in the fridge for something to drink other than milk, but nothing. Roger kept them in milk. He always went down to Haskins Dairy and got it.

"Remind me to tell him thank you," Maybelle told Bingo.

"Thank who?"

Maybelle closed the door and saw Roger.

"You," Maybelle said. "Thank you for getting us milk."

"Ah, no trouble."

"Did you hear if Rachel and Marybeth were up?"

"Yeah, I heard them moving around. They seemed to be arguing about something."

"Yeah, they can sure go at it, can't they? It's not the first time. And over the stupidest stuff. Shades up or down, who used which towel and when."

Maybelle set a pot of water to boil on the stove. She noticed the coffee pot was percolating away and smiled. There was nothing like that first cup of coffee in the morning—especially when someone else made it.

"Say," Roger said. "I know it's way too soon but . . . well, I was wondering something." He sat at the table.

"What's that?" Maybelle asked as she measured oats.

"Ahh, it's stupid. Maybe even rude."

"What?" Maybelle asked. "Just say it."

"Okay, but promise you won't get mad."

"I won't get mad," Maybelle said as she stirred.

Roger sat at the table and fidgeted with a spoon.

"Now tell me what's on your mind. I know something is wiggling around in that big head of yours."

"All right, well, I was wondering . . . something about Doris."

"Doris?"

"Yeah, I know it's only been a couple of weeks but . . . well, the world is so crazy and anything can happen and well, I was just wondering if you think she'd . . . have any interest in . . . me."

Maybelle swallowed as her heart raced. "What? Really? But she just found out about Mickey. How can you even think that?"

"I know, I know. I was wrong to ask. I won't give it another thought."

"Well, I guess it's wrong. I don't know. You're right. The world is a crazy place, but still."

Roger stood and started the coffee. "It's just . . . I've liked her for a long time. She's just so pretty and smart and . . . but I would never have said anything, you know, before." He smacked his forehead. "Ah, it's stupid. I'm sorry I even brought it up."

"Yeah, it is kind of stupid," Maybelle said. "It's kind of sweet, but . . . gee. Follow your heart, I guess. The worst to happen is she'll get mad and insulted or something."

"So you think I should at least try?"

"Can you wait? Just a while longer. Give it a month. It could make things kind of uncomfortable around here, if she gets really offended."

Rachel and Marybeth, who were still arguing over a blouse, entered the kitchen. "I told you I'd wash it," Rachel said. "It's barely noticeable."

"A ketchup stain? It's noticeable. And it might never come out."

"Morning," Maybelle said. "What's the trouble?"

Marybeth slipped into a seat at the table. "Ah, nothing. Rachel wore my blouse and got ketchup on it."

"I said I was sorry," Rachel said. "And I said I'll wash it."

"Morning," Roger said, as though he had just noticed the girls.

Rachel sat at the table. "Are we interrupting? You look a little upset, Rog."

"No, no," Roger said. "Nothing. I'm fine, really. Just thinking."

Maybelle noticed his dreamy look. It was plain as the nose on his face now. He had it bad for Doris. But he was correct. It was way too early to go courting Doris.

Marybeth poured herself a cup of coffee and leaned against the counter. She sipped and smiled. "Thanks for making the coffee, Roger."

"Yeah. It's nothing."

"It's a good thing. You are definitely a catch for someone." Maybelle grinned. It seemed to crack Roger's faraway mood.

Roger groaned. "I better get to the yard. See you girls later."

Maybelle smiled. "Are you coming to the launch?"

"Ah, gee, yeah, I almost forgot about that. I'll be there all right." Then he kissed Maybelle's cheek. "Be sure and really slam the bottle."

Rachel, who had apparently stopped arguing with Marybeth, started stirring the oatmeal. "Are you nervous?" she asked Maybelle.

"Nah, not really. I am worried if it is going to rain and I'll be standing out there getting all wet and stuff."

"Yeah," Marybeth said. "The wind is really kicking up and some dark clouds are moving in. But hey, the launch will still go off and you'll do fine. Just fine."

Bingo begged for his oatmeal.

"Just a second," Maybelle said. "It needs to cool."

Maybelle stayed near the warm stove while Marybeth and Rachel finished their breakfast. Then they packed their lunches, best they could do was tomato sandwiches, and headed out the door.

"You go ahead," Maybelle said. "I need to stop for Doris, anyway."

But for the first time this week, Doris was late. Maybelle thought she might have been falling back into her old worn path and it was kind of nice, although anyone would be hard-pressed to get Maybelle to admit tardiness was ever a good thing.

"Hey," Doris called from an upstairs window. "I'll be right down."

Maybelle waved and waited only a few minutes until she heard the door slam.

"Morning," Maybelle said. "You're late."

"Yeah, yeah, I overslept a little."

Maybelle smiled. Yep, Doris was getting back to her old self.

"Hey," Doris said as she plucked some leaves from a privet hedge. "Today's the big day." She sprinkled them over Maybelle like confetti.

"Yeah. I guess." She brushed some of the tiny leaves from her shoulder. "I don't know why everyone thinks it's such a big deal. So what, I smack a bottle against the ship and off she goes."

"Hey, sending a ship off to hunt Nazis is a big deal and you helped build it. Imagine that. Out on the high seas, carrying our men, our sailors. It is an honor."

Maybelle considered Doris's words. "You know what? You're right. When you think about it."

Doris pulled a pair of black, cotton gloves from her coat pocket. The winds had definitely changed. The fall had taken a grip and was not about to let go. "I think this is my favorite time of year." She pulled one glove on, and as she did, Maybelle saw her wedding band.

"Now don't take this the wrong way, but when do you take the ring off?"

"Ring?" Doris screwed up her lips. "Oh, my wedding ring." She shrugged. "I . . . I don't know. When the time is right, I suppose. Why?"

"No reason." She couldn't very well tell Doris about her conversation with Roger. "I was just wondering. For myself, too. I mean there's been no word about Holden in almost a month and—"

Doris grabbed Maybelle's hand. "Now don't talk like that. You haven't gotten any official word yet and until then you keep hoping. It's what you do. And it's all you do."

Doris's words came out a little forceful. But maybe it was what Maybelle needed to hear. She could so easily fall into despair.

"Okay, okay," Maybelle said as they picked up their pace. "I'm sorry."

"Good," Doris said. "Now, we are working on the quilt tonight, right? Speaking of hope and all."

"Yeah, as far as I know. But . . . well, I was wondering, when do you think you might be ready. . ."

"Might be ready for what?"

"Ah, never mind. Come on, we better run, the whistle is about to blow its stack and we don't need Logan breathing down our necks again."

"Not today," Doris said. "You're a VIP."

16

With still ten minutes to go before the lunch whistle, Logan approach Maybelle. He nearly startled the bejeebers right out of her when he tapped her shoulder.

"Whoa, sorry," he said, when she turned suddenly with her lit torch. "Don't singe my nose off."

"Logan," Maybelle hollered. "You scared me."

"I said I was sorry. I just want you to know you can skedaddle now if you want to get ready for the ceremony."

Maybelle turned off her torch and set it down. "Yes, great. Thanks."

She nodded to Doris on her way to the locker. She had left her suitcase there and was now wishing Doris could have come along. She pulled off her grimy work clothes, washed as best she could, and then slipped into the dress. She did her best to make her hair look like it had not spent the last four hours or so smashed under a welder's shield.

She wasn't alone in the locker room, but no one seemed to notice her or care until she stood in front of the small mirror and set her hat on her head.

"Well now," said a woman she didn't recognize. "Ain't you all gussied up for somethin'."

Maybelle smiled into the mirror. She could see the woman standing nearby. She really didn't want to have to explain, and fortunately, someone else came to her rescue.

"Ah, she's just got a dress on account of she's the sponsor today."

"Oh," said the first woman. "How come you rate?"

Maybelle shrugged and turned around. "Luck of the draw."

"Yeah, right," the first woman mocked. "I put my name in every time and every time I get passed."

"Luck of the draw," Maybelle repeated. "Now if you'll excuse me, I have to get upstairs."

"Sure thing, honey," the first woman said, but not before blocking Maybelle's way slightly. It made Maybelle feel terribly uncomfortable as she pulled on her coat and had to squeeze past the large woman to get out the door.

Maybelle found her way to the launching dock—slip number six. It was a huge place with miles of scaffolding surrounding the *Sharpsburg*. A massive T2 tanker had a deadweight of over 16,000 tons. It was gray and white and shiny and for some reason seemed a whole lot bigger than it did when she was working on it. Maybelle knew she had welded some of the seams and silently offered a prayer to God, "Don't let my seams leak."

She looked up and saw sailors walking around on deck. She waved. They waved back. And that was when she understood why some of the sponsors got attached to ships they launched.

"Safe travels," she called.

Then one of the members of the Pew family appeared. The family owned the shipyard and attended every launch. Mr. Pew was chubby with a huge paunch. He wore a white suit and white shoes and a dark tie even though it was well in autumn. And had a very nice smile.

"You must be our sponsor," he said, extending his hand.

Maybelle shook his hand. "Yes sir, I'm Maybelle Kazinski."

"Yes, yes," Mr. Pew said. "Crying shame about your husband, Howard."

"Holden," Maybelle said. "His name is Holden."

"Oh, right, sorry, honey. But you just listen to me. Chin up. He'll be home soon. You'll see."

"Thank you." Maybelle straightened her dress.

"Now there's nothing to it, just stand over here." Mr. Pew led her to a makeshift stage with a microphone. "Just tell the folks what an honor it is to be here and thank them all for their hard work. Then you come down here." He walked her to the ship. A bottle of wine was wrapped in a tightly woven net. Streamers were attached to the top. "You take the bottle and say, 'In the name of the United States of America, I christen thee the *Sharpsburg*,' and smack it as hard as you can. That's it."

"It doesn't sound hard."

"Nope. Whole thing should take less than twenty minutes. We want to get our workers back to work."

Maybelle smiled. "Of course."

A short time later, the area began to fill with people, mostly workers. The band was playing something patriotic, Maybelle was certain. But she couldn't name it. She kept trying to see Doris or even Janice and Lois or Roger. But she couldn't. Then, in a twinkling, she was led to the stage. She stood in front of the microphone with Mr. Pew.

"And here to sponsor this launch is Maybelle Kazinski, whose husband has been missing in action for nearly a month."

There was brief applause.

Maybelle said what she had to say only stumbling once over the words, "incredible honor." Then without a hitch she walked down the small platform, grabbed the bottle suspended from a rope, and said, "In the name of the United States of America I christen thee the *SS Sharpsburg*." SMACK! Maybelle hit the ship with the bottle.

Nothing happened. The bottle didn't break. Maybelle felt her toes curl inside her shoes as her stomach wobbled. How embarrassing.

"It's okay," Mr. Pew said. "Do it again."

She took the bottle and this time she slammed it as hard as she possibly could and wine mixed with water spewed everywhere including all over her coat. She hadn't counted on that. But she didn't even care as a resounding cheer went up and the ship slipped swiftly into the Delaware River as the men onboard cheered and waved their good-byes.

"I did it," she said. "It was fun."

"Good, good," Mr. Pew said. "Now, let's all get back to work."

"But I'm on lunch," Maybelle said.

"Of course, after lunch."

Maybelle found Doris sitting in their usual spot after she had changed back into work clothes.

"Were you there?" Maybelle said. "Did you see me?"

"Yeah, sure," Doris said. "I was there. Saw the whole thing. You did great. Even if you missed the first time."

"Thanks." Maybelle sat down and opened her lunch. She was starving for some reason and wasted no time downing her sandwich and thermos of milk.

"I don't get it. I smashed the bottle really, really hard the first time. How can glass not break?"

Doris shrugged. "It's not the first time. I've seen it before. It wasn't a big deal."

Maybelle bit into her sandwich. "I guess not, but I felt a little embarrassed."

"Sure. The important thing is the ship is on its way to sea."

"Imagine that," Maybelle said. "I'm gonna try to follow it, you know, maybe write to some of the guys onboard."

"See, I told you. I told you you'd get attached."

Maybelle swallowed and sipped her milk. "Yeah. I really care now. More than before."

Doris smiled. "I'm proud of you."

"Maybe you'll get a turn, someday."

"It would be nice. But I ain't counting on it."

A minute or two of silence fell between them. Maybelle could hear the band still playing. Only this time is wasn't patriotic. More like Tommy Dorsey.

"So, regular time tonight?" Maybelle asked.

"For what?" Doris said. She looked distracted.

"For the sewing circle."

"Oh, yeah, yeah. I guess. Except . . ."

"Except what?"

"Except you won't believe what happened on the way to the ceremony. Which is why I was a little late and had to stand way in the back. I had to stand on tiptoes to see you."

"What happened? Something more from the war department?"

"No, no. Roger."

Maybelle swallowed. "Oh that." She didn't need to be clued in. She was fairly certain what had happened. "I told him not to do it. I told him to wait."

"You know?"

"Well, he asked me what I thought this morning. I told him to wait, but also to follow his heart. Are you terribly miffed?"

"Miffed?" Doris bit into her sandwich. "I don't know what I am. I'm flattered, but geez Louise, Maybelle, Mickey hasn't been gone but a month, unless you count the fifteen months previous and then it's a long time, but still, isn't it too soon for me to think about . . . you know about . . . another man?" She could barely get the last two words out.

Maybelle shook her head. "I don't know. Who says what's right? Roger really likes you."

"I know. I like him, but not in that way. At least, I don't think I do. I never thought—"

"Could you?"

Doris stared off toward the river. The ship was still visible as it made its way to the Atlantic. "I'm like that ship. Up and down on the waves."

"I think you should follow your heart also."

"I don't think Mickey would want me to be alone. But still. It's so soon. So sudden."

"Of course not." Maybelle wiped her mouth on her sleeve. "I don't think Mickey would want it either, but—"

"I just have to think." Doris crumpled what remained of her sandwich in brown paper. She closed the lid on her lunch can. "I just have to think."

Maybelle finished eating. "We can talk more about it tonight, if you want."

"Will Roger be there?"

"Maybe. You know him. Comes and goes. Who knows, he might be feeling really embarrassed and won't want to face you."

"We can only hope." Doris pushed some stray hairs behind her ear. "We can only hope. I think I might die, just die, if I had to see him tonight."

"Hope is why we're calling the quilt that, remember? It's all we got. And maybe hope means different things for different people."

17

The first thing Maybelle did when she arrived home, besides let Bingo out, was to look for Roger. "I don't think it would be such a great idea if he was here when Doris gets here," she told Bingo as he loped down the back steps.

"Ahh, what do you care?" she said with a wave.

She turned around and stopped two inches from Roger.

"Hey," he said.

"Hey," Maybelle said. "I just got home."

"Me, too, but what doesn't Bingo care about?"

Maybelle squeezed past him into the kitchen. "Nothing. He didn't . . . seem too interested in my day. You know, the launch."

"Oh, right. Well, you did a good job, even if the bottle didn't break the first time."

Maybelle smiled. "Yeah, that was kind of funny." She pulled open the refrigerator. "Looks like wieners again. I sure wish we could get a nice roast someday."

"Hard to come by," Roger said. "Easier to get steaks down at Pat's."

Maybelle closed the refrigerator door. "Now that sounds good."

"I could go. If you want. We do get paid tomorrow. So we got money."

Now this sounded like the perfect way to get Roger out of the house for a while. "Sure, go ahead. Get four, maybe five."

"Right," Roger said. "And I guess it is a good idea if I'm not here when Doris arrives."

Maybelle leaned against the kitchen counter. "She told me, Roger." Maybelle felt a little frustration but thought it would be better to tamp it down. To take a higher route than hollering more at poor, lovelorn Roger. "I told you to wait, honey. It was too soon."

"I couldn't help it. The sun was glinting off her welding shield and she just looked so darn pretty. Like an angel."

Maybelle did an eye roll probably visible from the moon. "Even so, Rog, she seemed kind of bugged about it."

"I know. But a fella can hope, can't he?"

"Yes, but I would steer clear of her tonight."

Roger ran the water in the sink. "Okay," he said as he washed. "I'll go to Pat's. That should take a while. But . . . Do you think I might still have a chance?"

"I don't know. But I wouldn't under any circumstances try this again. Not for a while."

"Okay, okay." Roger stuffed his hand into his pocket and pulled out some dollar bills. "I guess I have enough for steaks. Want onions?"

"No, thanks," Maybelle said. "We get kind of close when we're working on the quilt."

—◦◦◦—

Janice and Lois were the first arrive. Janice was carrying strips of red, white, and blue material. Thin strips.

"Hey," Maybelle said. "Those look like the streamers on the bottle this afternoon—you know, at the launch."

"They are," Janice said. "I ran down and grabbed them from the trash. McFarley was about to dump them in the trash bin. I thought we could sew them into the quilt."

"What a great idea," Maybelle said. "Thanks for getting them."

"Yeah, I had to dig them out of his dustpan."

"You did a great job," Lois said.

Maybelle took the streamers and set them on the dining room table. "Did you guys happen to see Doris on your way?"

"No," Janice said. "We passed her house. The lights were on, but we didn't see her."

"Okay, she'll get here. She's late a lot, in case you haven't noticed."

Janice and Lois looked at each other. "We noticed."

"Hey," Maybelle said. "I can make popcorn, and we have Coca-Cola."

"Really?" Lois said. "What fun. I always like popcorn."

"Okay, why don't you get started, and I'll get the corn popping."

"Need help?" Janice asked.

"Nah, I think I can handle popcorn."

Maybelle grabbed a deep pot from under the counter and set it on the stove. Next, she dropped a lump of lard into the pot and set the flame. The popcorn was in a glass jar. She opened the jar and poured kernels into the pot, dropped on the lid, and waited.

Meanwhile, Bingo sashayed past looking hungry as usual with his tongue nearly scraping the floor. "I got a wiener for you," Maybelle said. She grabbed it from the refrigerator and fed it to the pooch, who nearly swallowed it whole.

Soon, the kernels started popping. Maybelle shook the pot as the popping got louder and more frequent. She watched it go for a minute until the loose-fitting lid began to rise and the popcorn to overflow.

"Oh dear," she said as she grabbed a large bowl.

Bingo was already batting hot popped corn around the floor like they were tiny white mice.

She turned off the flame and grabbed the pot handle without a potholder, singeing her palm slightly before dropping it. The popcorn fell to the floor.

That was when Janice flew into the kitchen. "What's wrong? Are you okay?"

Maybelle plunged her hand under the cold running water and turned only slightly. "Yeah, not as bad as some splatter burns, but I dropped the popcorn."

"Oh, it's okay, most of it is still in the pot." Janice pushed Bingo out of the way, grabbed the pot holder, and lifted the pot and most of the popcorn onto the counter. "See that. No harm done. Besides, your floors are clean enough to eat off of."

Maybelle dried her hands. "Maybe when Mom was alive."

Janice dumped the popcorn into the waiting bowl. "I'll just take this out."

Maybelle followed behind. Lois was already busy cutting and pinning, so Maybelle opened the Singer and set out the quilt. It was now large enough to fit a double bed, Holden and Maybelle's bed.

"It really is pretty," Lois said. "So many colors."

"And memories," Maybelle said.

Janice sat at the table and began going through pieces of cloth. "Any word on Holden?"

"No. Nothing."

"That's too bad," Lois said. "But I guess you have to keep up hope."

"I'll say," Janice said. "I finally got a V-Mail today."

Maybelle, who kept glancing at the door for Doris, said, "That's terrific. What's the news?" She sat at the machine even though it still looked like a big, scary monster with teeth.

"Oh, you know the censors. Poor Willy, he can't tell me a dog-gone thing. Just that he's doing okay and the C rations are terrible. And he'll be starting the discharge process soon."

"I'm surprised they let him say that," Lois said.

"Yeah," Janice said. "I guess the enemy doesn't care if guys are going home."

The doorbell rang.

"Must be Doris," Maybelle ran to the door and pulled it open. She enjoyed Janice and Lois all right but felt much more comfortable when Doris was there.

"Hey, I was worried about you," Maybelle said. "I was beginning to think you weren't coming."

"Yeah, I almost didn't come," Doris said. She hung her coat on a hook near the front door. She slipped off her shoes. Maybelle noticed she was holding a small envelope. "But then I figured why not," Doris continued. "I can't avoid him forever."

"Good girl," Maybelle said. "But he's not here. I sent him to Pat's. He feels kind of stupid."

"He should. I mean, what possessed him?"

"You. Apparently."

Maybelle followed Doris into the dining room.

Doris raised her hand as though she wanted to wave Maybelle's words away. "Yeah, yeah."

"Hey, Doris," Janice called. "Glad you could make it."

"Yeah, hi," Lois said with a bit of fabric between her teeth.

"How's it going?" Janice asked.

Doris moved closer to the women. She patted Bingo's side. "It's going," she said.

Maybelle could hear the sadness in her voice. "Hey, I think I finally sewed a straight line." Maybelle held up a piece of the quilt.

"You did?" Doris asked. "Will wonders never cease?"

Janice reached into her pocket and pulled out a small envelope. "I got mail."

Maybelle raised her eyebrows at Janice, but she didn't seem to get what Maybelle was trying to say.

"I hate V-Mail," Janice said. "I know it saves space and money and all that but still. They reduce the letters so small you can barely read them."

"All for the war effort," Doris said.

Janice opened it so gingerly you'd think she was performing surgery. She pulled out the small paper and read a few words before bursting into buckets of tears.

"What is it?" Lois asked. "Not bad news, I hope." She set her sewing on the table.

"No, no, I just miss him," she said. "He just says he's fine and will be home soon."

"That's terrific," Maybelle said. "I'm so happy for you." But she just felt like she had been kicked in the throat. She had to choke back her own tears. This was good news and maybe a good sign for Holden.

"I'm glad Willy is doing okay," Doris said. Then she looked at Maybelle. "See, your letter is coming, too. You'll see. Holden is probably safe and sound—somewhere."

But Maybelle knew Doris was doing all she could to hold back her own tears. Her own sadness. There would be no letter from Mickey. But would it send her into Roger's arms too soon? Maybelle took Doris's hand. "It's hard for you, too. I know."

Doris only nodded.

Maybelle smiled. "I forgot the Coca-Cola. I'll go get it."

The Coca-Cola was on the back mud porch. Maybelle had gotten eight bottles, eight girl-shaped bottles in her estimation. She took four.

"Need any help?" Doris, who had followed her, asked.

"I got it," Maybelle said. She sniffed. "Roger screwed this nifty bottle opener onto the wall. See?" She held a bottle under a funny-looking chunk of metal and then pulled up on it. The metal bottle cap slipped off and fell to the ground with the most pleasant ring.

"Are you crying?" Doris asked.

"A little."

Doris held the opened bottles as Maybelle opened them. "What will they think of next? It's like an automatic bottle opener."

"Genius," Doris said as Bingo sniffed around the fallen caps.

"Try not to be too sad," Doris said. "You're bound to get an answer soon."

"I know. It's just, just so hard. Some days I wish I'd get any news, even ... even bad news, you know what I mean. To get it over with. But don't get me wrong. I am really happy for Lois. Really. I am."

"War is awful," Doris said. "You just never know."

"I know. Look who I'm telling."

Doris and Maybelle headed back to the dining room. "Where did you get Coca-Cola anyway?" Doris asked.

"The grocer. Picked it up a little while ago."

"Here's to our GI Joes. It's what the sign over the display said. There was a picture of two pretty girls sitting between a globe. They were smiling."

"Yeah, I bet they were wearing pretty skimpy clothes, too."

"Kind of, but it was okay."

Doris set two bottles on the dining room table and Maybelle did the same. "Here you go," she said. "Some cold refreshment." She held her bottle up. "We deserve a treat, don't we?"

Janice was still glued to her V-Mail. Lois nudged her. "Come, drink up. You can moon over your letter later."

There came a bang in the kitchen, like a door slamming.

"Is that him?" Doris lowered her voice to a near whisper. "Is he home?"

"Roger?" Maybelle said. "Already? He had to go all the way down to Passyunk."

"Then what was that noise?" Doris asked.

"Probably just the dog," Maybelle said. "Don't be such a Nervous Nellie."

Janice looked up from her sewing. "Since when does Roger make you nervous?"

Maybelle looked at Doris who at that moment had turned the color of a persimmon.

"He doesn't," Doris said. "And . . . and it's none of your beeswax." She glared at Maybelle.

Maybelle mimed a locking motion on her lips. "Loose lips sink more than ships."

"Right," Doris said.

"Oh, come on now," Lois said. "You don't need to be a war general to figure out what is going on around here."

"Nothing is going on," Doris said.

"Maybe not yet," Janice said. "But it's no military secret Roger likes you."

"He's smitten," Lois said with a smile. "We've seen how he looks at you—coming and going."

Doris nearly slammed her bottle on the table. "Now stop it. I have no interest in Roger. He's just . . . just—"

"Handsome and strong?" Janice said.

"Now look," Maybelle said. "This is Doris's business. Leave her alone."

"All right, already," Janice said. "Sorry, Doris. We don't mean to be rude."

"Thank you," Doris said. "And I will kindly appreciate it if you would refrain from discussing my personal business again."

Doris glared at Maybelle again.

"I didn't say a word," she said. "Not a single word."

Maybelle grabbed the quilt and unfolded it. She spread it over the dining room table on top of all the scraps and sewing supplies. "My goodness," she said. "Look at this, why don't ya."

"Wow," Doris said. "The quilt is huge. Maybe we should think about calling it quits and start the actual quilting process?"

"It will fit my bed just fine," Maybelle said. She touched the fabric. Then her heart skipped a beat. "Hold on, did you say start the quilting process?"

"Yeah," Doris said. "Now we have to put the batting on and the backing and then we get to do the actual quilting."

Maybelle's head spun. She had no idea what in the world Doris was saying. Batting? "Actual quilting? What in the world have we been doing?"

The women laughed. Janice squirted cola out her nose. She had to wipe off a piece of yellow fabric.

"Well, this isn't all there is," Doris said. "You knew that, right?"

Maybelle shook her head so hard she thought it could spin off and go sailing around the room like a balloon. "No. I . . . I never thought about it, I suppose."

"Look," Doris said. "This is just the quilt top. The batting is the soft stuff in the middle and then there is a bottom layer. We sew them together and then quilt a pretty design on top to hold it all snug and nice."

Maybelle could hardly believe her ears. "How could I be so stupid?"

"Ahh, it's your first time," Lois said. "You're not stupid."

"So I guess we should stop and get some batting and a bottom cover," Maybelle said.

The girls grew silent. They sipped their cold Coca-Colas. Finally, Janice said. "I say we keep going. I say we keep going until Holden comes home and Willy comes home and Johnny comes home and make it as big as we want."

"Really?" Doris said. "Won't that be kind of impractical?"

Maybelle smiled as a giant lightbulb went on in her head. "I say we make it as big as we want and when all our guys are home—" she glanced at Doris who tried to smile. "When we're all together we have a picnic, and share one quilt."

"Good idea," Lois said. "I say we keep *Hope* alive. Keep her going."

Doris laughed. "Okay. It is a good idea. Let's keep going. Who cares how big it gets?"

"Plenty of material," Maybelle said.

"Plenty of memories," Doris said.

18

The month of October quickly melted into November, and Thanksgiving was hot on Maybelle's heels. No one, including Doris, who had managed to evade Roger for nearly three weeks so far, said anything about the holiday. As far as she knew, everyone would be home, including her tenants.

She sat in the kitchen, on a rare day off, patting Bingo's head as she ruminated on the situation. "I have never roasted a turkey. Mom always did it." Maybelle didn't know the first thing about roasting anything as large as a turkey.

"Doris is just gonna have to help me if she wants a traditional meal," she said with definite tones. "I can buy the stuff we need. Most of it, anyway. Roger will help get things."

She sipped her coffee. "Roger. This is one day I don't think Roger and Doris are going to be able to avoid contact. Best we can wish for is an air raid to keep them apart."

She laughed and rubbed Bingo's side. "You know what, maybe it's the perfect day to bring them together."

Maybelle sighed. She still had not received word of Holden. Still, she refused to give up on hope. The idea and the quilt. Doris had not gotten the day off so Maybelle was kind of enjoying the house to herself. Everyone, including the tenants, was at the yard.

Unfortunately, Rachel and Marybeth grew bored and tired with the quilt project and decided to drop out of the circle. They hung around sometimes, when there were brownies and Coca-Cola, but mostly they worked at the yard and hung out at Mackey's.

Maybelle had heard they were making quite a few friends down there. A lot of dancing and such. It wasn't what she really wanted to know. What they did on their own time was their business, as long as they didn't bring it home. And Maybelle was fine as long as they paid the rent and pitched in with housework from time to time. Rachel had been pretty faithful with helping out with the bathroom and Marybeth seemed to actually like to dust and sweep. Now if she could get someone to make Thanksgiving for her.

The holiday was still not celebrated by everyone in town. And she was fine with that. But Doris wanted to make a big meal. She had it mostly all planned and expected Maybelle to join in.

"We'll discuss it at the sewing circle tonight."

Maybelle whiled away the rest of the day around the house. She knew the weather would be turning colder so she made sure all the windows had tight shutters and heavy draperies. Francine liked to change the curtains on all the windows a couple of times a year. She had light, frilly curtains, along with blackout curtains, for the warmer months and heavier drapes for the winter. She kept them in the attic.

Fortunately, Francine was born organized, and Maybelle had no trouble finding the trunk with the heavy, green drapes inside. She lugged the thing down the steps with Bingo getting in the way. "I know you're trying to help, but please, downstairs." The dog dashed away. But it probably had more to do with the huge bang the trunk made when it fell down the last four steps into the living room. It burst open, spewing draperies and other whatnot, small nails, screws, and curtain hanger paraphernalia all over the place.

She also noticed her mother had pinned a note to each drape indicating which window they were to cover. Maybelle shook her head. "Sometimes I think I must have been an adopted child. Someone left me on Francine's doorstep."

Maybelle looked around the living room at the large windows. So much for good intentions. She would need help hanging the draperies. It now seemed there was precious little Maybelle could do on her own. She left the trunk in the middle of the floor and sat on the couch. "What good am I? What can I do? Except weld seams."

Bingo sidled nearby and whimpered.

"Oh, there must be something I can do. Maybe I should go to secretarial school or—" she laughed. "Me? A secretary? Nope."

And so she sat for most of the day missing Holden more than ever and contemplating a future without him. She did turn the radio on and allowed the sweet dulcet tones of the day to filter through the room. Frank Sinatra was beginning to grow on her. She did like music, even if she couldn't carry a tune in a bucket. And then, for a brief minute she thought about her father, the doctor. "I bet I'm more like him."

Bingo barked.

"Me? A doctor?"

It was as far as the thought got because the doorbell rang.

Her heart pounded as her mind jumped to a terrible conclusion. It was the army with bad news.

But no, thank goodness. It was only the man who read the light meter standing there in his crisp dark blue uniform and hat—similar to an army dress cap.

"Thank goodness," she said.

"Excuse me," the man said.

"Nothing, I was expecting . . . well, not really expecting—oh, please come in."

The older man squeezed past her and headed straight for the basement.

She had seen him before, many times, but this was the first time she actually greeted him. Quite often, it seemed Roger was around when the meter man came by.

And so, she waited some more. She waited for the day to draw to a close and for Roger to come home and the girls to come for the sewing circle. If only she could make a cake or brownies like Roger. It would help pass the time. But she was not about to attempt anything as adventurous, and possibly waste vital ingredients, especially this close to Thanksgiving. She did pick up the latest copy of *Our Yard*. She leafed through it, and her eyes landed on the section entitled "Strictly for the Girls." The column always had neat tidbits of information on anything from how to repair a cracked fingernail to the best way to blackout your windows. This month it even had a recipe for mincemeat pie.

"It sounds good," she told Bingo. "Maybe Doris and I can make a pie."

And then Roger came home. He was carrying boxes filled to almost overflowing with food items and other sundries like soap and shoe polish.

"Hey," he said, "I hit the jackpot. Everything but the turkey. I'll pick it up later."

Maybelle helped Roger unpack the boxes. There were potatoes and carrots, tomatoes and nuts, flour, sugar and cocoa, even cranberries for sauce, and an onion for the stuffing.

"This is going to be great, if I can figure out how to make it," Maybelle said.

Roger smiled. "Doris will be here to help. And so will I. I can peel potatoes like nobody's business."

Maybelle dropped the potatoes into a drawer under the counter. "Doris. But—"

Roger slipped into a chair at the table. "Guess who I ran into down at the grocer?"

Maybelle sucked air. "No? Doris? Really?"

Roger nodded. Bingo barked. "Yep, and we got it all straightened out. We got an understanding." He looked like he could he bust.

"An understanding?"

"Yep. And that's as good as a promise in my book."

Maybelle slid into a chair and looked Roger in the eye. "Oh, Roger, honey, don't go counting your chickens."

"Ah, chickens, schmickens. Like I said. We got an understanding. Now, if you'll excuse me, I know she's on her way over, so I'll just skedaddle down to Mackey's for dinner."

"But I thought you had an understanding."

"We do. Going to Mackey's tonight is part of the understanding."

Maybelle sucked even more air out of the kitchen. Oh boy, she dearly hoped Roger was not reading too much into this new . . . agreement.

Roger politely and sweetly kissed Maybelle's cheek. "See ya later." She couldn't remember when he seemed so happy.

She put all the groceries away and even found a package of turkey giblets obviously for Bingo. She unwrapped the innards and dropped them into his bowl. He came running, even slipping and sliding on the floor.

"Eat hearty," she said as his face landed in the bowl.

By then her own stomach was growling so she whipped together a quick "cream of" soup. This was pretty much whatever she could find, made quickly into a creamy, thick soup. Tonight it was cauliflower, tomatoes, cucumbers, and a few slices of already-cooked steak Roger brought home the day before. It smelled good and with some bread and butter, well, oleomargarine, but still. She was happy.

And even happier when Doris showed up at the back door with her own arms filled with groceries. "Hey," she called. "Let me in."

Maybelle pulled open the back door. "Whatcha got there?"

"All the makings for pie. We are going to eat like royalty this Thanksgiving."

"Okay," Maybelle said. "I think I might even be starting to get excited about it."

"Good." Doris pushed the box into Maybelle's hand. "Just the oleo and milk need to be refrigerated. And the eggs."

"Eggs? You got eggs?"

"A full dozen. Doc Pemberton gave them to me. Said someone paid him in eggs this week, and since he's not going to be home for the holiday he gave them to us. Oh, and we could have the chicken, too, but I didn't think you'd want her."

Maybelle put the groceries away and quickly filled two bowls with the cream soup. She was anxious to grill . . . speak to Doris about Roger and what in tarnation happened. Doris was looking a little happier than usual. And Maybelle hoped this was a good sign.

Doris said a blessing ending the prayer with, "And thank you for Roger and his big heart. Amen."

Okay, so now it was getting a little more than strange.

"What gives?" Maybelle asked. She stirred her soup and dunked a piece of bread into it. "Roger told me he ran into you and now you two have some kind of arrangement."

Doris ate some soup. "This is good. You always did make good cream of whateverisinthepantry soup."

Maybelle dropped her spoon in her bowl. "Now you are just being evasive. What gives?"

"We're engaged."

Maybelle swallowed a large lump of cauliflower. It nearly choked her. "You . . . you're . . . what?" she sputtered like an old automobile.

"Well, we're engaged to be engaged. Look, I like Roger. I could even go for him. When the time is right. I asked him if he could hang on for a while . . . until I felt like the time was right for me to . . . you know, get involved again."

"And he went for it?"

"Like a bear to honey."

"But he could be waiting a really long time," Maybelle said.

Doris shook her head. She sipped more soup and then smiled. "Maybe not too long. Just a respectable time."

Maybelle felt her stomach go a trifle wobbly. "How can you get over Mickey so fast? You seem so . . . so devil-may-care about it now. I thought you loved Mickey."

"I do . . . did love Mickey with all my soul and heart. But I also know in my same soul and same heart neither he nor God want me to remain single for the rest of my life. And if there is one thing I've learned from this war, it's . . . you never know. Life can throw you for a loop in an instant."

"Maybe," Maybelle said. "But back to you and Roger. Do you have any idea how long you expect him to wait?"

"No. But I'll know when I'm ready. Sometimes it's hard to believe Mickey is really, really gone and never coming back. Pastor Mendenhall said it might be because I never saw his . . . bod . . . you know."

Maybelle dipped more bread. "Yeah, it's got to be strange. And Pastor is probably correct."

"So Roger will wait," Doris said.

Maybelle finished her soup. She wanted more but thought it might be better to get started on the quilt.

Doris agreed. "Besides, in a couple of days, we'll have so much food you'll be wishing it would disappear."

"Speaking of that," Maybelle said as she cleared the table. "You are going to help?"

"If by *help* you mean cook the whole dinner, then yeah, I guess so. But you need to be here to help prepare things."

Maybelle stood at attention and saluted Doris. "Anything you need, General."

"Good." Doris pulled open the refrigerator. "Where's the turkey?"

"Roger is getting it tomorrow."

Doris nodded. "Okay, good. We'll need to get it in the oven bright and early Thursday morning. By seven o'clock."

Maybelle felt her knees buckle. "Seven? So early."

"It's a big bird. Takes hours to roast."

"Anyway," Doris said. "I think we should make a big, huge Thanksgiving meal. You know like the one on the cover of the *Saturday Evening Post*. I saw a copy in Doc's waiting room. The Rockwell fella sure can paint."

"I know the one. The same cover someone hung in the lunch room at the yard."

"Yeah, with that big turkey. Heck, I don't know if Roger got one that big."

"I bet he did."

The doorbell rang.

"I guess it's Janice and Lois," Doris said. "Tonight, we start the actual quilting."

"I'm not sure if I can."

"We'll teach you. Nothing to it really. And look, you learned to make straight seams and sew squares together. This will be easy as pie."

Maybelle followed Doris to the door. "I can't make pie, either."

"You know," Doris said. She paused a moment. "One of these days you are going to have to figure out what you are good at. And do it."

"Ahh, probably just being a mother, once Holden gets back."

"I don't know about that. At least for me. One thing Mickey and I always talked about was maybe I'd like to do something more than be a mother."

"Really?"

"Sure. Kids grow up. Then what?"

"Do you think Roger feels the same way, I mean, assuming you two . . . get married?" Maybelle swallowed.

"I'm sure of it. Roger would like nothing more than to have a wife and a mother for his children, but I think he would also want his wife to be happy. Maybe I'll become a teacher. I teach Sunday school."

"Oh, you'd make a great teacher."

The doorbell rang again. This time with a decidedly angry tone.

"Oh, the girls," Maybelle said. "We better let them in."

Maybelle spread the quilt, now sewn together including a nice wide purple border, onto the dining room table. The quilt was so large it hung over all four sides of the already big table.

"Oh my," Maybelle said. "It's as big as a tent. A great big army tent."

Doris laughed. "Yeah, but it would be the prettiest tent out there."

"Not exactly camouflage," Lois said.

"I'll say," Janice said. "It would attract Nazis."

They laughed.

"I think it will fit two beds," Maybelle said. But that was just fine with her. She liked how big it had grown and how she and her friends and family were represented. Now, it was easy to see the design, the crazy "quiltness" of it—of all those memories sewn together. Like community. Like friendship should be.

"Okay," Janice, who had carried a large box into the room said. "I sewed together about six big remnants . . ." Everyone looked at Maybelle.

"Well, I'm not that stupid. I know what it means."

"Good" Janice said. "I sewed together the remnants for the bottom cover. And I cut the batting also. It's nice and soft."

"Where did you get it?" Doris asked.

Janice smiled. "Oh, Roger isn't the only one around here with connections."

Maybelle shot Doris a look. She really wanted to tell them about the arrangement, but Doris gave her a look back. A look that clearly said, "If you tell, I will most assuredly kill you." She said nothing.

"Now," Doris said. "I guess it would be easier to machine sew the pieces together and then we can all work on hand-quilting the pieces together."

"Wait a second," Maybelle said. "Hand-quilt the pieces together? I thought you just said the machine will do that?"

Janice and Lois hid their snickers.

"Nope," Doris said. "We have to quilt all the squares down. That way the batting won't move and get all bunchy."

"And it will look so pretty," Lois said. "With all those tiny stitches. You'll see."

"How long will it take?" Maybelle said.

"Probably until Christmas," Doris said. "But maybe not. It all depends."

"On me, I suppose," Maybelle said.

"Come on," Janice said. "Let's get the pieces together and then we'll start."

Maybelle stood back and watched as the others expertly pinned together the top and the bottom with the batting in between. She was amazed.

Then Janice, who was probably the best seamstress in the group, set to work on the machine. Maybelle was enthralled at watching her work the monster. She filled the bobbin, threaded the needle, and set to work with the huge quilt like it was nothing. It took quite a bit of time to finish. In fact, Maybelle made tea and talked turkey stuffing with Doris.

"So Roger said he brought a bag of giblets?"

Maybelle poured hot water into a teapot. "A bag of what?"

"Giblets. The organs, hearts mostly, from the turkey. And livers."

Maybelle swallowed. What a disgusting thought. "No. I don't remember." She looked down at Bingo's bowl. "Oh, I thought it was for the dog. I fed it to Bingo."

"You what?" Doris said.

"I dumped the bag into Bingo's bowl. I didn't know."

Doris took a breath and blew it out her nose. "I can't believe it. The giblets. I needed them to make gravy."

"Oh, well, if it's any consolation Bingo practically inhaled them. They must have been delicious."

"Some say the best part of gravy is the giblets. Maybe Roger can get some more."

"It is kind of disgusting." Maybelle set the lid on top of the teapot. "Sure he can. I'm sorry. I really didn't know."

"It's okay. Come on. Let's go see how Janice is doing with *the Hope*. I'll carry the tray and you get the cookies."

"Cookies?"

Doris had her back to Maybelle. "Yeah, Roger said Mrs. Pomeroy gave him a tin of oatmeal molasses cookies today. They're really for Thanksgiving, but I say we eat them now."

"Oh, I thought I saw a red tin in the box."

Sure enough, Maybelle located the cookies and carried the entire tin, red with a clown painted on it, into the dining room. "Look what I found. Beats popcorn any day."

"Cookies?" Lois said. "I've been wanting something sweet."

"I don't know how sweet they are—" Maybelle lifted the lid from the tin. "But they sure look good."

Each of the women took a cookie and sat for a moment while silently savoring the treat.

"You know," Janice said from her seat at the Singer. "This cookie is making me look forward to Thanksgiving."

"Me, too," Lois said. "Are we having pie?"

"Mincemeat," Doris said. "All we could scrounge. But it'll be tasty."

Maybelle let go a sigh. "I hope so. I've never been responsible for Thanksgiving."

Doris gave her a shot in the arm. "I said I'd do most of the work."

"Sure," Janice said. "And we'll be here. You'll do great."

"Yeah," Lois said. "You said you couldn't sew and now look."

Maybelle looked at Janice who was adjusting the massive blanket so she could fit it through the machine. "I guess you're right."

Lois, Doris, and Maybelle continued talking and eating cookies while Janice finished the sewing the layers together.

It took Janice the better part of two hours to sew the layers together, including three bathroom breaks and a couple of cookie breaks. By the time she was finished, the women were so caught up in discussions about favorite holiday recipes, tips for what to do when the blackout signal sounded, and fond family memories, no one wanted to start quilting.

"Come on," Doris said. "Let's fold it up and go into the living room."

"Good idea," Lois said. "Did I tell you I got another V-Mail from Johnny today?"

"No," Doris said. "Tell us."

Doris and Maybelle sat on the sofa while Janice and Lois took the two comfy chairs. Bingo found his spot on the hearth and happily laid down to snooze or maybe listen to the girls thump their gums.

Maybelle thought it was nice they had grown quite fond of one another but was quite surprised when Doris all of a sudden and out of the blue told about Roger.

"Now if that don't beat all," Janice said. "He really proposed?"

Doris, who was still sipping a cup of tea, smiled. "Kind of."

"They have an arrangement," Maybelle said with pursed lips. "They're engaged to be engaged."

"Oh, I get it," Lois said. "When you're ready, right, Doris?"

"Right."

Janice leaned back in the chair. "I think Roger will make a great catch. Didn't I say so?" She looked at Lois.

"You said so." Lois grinned. "Janice can always call them. She really is quite the matchmaker."

"Yeah, I saw this one comin'. He is smitten with you."

Maybelle shook her head. "But isn't it too soon? What do you think people will say?"

Lois waved the comment away. "Pish-posh on that. Who cares? It's war times and anything can happen."

"Yeah," Janice said. "How do we know the Nazis ain't planning on invading Philadelphia right this very minute?"

Maybelle did not like the sound of that. "Impossible. They don't have the brains the US of A's got."

"But they're sneaky," Lois said.

"Hold on, hold on," Doris said. "I ain't doing anything until I feel it's right. Until the Good Lord taps me on the shoulder and tells me it's time."

"Oh, you're one of those, are you?" Janice said. "Believing God talks to ya?"

Doris set her cup on the end table. "No, but I know when He is tellin' me stuff."

Lois leaned toward Janice. "Leave her alone. People got to find solace wherever they can these days."

"So," Maybelle said. "What about them giblets?"

The three other women shared a glance and then laughed. "What?" they said together.

"Did you know they make gravy from giblets? That's the hearts and livers from the turkeys."

"Well, sure," Janice said. "And I always like to stick the neck in the mix, too. Great flavor in the neck."

Maybelle swallowed a sour burp. "Neck?"

"Sure," Doris said. "You'll see on Thursday. I'm sure Roger will be able to find more giblets. Not everyone likes them."

"More?" Lois said.

Doris chuckled as Bingo perked his ears. "Right, Maybelle didn't know what they were and fed them to Bingo."

Bingo let go a happy bark.

Lois and Janice laughed. "Ha, it's the zipper story all over again."

Maybelle tried to join in the laughing. And she really was okay with their fun, but still, it hurt just a trifle.

"Okay, okay," Doris said. "I guess we better get going. We have work tomorrow."

"Yeah, I'm surprised any of us got Thanksgiving off," Maybelle said.

"Roger is working the night shift," Doris said.

Janice put her arm around Lois. "Now ain't this sweet. She knows his schedule already."

"Ahh, put a lid on it," Doris said. "So he can be around for dinner,"

"I heard Logan has to work," Maybelle said. "Does he ever get a day off? He is always there."

The women grew quiet. "Maybe he just doesn't have anyone. Is he married?"

Maybelle started to walk toward the front door. "Not that I know of."

"Let's invite him," Lois said.

"That knucklehead," Janice said. "You want to invite your boss to dinner?"

Lois shrugged. "Sure. Why not? It might do us some good down the line, you know?"

"All right by me," Maybelle said. She opened the front door and handed the girls their coats. "But you invite him, Lois."

"Okay, I will." Lois slipped into her heavy, blue coat.

"Now be careful out there," Maybelle said. "Keep an eye to the sky. Never know when a bomb is gonna fall."

Doris hung back a moment. "So, I guess maybe people won't be so shocked if I start dating Roger."

Maybelle had to take a few seconds to get her bearings. "It doesn't sound like it. I think most people will understand."

Doris buttoned her coat. "I think I'll have another talk with Pastor Mendenhall."

"Good idea," Maybelle said.

Maybelle closed the door. It had been a nice evening. She liked the idea of Roger and Doris dating and maybe even getting married one day. But still, as she leaned against the heavy, oak door she couldn't help but heave a tremendous, molasses-smelling sigh. "What about me, Lord. When will I get news?"

19

Wednesday, the day before Thanksgiving, Maybelle and Doris hurried home from the yard. They were anxious to work on the quilt and to begin preparations for the next day's huge holiday meal.

The skies were overcast and threatening rain as they hurried down Ninth Street.

"Do you think it will rain tomorrow?" Doris asked as she skirted a stray cat in her path.

"Looks like it," Maybelle said. "I hope it doesn't rain on the parade tomorrow." She buttoned the top button of her coat as a chill wind whipped past.

"Macy's will hold the parade rain or shine."

They picked up the pace. "I hear it's spectacular," Doris said. "One year we'll have to take the train into New York and see it instead of waiting for the newsreels or pictures in the *Inquirer.*"

"Sounds like a great idea. Let's go next year. Me and Holden. You and Roger. We'll make it a day, maybe a whole weekend."

Doris stopped at her mailbox. "Let me just check." She pulled out a small stack of letters. "Oh, it's from the war department. Maybe Mickey's pay finally got to me. They give me six months', and I haven't seen a single month yet."

"Open it," Maybelle said.

"Yep. It's a check. Holy cow. Look at that." She showed the check to Maybelle. "A hundred dollars. Two months."

"Good for you," Maybelle said.

Doris kissed the check and stuffed it and the other letters into her purse. "Come on, we got a lot to do."

The first thing they did when they got to Maybelle's house was take off their boots and wash up. The smell from the yard was always on them it seemed. Maybelle suggested they change into blue jeans. Doris happily concurred.

Bingo was chomping at the bit to get outside, so Maybelle opened the back door and watched him take off lickety-split toward the back of the yard.

Doris opened the refrigerator and pulled out a brown wrapper about the size of a cheesesteak. She opened a small corner. "Will you look at this, giblets. And lots of them." She replaced the package and closed the door. "But no turkey. I hope Roger remembers to get it. He got a pretty big one, I think." Doris glanced around the small kitchen. "We're gonna need a lot of dressing."

"Okeydokey," Maybelle said. "Just tell me what to do."

"Later," Doris said. "Let's have tea and work on the quilt. We should start quilting. Gonna be a little hard without a frame, but we'll manage."

"Are you sure?" Maybelle said. She snagged two oatmeal molasses cookies after turning the flame on under the teakettle.

"Yeah, we got all night to cut up vegetables. I plan on spending the night. Figure I'll bake the pie tonight. Save time tomorrow."

"Good idea." They went to the dining room. "I was going to ask you to stay. But, well, will you be okay with Roger sleeping down the hall?"

"Sure," Doris said.

"No sneaking into his room, now," Maybelle said with a smile.

Doris punched her arm. "Now, cut it out. I'd . . . never."

"I know, I know," Maybelle said.

"It's nice it's just us tonight," Doris said.

Maybelle let go a deep breath. "Yeah. It is. Janice said she wanted to make something special for tomorrow and Lois said she's coming down with a cold."

"Too bad. Just so she doesn't spread it around. I hate colds. They take forever to go away."

Doris unfolded the now-larger-than-ever quilt over the dining table.

"You know, we'll need to get rid of all this sewing stuff for tomorrow," Maybelle said.

"I know. Will you look at it? It's the most amazing, colorful thing I have ever set my eyes on. Janice did a real good job sewing the layers together."

Doris opened the large sewing box.

"I still don't get why we need to do this by hand."

"Because it's fun for one thing, and for another it is plain impossible to work it around the machine."

Maybelle looked at the tiny Singer in comparison to the huge quilt. "Makes sense. So what do we do?" She felt so much more comfortable with just Doris there. Learning something new was always nerve-racking.

Doris threaded two small quilting needles and placed a small thimble on her middle finger. Maybelle wasn't sure why, but she did the same. It felt strange. But she liked the look of it. A tiny goose was embossed on the side. She wondered who would take the time to make something so utilitarian so lovely. Then she remembered something her mother had told her long ago. It was about a woman. A pioneer. One of the first settlers in the country.

"They found a small journal. She wrote about her family of five children and her quilt-making," her mother had said. "And inside was written, 'I make them warm to keep my family from freezing; I make them beautiful to keep my heart from breaking.'" Maybelle hadn't given it much thought until now. She understood about the quilt and about why they were made so lovely.

"We just make small quilt stitches around the squares and the designs," Doris said. "I'll start. Watch me and then grab a corner and start."

Maybelle watched for several minutes as Doris pushed and pulled and tugged and snipped. She was correct. The design was starting to come alive and the quilt was starting to get the quilted look. Padded but not bumpy.

With the thimble still on her finger, Maybelle took a deep breath and set to work. She was surprised at first at how hard it was to get the needle through all three layers of material. The thimble came in handy. And as she worked, she began to feel something she hadn't felt before. Kinship. Sisterhood.

"Thimbles will save your fingers," Doris said. "It can hurt and even draw blood if you don't use one."

They continued working for a few minutes, each lost in her own thoughts. Maybelle thought of Holden. At least she wanted to think about him. To remember him. But how? Where was he? Was he still even alive? She shuddered at the thought of his body, lost and decaying, in some deep forest or an unseen ditch.

Fortunately, her thoughts were interrupted when Roger burst into the kitchen. "Here you go," he called.

"What is that?" Doris asked.

"Sounds like Roger. Let's go see what he has now."

Doris set her work down. "You can never tell with him."

They entered the kitchen, and there stood Roger holding a large, dead turkey by the feet. A large, freshly killed turkey.

"Look here. One fine turkey. Got him myself not one hour ago," he said with a smile wider than the farm he probably shot him on. "Ready for plucking," Roger said.

Maybelle burst into the best laugh she had had in a while. "Are you nuts?"

"What?" Roger said. "Just pluck him and clean him, lop off his head and roast him."

"I am not plucking any bird," Doris said. "Take him down to the butcher shop."

"Ahh, you're kidding!" Roger said. "Can't you pluck a measly turkey?"

Maybelle was not sure if he was joking with them or not. "No," she said. "Now take the monster down to Sam's right now." Maybelle stamped her foot. "What was wrong with the bird we already bought?"

"Nothin'," Roger said. "Old man Wilton invited me to go shoot and—" he held the bird higher. "Here he is. Wilton got three."

"No," Maybelle said. "You take that bird out of here right now and get me the bird we bought."

"Okay, okay," Roger said and he left with his bird.

Maybelle and Doris, who was suspiciously silent through the exchange, waited until he was gone and then burst into laughter. "Can you believe it?" Doris said. "Do you think he actually thought we could pluck and butcher a turkey? I have trouble cleaning a bowl for oatmeal. I ain't no pioneer woman."

Maybelle smiled wide. "Francine would have done it. I've seen her pluck a pheasant or two when I was a girl. Daddy used to bring them home and Francine would have at it. My goodness the feathers would fly. She used to let me have the claw. I could work the talons by pulling on the ligaments, remember?"

"Yeah, yeah. You liked to scare us half out of our wits with those things."

Maybelle laughed more. "But that's as close I got to any kind of butchering. Could you do it? I mean what if you and Rog get married, and he starts bringing game fowl home for you to cook?"

"No way. The only thing I pluck are my eyebrows and not so much anymore."

"Yeah. He's a funny one."

Doris headed back to the dining room. "I think he did that just to fool us. It's probably one of Wilton's birds."

"You think?" Maybelle put the thimble on her finger and picked up the needle.

"Sure. He knows we'd never do it."

They were right. Roger burst into the living room laughing like there was no tomorrow. "Did I get you going?" he called. "I was only joking. It was Wilton's bird. He says Mrs. Wilton can pluck two turkeys at once."

"Fine for her," Maybelle called.

Roger sidled next to Doris. "You okay?"

She looked up at him. "Yeah, I knew you was only joking."

Maybelle watched as their eyes met. Doris quickly pulled away. But Roger lingered a second longer. "Look," he said. "I got the late shift again. But I'll be here in the morning, if you gals think you might need some help."

"Nah, we'll be okay," Maybelle said. "But Roger, where is our turkey?"

"He's already in the refrigerator. I snuck him in earlier before I brought the other one inside. He's a big one, twenty pounds."

"Twenty pounds?" Maybelle said. "Who is gonna eat twenty pounds of turkey?"

"We are," Doris said. "Just think of all those turkey sandwiches we can bring to the plant."

"Oh, yeah," Maybelle said. "Now that will be a treat over cucumber and mayonnaise."

"What do you say we work on the quilt for another half an hour or so and then get started on tomorrow's dinner?"

"Sounds like a great idea."

"I was meaning to ask," Doris said. "Where are the tenants? Haven't seen them."

"Oh, they've been on the late shift and then they are both going home for the holiday. Logan is none too thrilled about it, though."

"Oh, are they AWOL?"

"Yeah, I think so. I might be looking for more tenants soon."

They went about the business of the quilt as a wash of silence overtook the room. Maybelle was beginning to find these moments almost insufferable. Everything made her think of either Holden, lost somewhere in a war, or her mother, whom she missed more and more. And now with Roger's profession of love for Doris, and Doris agreeing to an arrangement, it made the whole thing even more strange.

"Are you okay?" Maybelle asked Doris.

Doris looked up from her sewing. "Sure. I'm okay."

"He really does love you, I think."

"What?" Doris jabbed the needle into the cloth.

"Him, Roger. He loves you."

Doris shook her head. "I know and I really don't want to lead him down a primrose path but—"

"You aren't sure?"

Doris stopped sewing and looked at Maybelle. "Yeah, I'm sure. I just wish I could let go of Mickey more."

"I don't think you'll ever let go of him completely. He'll always be part of your life."

"I guess it's what worries me. How could I ever make love to another man when I still got Mickey on my heart?"

Maybelle stabbed the fabric. "Wow, I never thought of it that way. But . . . maybe you'll need to talk to Roger about it."

"Yeah, that's what Pastor said."

"What else did the pastor say?"

"He said, love will find its way. It might be odd for a while, but he believes Roger is patient and kind and will even wait if he has to."

"Really?"

"But I don't want him to wait."

"You know, Doris," Maybelle said. "I think when you're ready, you'll know and . . . and the love-making part will be okay. You'll see."

Maybelle tugged at her needle. "Another knot. How come I keep making knots in my thread?"

"You have to let it hang sometimes," Doris said. "Now look, let me snip it. You'll never get that knot out."

"Knots," Maybelle said. "There are always knots. In everything. Even life."

"Yeah but we can get them out. We just have to know which string to pull first."

"How?"

"Well, God for one thing. You keep forgetting about Him."

Maybelle looked out the dining room window. The wind was rustling through what was left of the leaves on the oak tree. "Nah, I think He's forgotten me."

"You can't say that," Doris said. "God hasn't forgotten you. He never said life would be perfect."

"I know, but . . . but sometimes I think there can be just too much heartache."

Doris thought a moment. "Sometimes. Yes. Life is full of heartache. But seeing it as part of a better, wonderful plan helps."

"How can Mickey's death be part of any wonderful plan? How can Holden's . . . Holden's whatever . . . his 'missingness' be part of a wonderful plan?"

Doris jabbed the quilt and then brought the needle through to the front. "It just is. I have to believe it or I'd go nuts."

Maybelle made a few more stitches. They were slightly crooked and a bit too large perhaps, but at least she was doing it. "I still can't believe I'm actually sewing."

"Yep," Doris said. "Who knows maybe you'll finish that dress someday—the one with the zipper in the neck hole."

Maybelle laughed. "Nah, I think it should remain where it is." Then a lightbulb lit up in her brain. "Hey, you know what? We need to add it to the quilt."

"But we can't, we're nearly finished."

"Ahh, really, can't we just put a piece or a swatch on somewhere? Like a . . . what do you call it? Like Lois's lamb?"

"Appliqué? Maybe. Go on, get the dress. Do you know where it is?"

"Of course. It's my monument to shame. I've kept it in my hope chest all this time."

"Hope chest? Then it's only fitting."

"I just wish I had thought about it sooner."

"Me, too."

"Wait. I'll go get it."

Maybelle dashed up the steps. Her hope chest was sitting under the window. It was a large oak box, not too fancy, but with pretty inlay work around the lid and bottom. She pushed it open and a waft of cedar blew out. Maybelle riffled through some books, pictures, a couple of old newspapers announcing the start of the war. Then she found the dress rolled in a ball on the bottom. She pulled it out. The fabric was nice, seersucker, yellow with tiny white polka dots. The zipper still hung from the neck hole.

She raced down the steps. "Here it is. Sheesh, does it bring back a nightmare. Mrs. Leland was so mad at me. She threw me out of the class."

"I remember."

Doris took the dress. "Okay, we can cut a square and sew it here, on top of this square with your baby blanket."

"Oh, that's nice."

"Now I'll have to blind stitch it so it doesn't show."

"With your eyes closed?"

Doris rolled her eyes and chuckled softly. "No, silly."

"I'm joking," Maybelle said. "You always take me so seriously."

212

"Okay, okay, hand me the scissors."

A few minutes later, Doris was fast at work sewing a square of yellow seersucker onto the pink baby blanket.

"You know," Maybelle said. "It kind of makes the whole thing. It pulls it all together. A focal point even."

"It does," Doris said. "It really does. You see what I mean?"

"Mean about what?"

"The bigger plan." Doris pulled the needle through. "God knew this dress would fit into the plan somewhere. Nothing is wasted."

"So God wanted me to fail in high school?"

Doris shook her head. "No, no, I'm not saying that. You messed up the dress. But God found a way to use it for good. To give the whole debacle a greater purpose now. It's just the piece we need to bring *Hope* together."

Doris finished sewing the piece on. "There. Now what do you say we call it quits and get started on tomorrow's dinner?"

"I say it's a great plan."

They folded the quilt together. It took two of them now, four hands. They packed all the sewing stuff into the trunk and carried it into the living room.

"I think we should just leave it here," Maybelle said. "Then we won't have to lug it down the steps again."

"Good idea. What about the Singer?"

Maybelle looked into the dining room. "Do you think it'll be in the way?"

"Nah. I say we leave it there. We can close it up and use it as a sideboard. You know, it can hold the cranberries and stuff like that."

Maybelle draped her arm around Doris. "You, my friend, are a genius."

It took most of the night, well past midnight, before Maybelle and Doris had all the vegetables prepared and two mincemeat pies. She didn't use any meat, only raisins, apples, cinnamon, and other autumn spices.

Maybelle was amazed. It smelled just as rich as a traditional pie. It was sweet and luscious and even the texture was perfect.

"It'll fool the best of 'em," Maybelle said. Even Bingo didn't know the difference. He chomped the remainder of the concoction down like it was raw giblets.

"I know. I learned how to make them a couple of years ago. I actually like it better without meat. Especially after eating turkey."

Maybelle looked around the kitchen. She yawned wide. "What a mess. Do we have to clean up tonight?"

"'Fraid so," Doris said with an equally expansive yawn. "We'll be sorry in the morning, or when we get back down here. It's already morning."

"Okay," Maybelle said. "But you go to bed. I'll clean up."

"No," Doris said as she started gathering bowls and dishes to wash.

"I mean it," Maybelle said. "You'll be doing most of the work tomorrow."

"Okay. You don't have to convince me. I'll go to bed. But we're back here by six."

Maybelle glanced at the kitchen clock. "Four hours, holy cow!"

"You better hurry."

She actually liked being alone in the kitchen. She felt tired but surprisingly okay. She thought for sure her first Thanksgiving without Francine and Holden would be hard and horrible. Oh, it had its horrible moments. But Maybelle was thankful for Doris and Roger and good friends.

She had just dried the last spoon when Roger came home. He looked tired and in need of a shave.

"Hey," he said. "You still up?"

"We just finished pies and such for tomorrow. Doris went to bed already." She pointed toward the ceiling. "Upstairs."

"Oh, good idea."

"Now don't go getting any manly ideas," Maybelle joked.

"Me? Never. I am a gentleman."

"I know but—"

"But what?"

Maybelle wasn't certain she should spill the beans but did anyway. "Sit down a second. I want to tell you something. About Doris."

"Doris?" Roger sat at the table. He picked at the pie crust. "They smell delicious."

"Doris's own recipe. But you have to wait until tomorrow. And speaking of waiting." Maybelle took a breath. "And speaking of waiting. I think I know one of the reasons Doris is being so . . . well, why she's asked you to wait."

Roger stood and poured himself a glass of milk. "Oh, what is it?"

"It's . . . you know. The . . . physical part of marriage."

Maybelle watched Roger's face turn red. "Oh, but . . . she's been married. Why?"

"Precisely. She's been married. To a man she loved."

Roger took a breath and set the glass down. "Oh, sure. That makes sense. What should I do?"

Maybelle hung the dishtowel on a hook. "Nothing right now. But soon, try to get her to talk about it. She needs to know you'll do the right thing by her. Wait even."

Roger swallowed. "Sure. Sure, I will. I'd climb mountains for Doris. I'd give her the moon if it was mine to give."

"Then give her time."

20

The next morning Maybelle and Doris woke early. They had no trouble falling asleep. In fact, Doris was busy sawing wood when Maybelle finally made it to bed.

"Okay," Doris said. "Now the real fun starts."

Maybelle swung her feet over the side of the bed. "I don't know about this. I'm bushed."

"Come on," Doris said. "Throw some clothes on, work clothes, and we'll get some coffee."

"Okay, okay." Maybelle thought about the huge turkey. A wave of fear rushed over her. She had never cooked a turkey and hadn't the first idea how to begin. Even with Doris's expert help, Maybelle thought the success or failure of the meal was still her responsibility.

"All right. All right," Maybelle said. "You use the bathroom first. I'll be down."

"Don't dawdle," Doris said. "We have to get the turkey stuffed and into the oven if we want to eat on time."

"Okay, okay. Go."

Bingo sauntered into the room. He barked twice.

"Okay," Maybelle said. "Follow Doris. She'll let you out."

She wanted to just fall back and go to sleep but duty called. Somehow, Maybelle managed to rise and even shine that morning. After her coffee. Doris made it. She even made better coffee than Maybelle.

Watching Doris get to work on the stuffing made it obvious why it was a good idea to clean up from the night before. Doris was sautéing the onions and celery Maybelle had cut. She even had real butter. Just a little but still. Real butter. The aroma from the vegetables was so nice. Sweet, but earthy. Like spring.

Maybelle's job, after a bowl of cereal, was to keep close to Doris and start on the cleanup.

"Then we stay one step ahead of the game."

"Good idea. But when do I get to do something?"

"Later. When it's time to peel potatoes and carrots."

"KP duty," Maybelle said. But she was happy.

By nine o'clock, they had everything in order. Doris had assembled all the necessary ingredients and lined up bowls and pots needed for cooking.

They poured themselves second cups of coffee and headed into the living room to turn on the radio and listen to the parade reports. They didn't listen long before the doorbell rang.

"Is that Janice and Lois already?" Doris asked.

"Probably." Maybelle opened the door. Janice was there holding what looked like a lemon meringue pie. And Lois stood there holding a handkerchief to her nose.

"Come on in," Maybelle said. "We got coffee on."

Janice carried the pie through the living room.

"That looks delicious," Doris said. "Did you make it?"

"Sure did," Janice said. "I thought whipping the meringue was gonna kill me, but I must have developed some muscles working on the ships."

Lois flopped into a chair. "I'm sorry. I'm sick."

"Should you be here?" Doris asked.

Lois pouted. "But I don't want to be by myself."

"I know," Doris said. "I just wanted you to know you can go home, if you want."

Lois shook her head. "I'll be fine. Morning is always the worst. Ever notice how it is?"

"There isn't much to do for now," Doris said. "We were just listening to the parade news."

"Oh, that's a good idea," Janice said.

"Can we work on the quilt?" Lois asked. "We can just spread it out in here and each take a corner. It'll work."

Maybelle looked at Doris. Doris shrugged.

"Okay," Maybelle said. "But we might have to get up and down to do things for the dinner."

"Okay," Janice said.

Maybelle opened the trunk, and Janice helped her unfold the quilt. For a few moments, the women did nothing but stare at their handiwork.

"It's beautiful," Lois said. "Just beautiful."

They each touched the squares, particular squares, which held special meaning for them.

Doris lingered over Mickey's hunting shirt and his army stripe. She swiped at tears. Maybelle sobbed as she touched Holden's square, and Lois nearly passed out she cried so hard as she touched the pieces mattering most to her, including the little lamb that stood for her daughter, whom she missed more than she could say. Janice laughed when she saw the seersucker square bringing much needed levity to the moment.

"What's this?" Janice asked. She pointed to the square with the zipper disaster piece on it.

"It's the dress," Maybelle said. "The infamous zipper dress."

"That's a riot," she said. "I wish we had it sooner. But yeah, it kind of makes the whole quilt."

Lois sniffled and laughed. "I am so glad you thought to include it."

"My mother would be happy," Maybelle said. "I'm sure she had no idea about the possibilities when she started this thing. I'm sure she never intended it to be so big."

"Yeah, she would have loved this," Doris said. "She would have loved being part of the group."

"I'm sorry we didn't get to know her," Janice said. "She sounds like a marvelous woman."

Maybelle nodded. "She was. I loved her very much." She picked up a needle and set about threading it. The others followed.

The report from the parade route was not good. It had been canceled again because of the war.

"Ahh, it's too bad," Doris said.

"Yeah, I read about it in the paper. They just feel it's not the right thing to do what with all the rationing and salvaging going on."

"It makes sense," Maybelle said. She flipped the dial until Bing Crosby came on. "There you go. That's nice."

Janice and Lois could sew like they were on fire. Lois's stitches were so tiny and so neat they made Maybelle's stitches look like Dr. Frankenstein had done them. But this time, Maybelle didn't mind. She sewed how she sewed. It just wasn't important. The quilt, the sewing circle, doing something for the war effort, was what was important.

Doris got up a few times to check on the turkey and do things in the kitchen. She stopped sewing also when Roger came downstairs. She enlisted him in setting the table. Maybelle liked watching them work together. They did make a nice couple. Even if she felt kind of sorry for telling Roger Doris's secret. But still, it would be okay. Roger would use discretion. Then she felt her eyes roll. Roger was not really what you would call discreet. But as she watched him move around the table setting out flatware and making certain water glasses were just so, she knew in her heart Roger would do the right thing by Doris.

"You know," Maybelle said. "I've been thinking the quilt belongs to all of us. Not just me."

"Yes, but I say it stays here with you until Holden comes home," Doris said. "It started here."

"Good idea," Lois said. "And be sure and wrap him up tight in it."

"Oh, I will," Maybelle said.

Bingo was also enjoying the day, lying close to the fire after Roger got it started. Every so often, he perked his ears at the wind or when one of the girls laughed. Maybelle liked the look in Doris's eyes when Roger carried an armful of wood into the house. Wood he chopped.

"I wish every day could be like today," Maybelle said.

"Me, too," Roger said. "A whole day off and all these pretty ladies to share it with."

"Hey, hey," Doris said. "Watch it, buster."

"It's a shame so many folks have to work today," Janice said. She stood near the fire. "I love a nice fire."

"A lot of people are working," Roger said. "Mostly men though, so the women can be home cooking and stuff. They say they don't mind, the men that it is. They see it as part of their sacrifice."

Maybelle felt a twinge of sadness. She hoped if Holden never made it home, and was buried somewhere over there, at least his sacrifice was good, a part of God's larger plan.

"I like to think sometimes," she said, "if Holden is . . . you know, gone, maybe he died saving someone else's life. It would be just like him. He would throw himself on a grenade to save his buddies."

"He sure would," Doris said. Then she let go a huge sigh. "I sure miss Mickey."

Roger put his arm around her and kissed her head. "I know you do."

And then, Maybelle knew without a shadow of a doubt that Roger would take good care of Doris. All would be well.

———∞∞———

Maybelle and Doris excused themselves and got busy in the kitchen. Maybelle prepared the vegetables, the ones they had anyway. She peeled five pounds of potatoes, quartered them, and placed them in a big pot of salted water.

Roger carried in bottles of Coca-Cola from the porch. He had managed to get extra. And he happily set a sack of peas on the counter. "Someone will have to shell them."

"Where did you get peas?" Doris asked.

"Don't ask," he said. "Just be grateful. I forgot I left them on the mud porch yesterday."

Doris patted his cheek. "You are quite the scrounger."

The group worked hard until finally, everything was ready. Doris finished whipping the potatoes into a creamy consistency. Maybelle dumped cooked, emerald green peas into a white bowl. She put a small pat of butter on top. And saved the last of the butter for the potatoes. She would be doggoned if she was going to use oleo on her potatoes. Lois carried the peas to the table.

Then everything was set. The meal was ready, and the small group assembled around the table.

Maybelle asked the blessing. Not long, but sweet. Everything could be summed up in one prayer of thanksgiving. "Thank you for our fighting men. They are the reason we are here." But just before she said amen, Doris said. "And Lord, we ask you to bring Holden home."

Roger stood at the head of table to carve the delicious roasted turkey. The smells were wonderful.

"Here's to us," he said. "I am so thankful for you, my friends." He looked at Doris. She beamed. "Thank you for letting me be a part of your household, Maybelle."

Roger plunged the fork into the turkey, and juice ran from it. He sliced as the others passed vegetables, potatoes, bread, and gravy. He made many slices, taking a drumstick for himself, which he chomped into like King Henry. Doris laughed.

At first, the meal was boisterous and happy with everyone exchanging stories and even a few bad jokes. But after awhile the table grew quiet. Maybelle figured because everyone was missing their loved ones. Roger even took hold of Doris's hand. She let him hold it for a good long time. The sounds of Bing Crosby and Frank Sinatra filtered through the air, but every so often, the music was interrupted with news of the war.

"Very nice," Maybelle said.

But no one said anything. Mostly the mood had sunk very low.

"Let's break out the pie," Roger said.

"Good idea," Doris said. "Come on, we'll have pie in the living room. We can listen to *Burns and Allen*."

"Oh, just in time," Janice said. "I love them. They're so funny."

Maybelle let go a deep breath. She was glad the mood was lifting. She and Doris served the pies, both mincemeat and the lemon, on Francine's finest dishes—brought right from Dublin by her grandmother. Maybelle had always admired them, although they were seldom used.

"They are sweet," Doris said. "So delicate. No wonder your mother rarely used them."

"Yeah, a couple of pieces have broken over the years."

They carried the pie to the living room on the Coca-Cola tray and served it.

Maybelle turned up the radio. "Much better. They should be on after this advertisement. So many advertisements."

"I'll say. They'll tout anything, even pills for your liver," Roger said.

The remainder of the day went nicely; thankfully the mood never sunk too low again. The small group was enjoying the show and one another. Lois remarked, "I'm so glad to be with friends." Then she blustered. But only for a second or two.

"Me, too," Janice said. "Especially in times like these. I do hope they get Hitler soon and all our boys can come home."

"Oh, don't you worry your sweet little head," Roger said. "They'll get him."

"And I hope my Holden helps," Maybelle said. "I really do."

The conversation grew quiet as conversations had a habit of doing.

The doorbell rang followed by a loud knock. Maybelle's heart raced. Bingo danced and barked and ran to the door.

"Now who could that be?" Maybelle asked.

"Probably Logan," Doris said.

"Oh, yeah, right. We did invite him."

"You did?" Roger said. "That was really neighborly of you. You know, he has no one."

"No trouble," Doris said. "We got plenty of food. And for today at least, he's not our boss."

Maybelle pulled open the door. It wasn't Logan. It was an army officer holding a small yellow envelope.

21

Maybelle cried. She stood there and cried. Doris rushed to her side. "Maybelle, what is it?"

"I don't want to know," Maybelle said. "I can tell by the envelope. It's . . . it's bad news."

The officer held out the envelope. Doris took it.

"Thank you, ma'am," the officer said.

"Thank you," Doris said. "And Happy Thanksgiving."

The officer turned on his heel and walked back to a waiting black car.

Doris helped Maybelle into the living room.

"What is it?" Roger said.

Lois stood. She moved closer to Maybelle. Doris handed Roger the envelope. "You read it."

Roger removed the telegram from the envelope and read, "The Secretary of the Army wishes me to inform you Private Holden Kazinski has been located alive and well in Germany."

"What?" Maybelle cried. "Read it again."

Roger read the same words three times. "It's true. Holden is alive. He's okay."

Bingo perked up at the sound of Maybelle's voice. He barked and rushed to her side.

Maybelle patted his head. "Hear that, boy? Holden is coming home!"

Bingo sat with his tail wagging a mile a minute.

"But . . . but where? What happened?" Doris asked.

"No details," Roger said. "I'm sure Holden will write as soon as he can."

Maybelle took the telegram from Roger and flopped into the couch. "Thank God."

"Yes, thank God," Doris said.

Maybelle sobbed long and hard as her friends rallied near. She needed to read the telegram over and over.

"He's okay," she cried. "My Holden is okay."

Holden didn't come home that week or even that month. But Maybelle did get to talk to him via special transatlantic call set up by a few of the men at the shipyard. She couldn't talk long, only thirty seconds.

"It's really you, sweetheart," she said.

"It's really me," Holden said. "They're shipping me home on the next ship. I'll be home in a month."

"Oh, darling. I'll be here."

"How's Mom?" Holden asked.

"She . . . passed away."

"I'm sorry I wasn't there, honey."

"But you will be," Maybelle said. "You will be soon."

And he did come home, exactly six weeks after Thanksgiving. Too late for Christmas, but just in time for love. Maybelle could hardly wait to hold him in her arms, to hug and kiss him. But when the day arrived, Maybelle was met with something she did not know or expect.

A large black car pulled up in front of the house. Maybelle saw it from the porch. She ran to the car, but the officer stopped her. "Please, ma'am, let us handle this."

"Handle what?" Maybelle asked. "Holden Kazinski, you come out of that car."

The officer opened the back door, and Maybelle watched as Holden slowly climbed out of the car.

"Oh no." Tears streamed down her cheeks. "Holden." She reached up and kissed his mouth. He wobbled but the officer held him. Maybelle reached up a second time and touched his eyes. They were bandaged shut.

Bingo dashed down from the front stoop. He nudged Holden's hand.

"Hey, boy," Holden said. "How ya doin'?"

Maybelle looked at the officer. "What happened?"

Holden answered, "A blast. Too much shrapnel in my face and eyes. I'm blind, Maybelle. Forever."

Maybelle swallowed and tried to pull herself together. She tried to take his hand, but he wouldn't let her. "No, like this." He rested his hand on her shoulder. "You walk. I follow."

Maybelle slowly led Holden to the house. He handled the steps with little trouble. She led him to the sofa where he backed up and flopped like a rag doll into the cushion. The officer followed. He stayed near the door. "Are you all right, Private?" he called.

"Yes, I'm fine," Holden called. "Thank you." Then he reached out and groped around for Maybelle's hand. She let him pull her to the couch and he fell into her and cried. "Oh, honey, I'm so sorry."

She patted the back of his head. "It's okay. It's okay."

He cried a little softer. Bingo rested his big head in Holden's lap and whimpered.

"You didn't tell me," Maybelle said.

"I couldn't." He lifted his head. "I . . . I couldn't. Not on the telephone. Not from so far away."

———

Later in the afternoon, Doris arrived with Roger. They were stunned but did their best not to show it.

Roger shook his hand and hugged him. "Welcome home, man. Welcome home."

Doris had to keep taking deep breaths. She hugged him. Holden said, "Hey, Doris. It's good to . . . to see you."

Maybelle made coffee and she had pie, lemon meringue. Janice taught her to make it. Doris helped in the kitchen while the men stayed in the living room.

"Oh, Maybelle," Doris said. "I'm . . . so sorry. I don't know what to say. Are you okay?"

Maybelle nodded. "He's alive. He's home. He's mine."

Doris pulled her into a hug. "I'm so sorry. Is there anything we should do?"

Maybelle shook her head. "I don't know . . . yet. Just get used to it, I guess. That's what Mom would have said. Just get used to it."

"But you had so many plans."

"I still got plans." Maybelle plugged in the percolator. Doris sliced pie. "We're gonna get used to this."

"I know you will. But I'm here. Roger is here. If you need anything. Anything at all."

"I know." Maybelle carried the tray with pie. Holden told her how to serve him. The fork on the left, every time. She watched him eat. She fought tears as he fumbled a couple of times trying to find his mouth. He did okay, and he even managed to slip Bingo a bit of crust.

The four stayed together for a while, until Holden said he was tired and wanted to rest.

"Oh, we understand," Roger said. "Need help getting up the stairs?"

Holden shook his head. "No. May can do it. And I'll be doing it all by myself in no time. The doctors always said, no better time than the present to sharpen my skills."

"Say," Doris said as she and Roger stood in the doorway. "Maybelle has something to show you."

Maybelle glared daggers at Doris. "I . . . I do not. Not now."

"What?" Holden said. "What do you have?"

"It's upstairs," Doris said. "You'll see. Oh, I'm sorry. I got to stop saying that."

"It's all right," Holden said. "There are different ways to see. I can tell the difference between a general or a private walking past my bed just by the sound of his shoes."

Roger shook Holden's hand. "Glad to have you home. We need to get to Mackey's real soon."

"Mackey's," Holden said. "Sounds great. How is he anyway?"

"Still the same. Nothing has changed."

They waited a second until Doris and Roger were down the street. Holden seemed to be listening as they went. "Pretty soon I'll tell you exactly how many steps it is from this front porch to Doris's front porch."

"Come on," Maybelle said. "Let's get you upstairs."

Holden started up the steps one slow step at a time. "Just stay behind me, in case I lose my balance."

"Okay," Maybelle said. "I'm here."

"I know, darling. I know."

She led him to the bedroom. "So what do you want to show me?"

"It's on the bed."

"Oh, really?" Holden said. "You mean . . ."

"Not yet. But . . . look, it's a quilt. We made it. Me and Doris and some girls from the yard. We made the whole thing. I wish you could see it."

Holden felt his way to the bed. He touched the quilt, running his fingers over nearly every square. "It's beautiful."

"How can you tell?" Maybelle let go a soft a chuckle.

"I just can."

"It's a crazy quilt. Made from scraps gleaned from so many things." She picked up his hand and set it on his army stripes. "This is a square with your private's stripes."

"Oh, yeah."

He moved his hand around and stopped when he got to the infamous zipper square. "Seersucker. Your dress. The great zipper of shame."

"You are amazing," Maybelle said.

She put her hands on his shoulders and pushed him back on the bed. "Be gentle," he said. "I'm blind, you know."

Maybelle took the edge of the quilt and pulled it around them. "It's okay. We kiss with our eyes closed anyway."

Epilogue

As the days passed, Maybelle and Holden got to know each other in new and different ways. They learned many things. Holden learned about Francine's death and about his good friend, Mickey. He learned Maybelle wanted to go to medical school and figured his GI benefits would help with that. Marybeth and Rachel never returned and Holden and Maybelle were happy for that. She did, of course, quit her job at Sun Ship and Dry Dock.

Doris and Roger told Holden about their arrangement, and Roger promised when the arrangement became a reality, Holden would be best man. The quilt stayed mostly with Holden and Maybelle, and at last report, Maybelle was busy on a second quilt. A smaller one. Just perfect for a baby crib. But not to be used until they called her Dr. Maybelle Kazinski—hopefully she'd sew up patients better than she sewed dresses.

Author's Note

Writing a story like this might seem a simple task, but I wanted to paint as near a picture of what it was like for women to work at Sun Ship as I could. And for that, I must thank Dave Kavanagh, the Sun Ship historian who provided me with more than enough material. Thank you, Dave, for keeping Sun Ship and the thousands of employees alive and answering all of my questions. I also want to thank the Delaware County Historical Society for providing even more information about Chester, Pennsylvania.

In this story Doris's husband, Mickey, was killed in action, but his body was not returned home. This was not unusual at all. World War II posed a big logistical challenge, since American war dead were scattered around the globe. Nearly 80,000 U.S. troops died in the Pacific, for example, and 65,000 of their bodies were first buried in almost 200 battlefield cemeteries there.

Once the fighting ended, the bodies were exhumed and consolidated into larger regional graveyards. The first returns of World War II dead took place in the fall of 1947, six years after the attack at Pearl Harbor. Eventually, 171,000 of the roughly 280,000 identified remains were brought back to the United States (http://online.wsj.com/article/SB100014240527487042692045752708 41057314162.html).

Finally, I want to mention the first woman welder employed at Sun, Jeanette E. Swift. I named Doris Swift in her honor and in honor of the all the women who left children and family behind to work for the war effort. Thank you.

A Final Note about Sun Shipbuilding and Dry Dock

From *Our Yard—Victory Edition*

Women Made Good in Building Ships

Nell Drain

World War No. 2 marked the entry of women into the munitions shops and factories in a large way and Sun Ship was no exception to the general rule. A shipyard was about the last place where anybody thought women could make good because the work was regarded as heavy and hazardous. However, modern machinery and new methods already had created a change in the art of building vessels; women came into the Sun Shipyard, grew proficient, and soon they were in most of the mechanical departments.

The shipyard averaged construction of one ship a week during peak production. The focus for the shipyard, however, was not only on ship production but also on ship repair. From Pearl Harbor to the end of the war, Sun Ship repaired over 1,500 vessels damaged by bombs, torpedoes, mines, or other weapons of war. Because of the number of ships that passed through Sun's shipyard during the war, the contributions Sun Ship made to the war effort were monumental. Paul Burke, a member of the Navy's Armed Guard who worked at the shipyard for a brief time during 1943, explained to the *Delaware County Sunday Times* "to put out that many ships in such a short amount of time was miraculous—without them we couldn't have won the war."

World War II marked the peak of Sun Shipbuilding and Dry Dock Company's production. Over five years, from 1938 to 1943, the workforce grew from about 3,000 employees to the highest employment at the shipyard of 35,633 employees. This enormous growth made Sun Ship the largest single shipyard in the entire world. Of this large workforce, 2,681 were women, and they were respectfully referred to as "Tillie the Toiler" as opposed to "Rosie the Riveter." There were also about 12,000 African American workers employed at the shipyard. Richard L. Burke, vice president at the time, reported in a company publication that Sun Ship set a "notable precedent" with "every department thrown open to Negro workers on equal terms." Most of the African American workers were employed at the No. 4 yard, where the first ship built entirely by African Americans, the *SS Marine Eagle*, was launched.

Every effort has been made to contact the copyright holder of this article. If you are the copyright holder, please contact us at permissions@umpublishing.org.

Discussion Questions

1. This novel dealt with a lot of loss. Can you share about your own experience with loss or grief?

2. At one point Doris told Maybelle she would be standing in the gap for her. Have you ever stood in the gap or had someone stand in the gap for you?

3. The Sun Shipyard employed thousands of women during the height of World War II. Would you have liked to work there? Would you have been Tilly the Toiler?

4. Maybelle states from the outset that she can't sew. She tells the zipper story (which really happened to the author). She really had to step out of her comfort zone of the tomboy. Tell about a time you had to step out of your comfort zone.

5. What roles do you perform today that were considered a man's work at one time?

6. The women create a crazy quilt—full of memories. If you made a crazy quilt of memories, which memory would be in the center?

7. In the same train of thought as question 6, which memory would you like to hide and sew into a corner?

8. War is never easy. Has war affected you? How?

9. A strong sense of community was very important during this time in history. Is it still today? Has community changed, or are we all pretty much the same?

10. What do you think Roger's role was in this story? Was he a kind of big brother to all the women? Did he interest you?

Want to learn more about Joyce Magnin
And check out other great fiction from
Abingdon Press?

Check out our website at
www.AbingdonPress.com
to read interviews with your favorite authors,
find tips for starting a reading group,
and stay posted on what new titles are on the horizon.

Be sure to visit Joyce online!

http://joycemagnin.blogspot.com/

We hope you enjoyed *Maybelle in Stitches* and that you will continue to read the Quilts of Love series of books from Abingdon Press. Here's an excerpt from the next book in the series, Emily Wierenga's *A Promise in Pieces*.

~∞~

1

Noah looked like his father, and she hadn't noticed it before. But here in the backseat of a Dodge Caravan strewn with skateboarding magazines and CDs, there was time enough to see it in the young man whose long legs stretched from the seat beside her. To see the freckles dusting her grandson's cheeks, the way his hair poked up like a hayfield and his eyes grabbed at everything.

Up front, Oliver asked Shane to adjust the radio, the static reminding Clara of the white noise she used to make with a vacuum or a fan to calm her newborns. The first one was Shane, her eldest, the one in the passenger seat turning now to laugh at his father, who wrinkled his long nose as Shane tried to find a classical station.

Then, Vivaldi's *Four Seasons*, and Clara could see Oliver smiling, pleased, and she remembered the way he'd looked over at her in church so long ago with the same expression: as though he'd finally found what he'd been looking for.

Noah was playing a game on one of those Nintendo machines. He noticed her watching him, said, "Do you want to give it a try, Grandma?" He looked so eager.

Gone were the days of Hardy Boys and marbles. "Sure!" Clara said, mustering enthusiasm as she took the tiny gadget. Then she saw what he was playing—some kind of shooting game with uniformed men and guns—and she nearly dropped it.

"I'm sorry, it's too complicated for an old woman like me," she said, handing it back and turning to stare out the window, at Maryland passing by, wondering what a kid in high school could know about war.

They were taking the George Washington Memorial Parkway, one of Clara's favorite drives, which would carry them from her home state to Mount Vernon, Virginia. They were passing through Glen Echo, north of Washington, DC. And Clara remembered the story her Daddy had told her, on one of their summer holidays, about her namesake, Clara Barton, who'd spent the last fifteen years of her life here. The founder of the American Red Cross, Ms. Barton had tirelessly provided aid to wounded troops during the Civil War. She had dedicated her life to serving those in need, Daddy said.

On that holiday, Clara—only eight years old at the time—had decided she would do the same. After all, she had been named after Ms. Barton.

"Something wrong, Grandma?" Noah said.

Shane turned in the front seat. His green eyes met hers, and it seemed only yesterday she had brought him home wrapped in the quilt—the one cleaned, pressed, and folded, sitting in the back of their van.

Shane's eyebrows rose and Clara shrugged, feeling cold in her white cardigan even though it was late June. It had been more than fifty years.

"Fifty years," she said, more to herself than anything, and the van was quiet. She'd had these moments before, many of them. Moments landing her in the past, amongst broken and dead bodies, for there hadn't been enough beds in Normandy.

Oliver peered at her now in the rearview, through his glasses, and she should give his hair a trim, she thought. It sprouted silver around his ears, and when had her soldier-husband aged? At what point between them marrying and adopting Shane and giving birth to two others had his hair turned gray?

Noah was tucking the game away, now, saying, "I don't need to play this right now. What are you thinking about, Grandma?"

And she wiped at her eyes, moist, and cleared her throat and told herself to smarten up.

It was sixteen and a half hours to New Orleans, where they planned to visit the National World War II Museum, and she should make the most of the time she had with this boy who knew nothing of the miracle of the quilt in the back. Who knew nothing of loss, and this was good. But there is a need for history to plant itself in the hearts of its children.

"Do you know about Clara Barton?" she said. Noah shook his head.

"She was a woman of great character. The founder of the American Red Cross. This whole area is a National Historic Site in her name, and she didn't want it. All she wanted was to help people. In 1891, two men, Edwin and Edward Baltzley, offered Clara land for a house in an effort to draw people to this area. They offered her land, as well as free labor for building the house, believing people would come in flocks to see the home of the woman who founded the Red Cross.

"Clara was clever. As all women of the same name are," and here, she winked at Noah who laughed. "She had been looking for a new place to serve as headquarters for the Red Cross, so she took them up on it. She used the home originally as a warehouse for disaster-relief supplies, then reworked it and moved in six years later.

"A newly built electric trolley that ran into Washington brought in crowds of people to a nearby amusement park. When a new manager took over the park in 1906, he offered to buy Clara's home and turn it into a hotel. She refused, so he then tried to drive her out. Apparently, he built a slow-moving scenic railway right by her house, with a station by her front door. When it failed to work, he erected a Ferris wheel in front of her house. Can you imagine? It is said Clara loved the lights from the wheel. She served as president of the Red Cross until 1904, and kept living in the house until her death, eight years later, at age ninety. She said the moon used to always shine at Glen Echo."

Noah's eyes were fixed on her. "What a woman," he said.

Clara nodded. "I know. She's the reason I became a nurse. And went off to war when Daddy told me not to."

It was quiet in the car and then Shane said, "You can't stop there, Mom! Tell him the story!"

Oliver's eyes were shining in the mirror, Vivaldi was on the radio, and Maryland's fields of corn and hay were waving graceful good-byes.

"You sure?" she said to Noah.

He folded his hands in his lap. "I'm all yours, Grandma."

And so, she began.